PETTY OFFENSES
AND
CRIMES OF THE HEART

PETTY OFFENSES
AND
CRIMES OF THE HEART

Mitchell Waldman

International Standard Book Number 978-1-936138-36-4
Library of Congress Control Number 2011934402

— Acknowledgments —

The author thanks the editors who first published these stories.

"Bad Neighborhood" appeared in slightly different versions in *Innisfree, Rochester Shorts*, and *Long Story Short*.

"Catching up with Cartucci" appeared in *eFiction Magazine*.

"Chestnut Street" appeared in Red Fez.

"Fortunate Son" appeared in *Longshores Literary Magazine* and *Worldwide Hippies*.

"Glass Slippers" appeared in *new aesthetic*.

"My Life of Crime" appeared in *Rochester Shorts, Long Story Short*, and *(Short) Fiction Collective*.

"The Duke of Broad Street" appeared in *The Piker Press*.

"The Nazi Next Door" appeared in *Wind Magazine* and *Red Fez*.

"The Widow Across the Way" appeared in *Wilderness House Literary Review*.

To my wife,
my Love,
my best friend,

Diana,

who lights my fire
and
inspires my heart
every single day.

Contents

The Nazi Next Door

It all started with a package placed on Borglund's doorstep at two o'clock in the morning.

But, no, really, it started before that, when tilting his head over the picket fence, the smell of gin strong on his breath, he told me about his father, how he had collaborated with the Nazis back in Holland. I was speechless, but I must have had a telling look on my face because he stood back a step and, with watery eyes, said, "What else could he have done? He had a family, seven children to support." His father had been a railroad employee, had helped the SS route trains to the death camps. To Borglund, he was like any other man trapped in a job he didn't really like. But it was different—those trains were full of my people, my ancestors.

And that's when it really began.

A bag of shit, a bag of cat shit left on his doorstep. What is it really? Not much, in light of the number of ancestors of mine who were gassed in the war, whose names I don't even know. Not much in light of the dreams, the nightmares that have started to visit me ever since talking to Borglund that night. Sometimes it's every night, sometimes weeks go by without one, but when they come, it's as clear as day—the gray-helmeted men with spatterings of Nazi red, the blood of their victims, as decoration. Some of them so young, so very young—pimples on their faces still, gangly teenage postures, rifles over their shoulders or held firmly in the creases between their arms and chests. But no children these—the eyes cold, metallic, the eyes that don't look at you, they look through you, the "superiority," arrogance, trained into them.

I'm standing there, behind a wall, watching as they pull my proud but faceless ancestors down a flimsy attic ladder, or sometimes down from a hay loft (the place changes, but the events never do), march them along in their baggy creased trousers and yellowing button down shirts, their aging flowered dresses, heavy woolen socks, and clunky black shoes. I wonder what they're thinking as they do these things, these wunder boys who have learned their lessons of hatred with such zeal—do they reminisce about a certain young Fraulein back in Hamburg or Bremen, or about their days back in school, skipping home with strapped books swinging? In their brown knee knockers and caps, peering into the baker's window with hungry eyes? Thinking these thoughts, even as they carry out their orders, thinking nothing of the crime, the genocide they've initiated? Innocent (in German: unschuldig), a word that will never again apply to them. The crime: the wholesale destruction of families (my family) and most of a race.

"Shnell! Shnell!" the young men shout, their rifle tips prodding my relatives—the children among them—forward, as I tremble, want to scream out, but know I can't make a sound, can't even breathe, as, grim-faced (the victims have faces now, or maybe just eyes), even the children stare hopelessly with the looks of the condemned, the already dead, as my tears start to fall—tap, tap— onto the floor, and a gray-helmeted head turns, the fiery eyes searching in my direction, the black boots creaking, the rifle aimed toward me, a shot ringing out, and I scream (or is it just in the dream?), my heart racing, body drenched in sweat. I prop myself up in bed, sit up against the wall, don't ever want to sleep again—but it's still, silent, crickets singing now, cicadas screeching outside in the darkness, the breeze coming through the window, lightly sweeping the blinds forward, then sucking them back so they slap gently against the window pane. An occasional car swishing on the street below.

And across the yard, Borglund's light still on. It's two o'clock in the morning—is he devising these dreams somehow, does he have some sort of evil machine to put them in my head?

His words come back to me long after our conversation at the fence, not only what he said but the way he said it, with wide-eyed innocence, that open-palmed gesture of defeat—what else, indeed. For weeks I mull over the words, knowing that they slipped out, that he never meant to tell me at all—it was the booze that lubricated the tongue, let the words come, almost of their own volition, like a confession.

Borglund is a man who goes to church with his wife Helen (his second wife) every Sunday morning. He never misses it. He helps his neighbors plant their gardens. He's retired and doesn't seem to know what to do with himself. He has two grown sons who come to visit him once or twice a year. He spends hours on his knees, digging holes, shoveling dirt. His yard is a sanctuary for birds and, though small, he has squeezed every space full of exotic plants and flowers.

And there's the grass. He's obsessed with it, cuts it every day.

Even my wife, Donna, has noticed it, and she's the forgiving kind. She heard the motor first, then looked out the front window to see Hans cutting his grass, and a neglected strip in front of our house, yet again.

It's almost as if he wishes time would stand still, keep the blades from growing. Or is it his love of order, of neatness, picked up from the Germans maybe—the way they neatly organized us, like sheep, fifty years ago, and took us to our deaths. And the theory behind it, that only the superior genes should survive. Neatness, order. That was behind it all, despite the lunacy behind the theory, the horror behind its application.

We used to talk over the fence, Hans and I. I would be walking home. I would wave, say hello. He would ask me about work. I would tell him how it was. "So, so." He had had work problems too. A commercial artist for a large company, he had given it up because, like me, he couldn't take all of the crap, the bosses telling him to do this, to do that, running him ragged. (I still do take the crap—I have a family to support).

But after his revelation about his father, the chatter stopped. I started to avoid him. I'd pretend I didn't see him. And his attitude was similar. He'd go on puttering in the yard, digging a new hole for this or that. Either he was embarrassed for telling his little secret, or he was ignoring me because I was one of them, a Jew. But could that really have been it? There'd never been any evidence of anti-Semitism in this man. But, on the other hand, having been a child in the time of the Nazis, and having a father who helped them, willingly or not, how could some of that not have rubbed off?

Then there was the incident with my girls. They were innocently chalking a group of hopscotch boxes in front of his house. The girls—three-year-old Lucy and six-year-old Lainie—came running back to our house, tears in their eyes, telling my wife how mean Mr. Borglund had scolded them for messing up his sidewalk.

"So, what are you going to do about it?" Donna asked me that evening, hands on her hips, giving me one of her looks.

I threw up my hands. "What am I supposed to do about it? It's his property, he doesn't want it to be dirtied. You know how he is, like an old lady."

But I did do something about it. When everyone else was asleep, snoring away, I snuck to the basement with a small box, then scooped some choice tidbits from the cat box into the small box, sealed it, climbed back up the stairs, opened the door and, walking very quietly to Borglund's, laid the package on his doorstep. Stealing back home then, feeling electric, a dangerous thrill running through my entire body. Smiling to myself as I took off my coat and hung it on the rack, thinking about the horror on Borglund's face as he would open the box the next day. Feeding on that horror, the payback, just a small one for what he had imposed on my people—though I'm not religious, they are still my people, were my ancestors, great aunts and uncles, and cousins, how many cousins, who I will never know, whose names have long been forgotten, all of them liquidated, murdered, in that war, in that Holocaust.

But in the days that followed, avoiding him at all costs for fear that he would know who had left that package, I had second thoughts. Had I been unfair? After all, it was not him, it was his father.

Yes, I thought, but descendants should be made to pay for what their predecessors did, shouldn't they?

But, no, that wasn't it at all, really. I had two German-American roommates in college and I never felt that way about either of them with their pale blue eyes, their straight blond hair and their prominent chins.

I peek at him sometimes from behind the blinds in our bedroom. He lives on the top floor of the house just across the way from our bedroom, rents the first floor out to a young couple—it keeps him in seeds. Behind the blinds, from our darkened bedroom, I can see him over the bushes—there are no curtains over what is their living room. The sound of the television blares and, on rare occasion, the raised voices between him and his wife, Helen, although the words don't quite come through.

"What are you looking at?" Donna says from the darkness.

"Nothing. I thought I heard something." But it's just him, Borglund, just beyond my view, but never quite out of my mind.

I take to diving into my work to avoid thinking too much about it. But, no matter what, I always return to this new obsession, wondering, scheming about what new package to leave him next. It becomes a time-consuming task after that first one. You can't easily leave him something obvious, like a picture of Hitler; that way he would know who had planted the present, wouldn't he? It has to be something fairly ambiguous, but clear enough to let him know. But nothing threatening enough to bring the police into it.

The second gift contained a package of dead goldfish floating around in water in a plastic bag. "How much for them?" I'd asked the boy at the pet shop.

"But they're dead." What would you want with them?" he asked.

I'd insisted: "How much?"

He'd taken his net and swept them out, put them in a bag, twisted the top around and tied it. Then he'd handed the bag over, looking at me for an instant too long before jerking his head away. Before I could thank him, he'd already moved away toward the tanks, in pursuit of his next customer. And, after I walked out of the store, I imagined the boy telling his coworkers about the crazy man who had wanted the dead fish. I heard them all laughing, talking about the "types" that walked into their store.

Another time it was a piece of a headstone that had broken off. I'd been walking in the cemetery near us. (I'd taken to doing this lately, thinking more and more about my dead, nameless, ancestors) and had stumbled (literally) on what I had thought was just a chunk of rock. But when I had picked it up I had seen the words Died 19...and that was where the letters met the jagged edge.

And last night it was a dead baby bird. I'd found it on the side of the house—it must've fallen out of its nest—picked it up with a doubled up piece of paper toweling to get it before the neighborhood cats sunk their teeth into it.

I caught our own cat once, she'd trapped a living bird. I don't know what kind of bird it was—a sparrow maybe. It was gray and wasn't moving, was in shock, I guess, scared stiff. I only knew it was alive because it blinked and its tiny yellow beak quivered. When I found it, found them, the cat, Natasha, had trapped the little bird between her paws. She'd let it go, then jump on it again, playing with it, the game of death. I yelled at Natasha "Stop! Let it go!" She looked at me with her crescent green eyes wide, questioning, but not moving.

"Dammit!" I yelled, bolting toward her, jerking her paws away from the little bird, which sat there still, shivering—perhaps it had given up hope and now was too weak to even save itself. I waved my arms at the bird. "Go now, you're free," but it just sat there looking at me until I bent down, as if to grab it, and it shot straight up into the air for home, my heart flying with it. All that it left behind was a single gray feather, about two inches long, that had fallen back to Earth as it had taken flight. And, of course, there was Natasha, who stared at me with a look of hurt.

So: a dead bird for Borglund, one that couldn't be saved, in a plastic bag. Seven children, what could he do? Maybe he would think about it, maybe he would know.

I see him occasionally, say hi to avoid suspicion. He comments on the weather, that's about it, and I walk on.

It goes on for weeks, months, the friendly but distant greetings by day, the parceling out of my little gifts by night, first the more innocuous ones—dulled, discarded razor blades, carefully wrapped pieces of burnt toast, discarded chicken bones, the meat chewed off, or, sometimes only the skin, like the skin of my ancestors which they made lampshades out of, and then it gets worse, more threatening—crumpled newspaper clippings of car bombings, of gruesome murders, a picture taken from a magazine of young children with an X neatly drawn in black magic marker from corner to corner, poems about faces who are no longer there....

But sometimes it's all too much.

One night, in the fall, I'm walking by his house. I'm out for a walk to escape the need to sleep. The fear of sleep. Three dreams in three nights because of him. The sky dark, but clouds up high, gray veils passing before a bright full moon. And from Borglund's second floor window the sounds of a television and of people laughing.

I notice he's left his car lights on, try the doors. Go to his house and ring the bell. The voices upstairs stop.

A minute later his face appears at the little frame of a window. He opens the door and steps out. He's wearing a striped knit shirt and military green shorts (the kind everyone wears these days), the remains of a drink in his hand, the tiny chips of ice tinkling.

"Hi" he says too loudly, beaming at me. Two of his bottom teeth are brown; they're long and narrow, and bent toward each other. "What can I do for you?" he asks.

"Your lights," I say.

"Huh? What's that?" he asks, tilting his head like he did that night at the fence.

"Your car lights. You left them on. I tried the door but..."

"Son of a bitch." His face wrinkles into a frown, and he moves in his thongs toward the car door, twisting back around at me with a smile, shaking his head. "Now, how the hell did I do that?"

I shrug, but he's already opening the car door, taking care of the problem, slamming the door, and smiling. "All set," he says. "Thanks a lot. I'd hate to have come out here in the morning and... and..."

"No problem," I say.

He puts his hand on my shoulder, squeezes the round bone a little too hard between his thumb and forefinger. I'm staring at him, his smile, studying the long jagged brown teeth. The sour smell of old alcohol on his breath.

"Why don't you come upstairs for a drink."

"Well, I don't know...." I say, avoiding his eyes.

"I insist," he says, "you must be rewarded."

In his apartment—it's smaller than I imagined—Helen is sitting on the couch in her shorts and sleeveless blouse (they're both in good physical shape for people in their mid- to late-fifties) watching me with tentative eyes, as Hans tells her "Rich here just saved us a call to the garage in the morning. I left the car lights on, can you believe it!" She laughs loudly. It's the same loud, but not unpleasant, laugh that I've heard through the air between our houses on warm summer nights. "Thanks a lot," she says. "It would have been hell tomorrow to rush to get out the door and then find a dead battery. But, he always does that!" she says, looking at her husband now, waving a finger at him, while he laughs good-naturedly, shaking his head, saying "I don't know what gets into me sometimes!"

Hans turns his back now, facing his small bar. "So what'll you have, Rich? Gin all right? You look like a gin drinker to me. What do you think, babe?"

Helen laughs again, a quick burst, then says, "Oh yes. Gin definitely, I'd say."

"With tonic? How's that sound, Rich?"
"Oh, fine, that'll be just..." He's already handing me the glass. I take it, thanking him, then begin to sip and watch them both, the inevitable question playing in my mind.

Then, in looking around, I notice: on a low table in the corner of the room are a number of my "presents." When my eyes come across them I stay calm, try not to look away too quickly, nor linger on them too long, just let my eyes glide slowly across them, at the same rate as I take everything else in.

"Nice place you've got here," I say, barely aware of my own words.

"Thanks," Hans says, watching me. "Of course, it was a lot of work, but we've made it home."

On the television, a baseball game's on. There are runners on first and third.

"You follow the Yanks? Quite a season they're having."

"No," I say. "I'm not really into sports much."

"You still running? I see you sometimes in the mornings. How far do you go?"

"Oh, five miles generally. Every other day."

"You know, I used to run two, three times a day."

"Hmmm." I sip, then, thinking better of it, trying not to prolong this, gulp the last of my drink and say, "Well, thanks for the drink. I guess I'd better be going."

"So soon?" Hans says. "How 'bout another little one? As a night cap. It'll help you sleep," he says, staring right at me.

"You see this stuff over here?" he says suddenly, pointing, walking towards the table with the gifts.

"Hmmm? Yes?" He's blind-sided me.

"You wonder, what is all this stuff."

I play it nonchalant, trying to look mildly curious, shrug, laugh, say, "What is it?"

He picks up a little white box with a small broken glass mirror in it, my most recent gift. Only the day before I'd taken my hammer and smashed the little dime store mirror, then carefully glued the glass fragments back together like a puzzle on the cardboard backing, before laying it in tissue in the box—a little coffin—and, putting the lid back on, all the while imagining him looking into it, seeing the cracks in his own reflection.

 He hands the box to me.

"You think I collect junk?" he asks.

I shrug again and smile at him, let him know I'm indulging him, playing the gracious guest. "People collect all sorts of things," I say.

"Yes," he says, looking at me, but not smiling now. "But I'm not one of them. You see, Rich, I have very little use for most things."

I say nothing.

"No," he says, "I've been getting these... things..."—He sweeps his arm over the table—"for many months now, and I don't know who or why."

"You've been getting them...how?"

"On my doorstep. I wake up to them once, twice a week sometimes. They're my little morning surprises." I take another swallow of gin. His face is red now and he suddenly strikes out, grabs up the car bombing story, slightly yellowed now, and thrusts it toward me, on top of the box with the mirror—"I mean, what kind of sick mind would leave me this?"

I pretend to read the story, doing my best to keep from shaking.

"The only reason I haven't called the police is because it's just been...this. Nothing else. No phone calls. Nothing."

I try to hand the things—the box, the article—back to him, but he won't take them.

Helen coughs on the couch behind us, but I don't turn around.

"I was thinking about it," he says, "trying to remember when it all started ... and then one night, not very long ago, it struck me."

I'm paralyzed, unable to take another breath.

He stares at me. "You know, Rich, I can't sleep at nights. It's that bad."

I'm visibly shaking now. It's all I can take. I slam the box and the newspaper clipping down on the table. "And you think I can?" Behind me, from the couch, a thin gasp, quickly stifled, and I continue, "Ever since that night, that night when you told me about..."

"About my father, that's what it's about, isn't it?"

"You said, 'What else could he have done?' I was outraged! And the dreams. I have them all the time! The storm troopers come. Sometimes with a man who looks like you. Lately, he's become you. They're coming for my family, they're coming for me."

"I'm sorry, Rich," he says, putting his hand on my shoulder again, but gentler than before. "I know how that must have sounded, 'What could he do?' But, really, what could he, what would you have done?" He takes his hand off me suddenly, sweeps it quickly through the air, and then back at me. He presses the tip of his index finger against my chest. "You think it was easy for him? You think I'm proud of him for what he did? He was just trying to survive, too! They would have put him to death just as easily as they'd put the Jews. Those people were monsters!"

I feel like crying now, can't look him in the eye.

"You know, Rich, I was just a boy then. I was there. I saw it. You think that's easy for a child, to experience all that horror, to witness it?"

I look up at him. He's no longer angry, but wears a sad smile now. "God knows my nightmares have never stopped."

From then on the dreams fade—there are one or two more, but, the last time, just as the gray-helmeted machines are dragging my relatives down the stairs, just as they're about to turn to where my breath, my pounding heart is giving me away, Borglund comes right into the dream, stands in front of the soldiers and says "Stop. Enough now. Go home to your families." And the blood in their eyes fades. They turn into little boys who drop their heads in shame and walk silently out of the room, the last closing the door behind him.

And the next night, I leave my final gifts on his doorstep—a bottle of wine, a rose, and a two-inch gray feather from a sparrow, the one that got away.

Fortunate Son

Delores Leary picked up the baseball mitt from the undisturbed blue cover of the single bed. It was one of two beds in the room, the one that her son, Andy, had occupied when he'd been there. She stroked the worn brown leather palm of the mitt and brought it close to her face to smell its musky scent. Then she closed her eye and found herself traveling back, back to those innocent days, driving Andy and Ricky to little league games, sitting in the bleachers, watching the two of them running across the sun-bleached field in their Dorsey Dodge uniforms. She'd been so proud, watching her little guys, cheering them on every time one of them came to bat or a ball was hit in their direction. And she'd always been there to encourage them with a smile or a pat on the back when one of them dropped a ball, struck out, or was thrown out trying to steal a base.

She buried her face in the leather, fell across the bed, and wept silent tears. She remembered his face, those eyes, that smile, that beacon of unadulterated light that seemed like it would burn forever. But that was then.

A car commercial was playing on the television. Delores lit a cigarette and winced. When it had happened she'd taken up smoking again after having quit for ten years. The tune in the background was Creedence Clearwater Revival's Fortunate Son. Ironic, she thought. A large flag, ghostly, superimposed in the background, was waving in the wind as a midnight blue sports car drove by fast, dust flying up by the roadside. The advertisers missed the point. It was an antiwar song but they'd distorted it for their own use, to sell cars, all-American cars, made to a great extent in Japan.

She thought of Andy, her very own unfortunate son.

Another ad came on, this one for the Marines. A line of strong, iron-jawed men in dress blues marched and saluted while the crowd clapped and cheered in the background waving flags. Patriotism— what was that? The heading ran across the screen: A few good men. Are you man enough to fit the bill?

Man enough. She couldn't take it. She felt dizzy, grasped for the remote and hit the red button. And then there was only silence in the house. A strange, reverberating stillness. And the swishing of cars outside in the rain.

What had he been thinking when he'd decided to join up? Had he been caught up by the flag-waving, the propaganda? A few good men, a few good men for what? To die? It was bullshit, pure bullshit. It wasn't the advertisers' sons going over there, still children, scared children, not knowing what the hell they were doing, acting like men, prey to their macho preachings. Boys wanted to be men. Of course. So this was how they could prove themselves. Is that what Andy had thought? That this would make him a man?

He was sitting next to Ricky at the dinner table playing with his peas, moving them to the back of his plate. He hadn't touched his lamb chops. It wasn't like Andy not to eat. He was just sitting there, staring at his plate. Meanwhile blond-haired Ricky, a year younger than his brother, was shoveling the last bite of his chop into his mouth, chewing greedily smacking his belly and belching, this big goofy smile on his face.

"God, Rick, that's gross!" Delores said. "Where did you learn your manners from, the zoo?"

Ricky laughed but Andy wasn't reacting at all, still staring obliviously at his plate. The younger boy stopped laughing and stared at his brother.

"Okay, Andy boy, what is it?" Delores asked. What's wrong with my little boy?"

Andy looked up at his mother, his eyebrows pulled together, his eyes narrowed to two small slits. "Maybe that's it, Mom. I'm not your little boy anymore. I'm eighteen. Or haven't you noticed?"

"Yeah, yeah, you're eighteen. Let me tell you something. You'll always be my little boy, even when you're eighty and I'm dead."

"Oh, very nice, Mom," Ricky said, and started laughing.

Andy was still staring at her with his deadpan look. Then he spilled it: "Joe Martin's joining the Army." Joe Martin was his best friend. They'd been Cub Scouts together, gone fishing together, then, when they were older, had gone on double dates together.

"He is? What does his mother say about it?"

"Jesus, Mom, that's the whole point. What can she say about it? Joe's a man now."

"Just because you're eighteen and you've had a smoke and a beer and maybe got laid doesn't necessarily qualify you for membership in the Man Club. Does his mother still cook his meals, do his laundry for him, pick up after him?"

"You're missing the point, Mom. Joe's joining up, and...I think I might, too. What with all this terrorist shit happening and 9/11 and all the Arabs...?" There was a moment of shock—her heart was racing and she couldn't breathe, couldn't move or say a word. She thought of how he had looked dressed in his blue Cub Scout uniform with the gold neck kerchief. There was a picture in their foyer of Andy and Joe in these uniforms, arms around each other grinning. Joe freckled and missing one of his front teeth, Andy, hat on crooked, covering a brown mop of hair, crossing his eyes, acting generally goofy and bright like the star that he had seemed to Delores in those days, the brightest star in her sometimes ink black sky. It seemed like only yesterday. How could she be listening to the same boy now, grown up, or almost grown up, talking about "plans," things that no mother could listen to without her heart palpitating, words that no mother could bear to hear?

"I've got to do my share," he said, jaw set. "For all of us." He sounded like some stranger who had walked in the front door and sat himself down at her kitchen table.

"Dad served. I want to do my part, too."

Dad, who in Andy's more bitter moments he referred to as "the Sperm Donor." What could she say while the voice inside her head was screaming "No!!!" She took a deep breath and spoke, trying to battle with him, reason with him. "What about college? You were talking about that, about getting an athletic scholarship, going to college, maybe becoming a doctor. And what about how you've always wanted to help people? How are you going to help people by shooting at them?"

"God, Mom, you don't understand! This is doing something for people. For our people. We're talking about our survival here!"

Delores couldn't believe what she was hearing. She shook her head, and put her hand on his cheek. "You really believe that?" Andy pulled away from her.

"Yes, I really believe that." He looked right at her, firmly, not batting a lash. Then he softened some, turned his gaze down, and stared at his hands, his long slender fingers stretched out on the table top. Suddenly he didn't look so grown up, he didn't look quite so sure of himself. "And, as for school, that can wait. Anyway, I don't know, my grades generally suck and I have no idea what I really want to do. Plus there's the New GI Bill. Sergeant Conners said that would help out financially when I get out."

When I get out. It echoed in her ears.

If you get out, a voice in her head corrected. This thought came out sooner than she could process it, making her whole body shudder. This was her baby she was thinking about. She felt sick to her stomach, like she was going to vomit. Delores rose from the table, bolted for the bathroom, and slammed the door behind her.

"Mom, you all right in there? You didn't die or anything, did ya?"

She got off her knees, flushed the toilet, smoothed down her blouse and looked at herself in the mirror, trying a smile on for her boys. Not a very convincing one, she was sure, but it would have to do.

"I'm fine, Andy, just must've been something I ate." Then she opened the door and tried that smile out on them—Andy standing there with the concerned look, hands on his hips, and his "little brother," the body builder who was at least twice as wide as Andy, bending over, putting his hand gently on his mother's back, saying, "Are you all right, Mom? Are you sure you're all right?"

The phone call came on a Tuesday evening. She was watching a game show, Hollywood Squares. She watched anything other than the news these days. Comedies especially, love stories. Even cartoons and game shows. Anything to keep from hearing the real stuff, the news about the war.

It was a Sergeant Young who called. He didn't say why but he wanted to come see her. Personally. She was terrified when she heard him say that. It could only mean one thing, couldn't it? Or maybe she was just jumping to conclusions. Maybe she'd seen one war movie too many.

When the knock came at the door she didn't know what to do. She continued to sort the mail and papers lying on the table in her kitchen, afraid to move. Again the knock. The vibrations of the BOOM BOOM BOOM reverberated through her body like an electrical shock. She stacked her papers and envelopes neatly, brushed back her hair, and walked slowly, feeling her insides quiver as she approached the door. She felt like she was watching someone else as she turned the bolt lock, pulled open the door and stared at a soldier in dress blues standing there with a somber look, hands clasped in front of his belt. She sighed, while the woman she was watching asked the man to come in.

He was sitting on the couch, a good-looking twentyish man with a brush of blond hair on the top of his head. What was he doing here? Why wasn't he sitting somewhere in some office, staring safely at some computer screen, or working at a toy store customer service desk, shining those blue eyes on unhappy customers, apologizing for the air gun that didn't fire right, rather than sitting here now doing what he was about to do?

Andy was eight years old preparing for his role in a class room production of Sleeping Beauty. He was playing the part of the Handsome Prince mainly because no other boy in the class had had the courage to do so. Delores tried to imagine him sticking his hand straight up in the air while the other boys tittered behind their hands or stared down at their desks, trying to avoid the gaze of their teacher, Mrs. Bowman, after she'd called for volunteers to fill the role. How proud she'd been of him when he'd told her about it. Not that he hadn't been afraid to. He had never been one to shy away from his fears. He'd learned his lines the week before the play and when time came to deliver, he'd strode right up onto the stage and delivered the lines expertly, without flinching.

And when the time had come for him to "do his part," as he'd said, he hadn't flinched either. She wished he would have flinched a little sometimes. But, with Andy, it had always been charge right into it, without question. He never lacked decisiveness, that was for sure. And look where it had gotten him. Just look.

The young man sat on the sofa across from Delores. She had her manners on, asked him if he wanted something to drink. He smiled and said a glass of water would be fine. It was a hot day. One of those ninety-five-in-the-shade types of days.

She walked very carefully into the kitchen, maintaining control, opened the refrigerator door, poured the water from the jug, closed the refrigerator door, and walked just as carefully back to the living room. Her hand shook only slightly as she brought the glass to the young man.

She'd forgotten his name, although she was sure he had told her when he'd appeared at the door. Suddenly, it seemed so important to know his name, like her son's very life hinged on knowing it.

"I'm sorry," she said, leaning over, handing the trembling glass to the man, "your name was... ?"

"Just call me Derron, Mrs.Leary."

"Derron," she said, feeling nothing at all. Just numbness. Like this was some sort of strange dream, not quite real.

He took the glass from her, took a long drink from it, wiped his brow, and set the glass on the end table next to the couch. Then he folded his hands together and looked across at Delores. "The reason I'm here, Mrs. Leary, is that your son, Andy, is what we call Missing in Action." He paused for a moment watching. She sat in her chair, hands neatly folded on her lap, staring at the young man, watching his mouth move. Feeling nothing still, numb from head to toe. Staring at this man, this boy, because that's all he was, a boy who'd been given the task of telling the unspeakable to the mother of another boy he probably never even met. While older men, politicians and rogues who planned all the wars, the attacks, sat in comfy leather chairs, she imagined, smoking cigars, and drinking twenty year old brandy, thinking up their next stratagem, not thinking of the lives of these boys and their families that would be affected by what to them were games, mere games. In her mind she saw them laughing and carrying on, maybe tossing in a dirty joke or an ethnic joke here or there. Maybe one about Arabs, no doubt one about Arabs, Iraqis. There always had to be someone to kick around, to blame for things, to look down on. Someone to feel better than. To stomp on. But we're all people, she thought, aren't we? If we kill one of theirs, if we kill fifty of theirs, there are still fifty sets of parents on their side who have lost a son. Just like her—Missing in Action. She knew what that meant, even though he went on to explain: "This means nothing more than that his whereabouts are currently unaccounted for."

She nodded stiffly, only because it was what he wanted her to do. But, then, she put her head down and she couldn't help herself. She started to weep. Sitting straight upright, her hands positioned along the blue denim covering her upper thighs, she cried like a fountain, silently spouting the tears she'd held for hours, since she'd gotten the call and had seen what was coming.

Andy was dead. She knew he was and nothing that this or any other person could say would change that. Missing in Action just meant they hadn't found him yet. She showed the Sergeant to the door. He turned sharply when she opened the screen door and shook her hand. "We'll let you know when we have more information. And don't be overly concerned. He may just be misplaced for the moment."

Misplaced. What a strange way to put it and what a terrible, cowardly thing to do, to lie to a dead boy's mother. She felt like saying something, the anger building in her, but said only, "Thank you, Sergeant," and watched him walk stiffly, cap in hand, to his waiting car.

Just misplaced. She almost wanted to laugh aloud, cackle rudely at the boy, but the hollow pit in her chest prevented her from doing so. It was the place where her heart had been—her misplaced heart.

She had started working at the high school when Andy had just entered his freshman year. Why had she taken the job there after losing the job at the real estate agency? Because she couldn't stand to be too far away from him, to lose a grip on her little boy?

In four short years that probably felt like decades to Andy, she'd watched him mature into a young man in the halls of that high school. She'd seen him gain confidence and muscle and add a swagger to his step as he approached the girls his age, who all seemed to adore him. He'd been the quarterback on the football team, a pitcher in baseball. Some college was bound to pick him up, award him a sports scholarship, despite his grades, which hadn't been too bad, really. He was good. So why had he shut the door on them, shut the door on his education and gone the way he'd gone?

Some mistakes you can change, some things you can go back and fix but this, as it seemed to turn out, was not one of them. But one life to give to my country. Nathan Hale. The fabled phrase being that he'd regretted that he'd but one life to give to his country. Only twenty-one when he was hanged by the British. She wasn't sure why she remembered these facts all of the sudden, this remnant of her own studies long since past, but the words rang with a shrill clarity through her brain as she sipped her morning coffee and read the headlines about the war, about Iraq, a place no one in their right mind would go to of their own volition. A hostile land, but a land filled with people, people like she and Andy, with mothers and sons and brothers and fathers. Who breathed the same air, needed food and water, love and understanding. Killing each other for what? Some political agenda? Differences of opinion? For private capitalistic interests of certain politicos afraid that they and their buddies might lose a share of their profits? For the flexing of the almighty male muscle? Aggression, ape-like shows of brutality? King of the hill politics? Terrorizing a country because of a few bad apples who just so happened, unfortunately, to have been in power at the time and had been, ironically, terrorizing their own citizens? Not clear. Made no sense. Police force of the world USA. Andy wasn't a Fortunate Son. And Delores sure as hell didn't feel like a Fortunate Mother these days either. No way, not at all. All she saw of the world now was through tear-stained eyes. it was like gazing through a glass of water, a river of tears.

She didn't know why she called him—Jerry, her ex, the role model for her boy to sacrifice himself for a war he knew nothing about. He, like his father, had gone to fight other men's battles, fighting for secret political and businessmen's agendas behind the red white and blue shining in the sun as a facade for the real reasons for these battles of power. Why did men always start wars? To overcome insecurities about the sizes of their penises? To show that their muscles were bigger than those of the other testosterone-laced warriors?

When Jerry pulled up to the door in his beat up Chevy Blazer, she was almost sorry she'd called him. What had she been thinking? Their marriage had been a sham for a long time. Ever since the war, since he'd come home with the severed arm. He'd lost more than an arm then. He'd lost his humanity, his spirit. He was not the man he had been, but seemed, after Vietnam, to be just a shell of that person. Still she had stayed with him for a long time, too long. Long enough to give birth to Andy and Ricky. She'd felt guilty about it, somehow, that he had gotten injured. She took care of him. But why? After twelve years of marriage she asked herself that question and realized how ridiculous her guilt was. She had not committed war, she had not ripped off his arm in the middle of a fire fight. She had done nothing but absorb his pain for twelve long, sad, empty years. And, after twelve years she had packed Jerry's bags one sunny autumn day and told him to move out. He must have seen it coming—he knew they didn't have a functioning marriage any-more—because all he did was nod and pick up the bags, a hang-dog look on his face, and walked out the door.

And this was the man that Andy had been inspired by. He hadn't known his father before the shell shock of war, how he had smiled and laughed and imitated his high school teachers. He had, in fact, been the class clown. And after the war, if he cracked a smile once in a month it was something of an aberration, a miracle almost, the ghost of the Jerry she had known in the past.

She stood by the front door, peering out the little window, watching him, in his Cubs cap, slam the door of his Blazer, walk around the car slowly, and trudge up the walk. When he got to the steps, she opened the door before he could ring the bell. He almost fell into the house, but caught himself, his good arm swinging in the air—he looked like a high wire walker, catching his balance and straightening his body in one fluid motion. Jerry could be more graceful looking than she'd ever suspected, but after years of doing the one-armed-man routine, she figured he'd mastered it pretty well.

"Got a beer?" were the first words out of his mouth. Not "Hello," or "How're the boys?" or "How are you?," nothing as cordial as that. Just, "Got a beer?"—like he stopped over there every other day.

"Uh, no, Jerry. Sorry about that. No beer." He pulled his cap off and stared at her, looking confused for a moment, then shrugged. "Okay," he said. His reddish hair was thinning and mussed, he had what looked like two days of stubble on his face, and was wearing one of those red checked flannel shirts that he seemed so fond of. It could have been the same one she saw him in the last time he'd been there—what had it been, two, three months ago when he'd actually shown up to visit with Ricky, and taken him to a baseball game?

He walked into the living room and dropped down on the couch, like he belonged there, like he still lived there. Delores just stared at the man, wondering who he was, who he had become, and wondering why on earth she had called him here, why she had thought, in a moment of insanity, that he could somehow calm her fears, soothe her sorrows, her feelings of loss.

"If you wanted some beer, you should have brought your own," Delores said, hands on hips. "Anyway, this isn't a fucking social call. It's about our son. It's about Andy. He's missing."

She was staring at him, looking for some reaction in his face, in those foggy eyes. "Missing?" was all he said, like he hadn't served in Nam, like he had no understanding of what the word meant.

"Yes, Jerry, missing, like Missing in Action, MIA, gone, gone, gone." She raised a hand to her face to cover the tears and to block out everything—she didn't want to see the world right now, and certainly didn't want to see Jerry's reaction, him feeling sorry for her, he of all people. In a moment though, through the silence of the room, the heaviness of her sobs in a room decorated with cheery daisy covered wallpaper (what had she been thinking when she did that?), she felt his thick hand on her back tentatively, and he said in his breathy voice, "It's okay, Delores. It'll be all right." To which she reacted violently, shaking his hand off of her, staring at his dumb, emotionless face, and shouting, "No, Jerry, it will not be all right, it was never all right! You are not all right—look what they did to you—your son is not all right, this world is not all right as long as we're sending our boys to be slaughtered for no logical reason!"

He was staring back at her now, arms by his sides, his amputated limp hanging there in the tied off shirt, a hopeless, useless appendage, a reminder of what Jerry seemed to have become—a hollow, hopeless, defenseless man. He looked like he was about to cry, and Delores was immediately sorry, but she wouldn't, she couldn't say it, just held her breath waiting for him to go, just go. After a few minutes he got the idea, picked up his baseball cap off the couch, and mumbled, "I'm sorry, I was just trying to help." He stood there, looking at her and stumbled toward the door without another word. Delores watched him and calmly said, as he was opening the screen door, "He's dead, Jerry. Our son is dead." He didn't seem to hear it or chose not to as the screen door slammed behind him and he walked stiffly, like some sort of slow monster, long since robbed of his powers, back to his car.

Days went by, then weeks without any further word from the Army, from Sergeant Young. The war went on, more reports of the constantly increasing death toll of American soldiers, and of prisoners being beheaded, coming every day. It got to the point where she didn't want to hear any more. She just wanted to stuff her fingers in her ears, and shut her eyes tight, not hear or see another word about war. Everywhere she went—the grocery store, the hairdresser, the gas station—people were talking about it. How many more of their kids would die? The argument over whether the President had been right in invading the country and whether it was unpatriotic to question his intent in getting the terrorists. She wanted to move to a different country, a place where her son would not have been sent to such a place to lay his life on the line. But it was too late for that now anyway. Too late, too late, too late.

So what do you do when you think your son is dead? What can you do is the question? You go on through the motions, throwing loads of laundry into the washing machine, clearing dishes from the dishwasher, sweeping the floor, cutting the grass, making coffee, reading the newspaper, like everything's okay, everything's normal.

But nothing's okay, nothing's normal, nothing's the same. The world has been spun on its side, and it's like you're a top spinning, looking for something to grab onto to regain your balance, but there's nothing to grab, nothing at all. You close your eyes and listen to the cars swish by, hearing the rain water splashing in the street. And, as the sun falls and the shadowy lines of night creep into the solitude of your room, you wonder if the next person who knocks on the door, or the next voice on the phone, will be that of your son, your missing son.

She heard nothing, but was afraid to call the Sergeant, afraid almost to breathe. She played a game, acted as if Andy were on a vacation somewhere. She even imagined where he was, at a beach somewhere, Florida maybe. She would close her eyes and imagine watching him lay a towel on the hot sand, see the perspiration sliding down his cheek and chin. Imagine him with his buddies, sneaking beers out of a small cooler and making cracks about some of the girls walking by in their skimpy bikinis. "Get a load of that one," she could hear him say, tipping his head towards a blonde-haired girl in a hot pink bikini, hitting his friend, Joe, with the back of his hand. "I'd love to get a load of that, are you kiddin?" And then they were laughing, crazy carefree laughter, the way they had used to, the way he had, before...before....

It was just after their last football game of the season. Their senior year. Their last football game. It was one o'clock in the morning when she'd heard a ruckus outside, swept back the lace curtains in her bedroom and peered out the window to see Andy and Ricky and Joe walking arm in arm, laughing and singing the lyrics to "Satisfaction" at the top of their lungs, slipping and swaying down the sidewalk, this huge six-legged drunken teenage monster boy. It was a wonder people weren't yelling out the window and that a police car wasn't rolling up beside them to give them a talking to. It was all she could do to get her robe wrapped around her and hop down the stairs when she heard the front door open and the three boys tumble into her foyer laughing and singing and falling onto the floor. Punching each other and howling and being boys. Andy among the pile on the floor with his broad grin and deep laugh, long arms and legs sprawled by his side like a helpless infant. Not a fragment of anything but innocence in his big brown eyes. She'd meant to yell at them, scold them for drinking, tell them they were being way too loud and disrespectful, that people were sleeping. But seeing them, seeing Andy like that, she'd just melted, stood there in the doorway watching them with her arms crossed in front of her, a stern look painted on her face. It was all she could do to stop from laughing. Taking it all in, their youth, their innocence, their exuberance. Drinking it in with her eyes, this wide smile on her face, feeling like her face was going to crack she was smiling so widely then.

And that moment was so brief, just a minute sliver of the pie, a sparkling fleck of dust in the nighttime, a single moment in the infinite moments of time.

She trudged to work every day at the high school, where she worked in the office. She no longer felt like the young woman she had once been, who rushed headlong into the new day, excited to meet the challenges awaiting her. Now it was like life had become a series of motions repeated on a daily basis. There no longer seemed to be any point in any of it. And her mind was always on Andy. There was a hole inside of her. It wasn't just her son, but it felt like her heart was also missing in action.

She was driving to work on a lightly traveled road when she saw a fuzzy gray object streak in front of her car. She swerved to miss it, almost running off the road, and squealed her brakes. She got out of the car, shaking, looking back at the space where she had been. The sun was shining and the birds were chirping from the overhanging trees that swayed in the gentle summer breeze. In the middle of the road lay a small squirrel motionless on his side, his eyes closed, his tiny little paws curled up under his little jaw. And then there was the shock—his snow white belly. It was totally unexpected. She had assumed squirrels were all just gray or brown or something in between. She had never really given them much thought. She walked toward the animal cautiously, shaking at the thought that she had killed this innocent creature, tears running down her cheeks, then she was sobbing.

There was the sound of a car approaching. The little animal was lying right on the double yellow line. She couldn't let the remnant of her violent act be made even worse. So she stood like a guard in front of the little animal, her feet planted firmly, her arms raised, palms forward as a small red sports car approached and squealed its brakes to a stop, just a foot from where she was standing, where she would not budge. Two young men in business suits yelled at her, one yelling "Get out of the road, crazy lunatic!," the other yelling "Loony bitch!" Okay, she was a lunatic, a loony bitch and she was sure she must look like a sight, a fright, her mascara all running down her cheeks now from the tears, but she didn't care. She had murdered the little squirrel with her monster machine and the least she could do was give it a decent burial. The tremors ran through her body as the tiny red car sputtered off. She pulled off her sweater and carefully bent down to the spot where he lay, so peacefully, so sadly, the birds singing his eulogy, the sun warming the remains of his soul. Did animals have souls? She didn't know, but she assumed they did. She got right next to the gray squirrel. She was not afraid, bent down and stroked its soft white belly, so naked looking in the daylight, in the bright sun, the tears streaming down her cheeks now. She stared at him for thirty seconds or so, then wrapped him up like an infant in her sweater and held the tiny animal close to her breast.

Once inside the car, she put the sweater on the passenger seat beside her and pulled her cell phone out of her purse. She dialed the school's number and told the vice principal, Anne McCoffrey, that she'd had a little accident. No, she was all right, she said. Just a little shook up. She would be to work a little late. Then she turned the car around and, her hands still shaking on the wheel, headed back home. There she would get out her shovel and, the tears still flowing, would try not to think about what she was really thinking, dig a three foot deep hole in her garden behind the tomato plants and plant her little friend, the innocent victim, the one who hadn't known, who hadn't seen her coming. Lying him in a place of peace and, she hoped, eternal rest.

Two months after Sergeant Young came to her door and shattered her world, she still could not think straight, could not go an hour without crying or feeling like she was about to cry. She called the Army every day, sometimes twice, three times a day and the answer was always the same: No news.

She was falling apart.

Sometimes it didn't seem like she could make it through another day.

At night she would awaken three, sometimes four times for, it seemed, no reason at all. But there was a reason. A waiting, an expectancy of something. Something like Andy rushing through the door, that big wide grin on his face as he would throw his muscled arms around her and she would say, softly, almost to herself, patting his back lightly: "You made it, you finally made it home."

Other times there were nightmares. Grotesque images of someone who looked like Andy, starting as a teenager, with the gleaming smile, the bright clear eyes, the reddened cheeks from spending a crisp winter day playing out in the snow and ice. And after that the face would change before her eyes, melt almost so that it was dripping, misshapen, like a melted candle and the smile would turn downward, disappear altogether into the bottom of his chin. And his body would become deformed, parts of limbs hanging, looking more like a tattered scarecrow. It was sort of a theme, a recurring dream. The most terrifying of all was when, instead of flying through the door to greet her, wrap his arms around her, he came through the door and reached out for her but had nothing to reach with, lacking arms, only the sockets where they should have been remaining, and, as he reached over to hug her, he fell face first to the floor, and smashed his face cracking like glass, while she helplessly bent down, weeping, shaking, crying "Andy, are you okay, are you okay, Honey?" And in the midst of all this Ricky would show up with a broom and a dust pan, seemingly without emotion, and sweep the cracked shards of his brother's face into the pan and toss them into the trash, only his brother's torso remaining, lifeless on the floor, a hunk of useless flesh which she clung to, her heart nearing the breaking point, wailing to the ceiling, but there was no one there, no one was listening. What of God, where was he, if he was, and why wouldn't he do something to bring her child back to her?

She would wake up, her body drenched in sweat, her heart pounding and her mind racing, it taking a minute to realize that no, this had not actually happened, it was just a dream. She would sit up in bed, her arms wrapped around herself, holding herself like a baby. Then, unable to sleep, she would fix herself a cup of tea, turn on the tube, drape a blanket over herself, her cold sweat bringing a chill to her body. If she was having a lucky night she might doze off an hour or two before it was time to wake up again and go through the morning drudgery of getting ready for work. Other nights she wasn't so lucky and would never fall asleep at all, but would prepare herself to work, and drag herself through the day like some sort of awakened corpse, one of the faceless nameless creatures in that old movie, Dawn of the Dead, walking around that shopping mall aimlessly reaching, reaching, reaching for something, for nothing, for everything.

She told herself that she was strong, but no one could be this strong. She would talk to friends. Her oldest, dearest friend, Becky, would sit there and hold her and cry with her. They had grown up together, gotten married and had children together and had been close always, sharing their secrets, loves, and hates, their fear and their pain. The pain and fear that comes from raising a child in this world. And when you lose a child—what greater pain does a mother have than that? They were like sisters, holding each other, Becky comforting Delores through the night. But when Becky left the pain was still there, there was no getting rid of it. And Jerry—Jerry was Andy's father, but he was more like a child than anything. He just didn't seem to comprehend. Ricky—you couldn't even talk to him about it.

When she had first told Ricky that Andy was Missing in Action, he had just smiled and wrapped his arms around his mother, saying, "Don't worry, Mom. He'll be back. He's just missing. Don't go worrying for nothing." Then, with a smile reminiscent of Andy's but not quite as broad or convincing, he had walked off to school, whistling, actually whistling, as he'd picked up his books and pushed open the screen door.

And after that there had been little scenes. He was in a total state of denial, it seemed. One time sitting next to each other at dinner. The silence heavy between them. Delores watched as Ricky ate, looking at the empty seat beside him. She'd started crying then, and Ricky had looked up at her for an instance, seemingly annoyed. Then he'd returned his attention to his steak, his knife and fork poised for attack.

She had said then, "He's not coming home, Ricky. Your brother's dead." In response to which Andy had thrown his utensils across the room, hitting the wall, then stood up and yelled at her, "I'm not going to take this, you acting like this. My brother is not dead. He's missing, missing, missing ... that's what the man said, right? Do you know what missing means? They don't know where he is right now, that's all. They didn't say he was dead!" He stormed out of the room then, and out of the house. She would have liked to console him, put her arms around him, and let him sink against her, like he used to, but he was becoming a man in his own right now, seventeen years old. He was no mama's boy anymore. He was at the age where, in the world of boys, showing his feelings was not allowed, was subject to the ridicule of all his peers.

But that wasn't what bothered Delores Leary. What bothered her most was the thought that maybe he wasn't feeling anything but anger. That maybe he really believed that Andy was still alive. Maybe Ricky was just in a state of total denial. And what would happen when he came out of it? Would he fall, would he break down? Would he, could he ever be the same without his big brother?

She tossed and turned at night, woke up staring at the clock, dragged herself to work, trying to find any information, any information about Andy, only to find nothing, an emptiness growing inside of her, like a black hole, threatening to swallow her up from the inside out. That was how it felt.

She woke up one morning and she just couldn't go on. Couldn't even get out of her bed. She reached for the phone on her night stand and called in sick, gave her excuses and her regrets. Then lay there without an ounce of energy to move, without an ounce of motivation to do so.

Her son stopped in for a moment at her doorway and stared at her, just stared. "You're not going to work today?" he asked, to which she replied. "No, what's the point?"

"Is there anything I can get you?"

"No, nothing." To which he shrugged, shuffled with his hands in his khaki pockets, stared at his feet and mumbled, "Well, guess I gotta go."

"Okay, Sweetie," she said, and then, as he was walking away, without knowing why, said, "Be careful out there." Because that was how she felt. That it was a dangerous world. You couldn't take anything for granted anymore, not a thing.

She spent the day watching television and eating Oreos, dropping napkins and wrappers on her nightstand. A tiny mountain of paper would be there by the end of the day. The television voices, the inane smiles of its subjects, numbed her. It was a make believe world, a world of fantasy. The phone rang several times but she wouldn't answer it.

When Ricky came home from school and stopped in on her he came in slowly, cautiously. "Mom," he said, "are you all right?"

She sighed, as he stood at the side of her bed. "No, Honey, I'm not all right, I'm not I'm not I'm not." She broke down then, crying, and he bent down awkwardly and put one arm around her as she wept in his arms. After a few minutes she took a deep long breath and said, "I'm sorry, Ricky for not being strong for you, for disappointing you." To which Ricky said, "No, Mom, it's all right, you know it's all right. You've been taking care of me, of us, for so long, sometimes we forget that you need taking care of, too." She smiled at him and put her hand on his face. Palm to cheek. "I love you, Ricky, I love you so much," she said, wrapping her arms tightly around her son, closing her eyes as the tears dripped off her cheeks.

And that night she slept, exhausted by it all, by the endless days of thinking, the endless nights of hoping.

It was that night that her son appeared in her dream, not a grotesque facsimile of Andy as in past dreams, but the perfect face of Andy, with all the lightness and clarity of his soul surrounding him as he walked out of what seemed like a foggy mist. She was sitting on the top of a hill for some reason, and out of this cloud appeared Andy, fresh as the morning sun, not a care in the world written on his face. Walking so calmly toward her, that wide smile lighting up the sky it seemed. He walked right toward her and paused, looking her right in the eye. Then he bent down on one crooked knee, grabbed one of her hands in his and said to her, "I'm fine, Mom. I'll be fine. There is no more pain anymore. I'm in a good place and you don't have to worry about me anymore, do you understand?" She started to cry in the dream, but he put his hand on her face, much like Delores had placed her hand on Ricky's face that same evening. And Andy said, "Don't cry for me, Mom. I'm all right." She stopped crying then and stared at him, her beautiful boy. For a second there was a flash of a body—his body—lying motionless in a field, eyes closed, arms lying beside him, his rifle laying on the hard dirt beside him. The image passed and it was Andy again. He nodded at her, smiling, then got up, turned and walked back to the cloud. He moved calmly into it and disappeared.

At that instant she awoke and felt a presence in the room. She looked around in the dark and seemed to see tiny lights. Or was she just imagining it? Imagining that the spirit of her son was there with her now, trying to console her, to make her feel at peace. And, oddly, she did feel better somehow. The pit of emptiness, of the unknown, of trying to understand it had been replaced, it seemed, with a calmness. Like the waves of the ocean washing gently upon the shores of time.

The next morning she got out of bed and felt different.

She was sitting on her porch, looking out at the day, waiting for him. And at ten to nine in the morning, Sergeant Young appeared right on schedule, pulling his car up to the curb, shutting his door softly, and walking toward the house, jaw set, to give her the news, the news she already knew.

An hour later, the Sergeant long gone, there was another knock on the door. Delores wiped her eyes, and got off the couch where she lay. When she opened the door, a young cub scout was standing there with bags of caramel corn to sell. She smiled at him as he said his name—Matthew Stevens—gave his learned spiel about raising money for the troop. "Okay," she said. "I'll take two, no wait ... give me three."

"That'll be six dollars," the boy said.

"Oh, wait," Delores said. "I left my money upstairs. Can you wait for me for a second?" The little brown-haired boy nodded. She invited him into the foyer, then ran upstairs to her sons' room.

When she came back down she said, "Oh, there's my purse," as if she had forgotten it, headed for the living room and pulled a five and a one out of her wallet. Then she walked toward the boy and handed him the money. He handed her the plastic wrapped bags of caramel corn. Then she pulled out the thing she held behind her back, and handed it to the boy.

"Umm, we generally only accept money, M'am."

"No, you don't understand," she said, this is for you. I want you to have it. It's very special. It was my son's. He was a Cub Scout, too, but he would want you to have it now."

"Well," he said, looking down at the baseball mitt, putting it on his hand and pounding it lightly with his fist, "if you really think it's all right ..."

She reached over and brushed the boy's hair out of his face quickly, and looked deep into his eyes. "I know it's all right, Matthew. Just think of it as a present from Andy."

"Andy?"

"Andy was my son."

"Thanks, M'am. It's a nice mitt." He smiled, picked up his bag with his other hand and walked back down the walk, looking back at Delores, the mitt under his arm, and waved.

Delores smiled at the boy and waved back. In a moment, she thought, he would be walking down the street, out of sight, gone, gone forever.

Lessons and Lies

It was the year the Nazis were threatening to march in Robert Friedman's hometown.

It was the year that the Cubs wouldn't win the pennant (again). And it was the year that Robert Friedman's interest in the Cubs was starting to be overshadowed by something else....

Robert was seventeen years old and had never been on a date. It wasn't that he wasn't interested in girls. It wasn't even that he couldn't imagine why any girl would even think about going out with him. It was that he didn't know if any girl on earth even knew he existed. Earth, for this purpose, being the country of the United States, State of Illinois, Village of Skokie, and school, Niles North High School.

He didn't know how to act with girls, didn't know what to say to them, got flustered, sweaty palms, knocking knees, pink cheeks, just being around them. It was nuts. While other guys in the neighborhood were hanging around with all the local girls and taking them out on dates, then talking about their exploits in the park at night, smoking their cigarettes, strutting and spouting off about what base they got to with Martha Wasserman or Sharon Silverstein or Penny Moskowitz, Robert would smile nervously at them, remaining on the fringes of the group with his hands jammed in his pockets. He feigned understanding what it was all about, while Steve Bittermyer and Ralph Goldman went on and on, showing what big men they were.

"We were at the drive-in, see," Bittermyer was saying. "You know about drive-ins, right?" The five other guys circled around them as Bittermyer smoked his twig, bounced the basketball in the dark, and then broke out laughing. "Yeah, drive-ins."

"Sure, who doesn't know about drive-ins?"

"Well, anyway, Sharon spilled her drink on her blouse. And, like, I gotta tell ya, I almost think she did it on purpose. So, I say to her, 'Why don't you just take it off and let it dry. Nobody'll see, it's dark out here. You don't want to be sitting soaking wet like that all night, do ya?' And she gives me this look, sorta like, I know what you're doing. But it was only for a second, and then she's got the little Miss Innocent face on again. So I say, 'Come on, we can get in the back, nobody'll see us back there for sure.' I mean, we were in my dad's Olds 98. It's like a boat, y'know? And Sharon, she says, "Okay," slides out of the car on her side and climbs in the back. And me, I slide in the back with her, and help her unbutton her shirt, and next thing you know, we're goin' at it—damn was she hot to trot—and in a matter of minutes I've got the shirt off and the bra off and I'm sitting there holding naked breast. God, is anything so glorious as naked breast?" Then all of the sudden he turns to Robert. "What-taya think of that, Friedman? Whattaya think that feels like?" And all the other guys started laughing again, only this time even harder.

He didn't move, just stood there, until the story continued. Then he slipped back, slipped away, until he was halfway back to his house, not one of them even noticing, the echo of their ghostly laughter in the dark of the park ringing in his ears.

Sandy Auerbach had the most beautiful hair Robert Friedman had ever seen. It was golden like wheat and shimmered in the sunlight. It flowed down her back like a brilliant light waterfall. Sandy Auerbach had the most beautiful blue eyes, the most beautiful smile, the most beautiful little pug nose, the most beautiful long legs and ass and breasts, and that smile, and her teeth and that hair—she was like a dream, and she infested his mind, he couldn't shake her out of it. Not that he'd had the courage to say anything to her, not even a word.

He would get to his psychology class early, rushing through the halls to get to room A-212 ahead of the crowd, just so he could be there to watch Sandy walk into the classroom with that long stroll and sway of hers, smiling and chewing her gum and walking and smelling ... God, she smelled like a garden of lilacs, she smelled so good walking past him and taking her seat behind him. Occasionally he'd let the pencil roll off his desk and, bending down to get it, would glance back in her direction. Sometimes she'd wear this short black skirt and these long black boots.

When the teacher got in front of the class and started talking, it was all Robert could do to keep his mind on his words because all Robert could think of was Sandy Sandy Sandy, wondering what she was doing there behind him, crossing her legs, smiling, looking intently at the teacher, filing her nails...what?

"Why don't you talk to her, you twerp?" Warren Feingold said, pulling his Saran-wrapped sandwich out of his paper lunch bag. "God, bologna again. Jesus, I told my mom I'm sick of bologna, but does she listen? What you got, Robert?"

"Tuna. Want to trade?"

"Yeah, sure." They swapped sandwiches and began unwrapping them.

"Mayo, she put mayo on it, too. Whatta I look like, a goy?"

"Maybe she was out of mustard."

"No, no, we're never out of mustard. My dad uses it for everything. His salami, his steak, his eggs. I think he even shaves with it. Believe me when I tell you if we were ever out of mustard, my dad would have a major fit like you wouldn't believe."

"I don't believe it," Robert said. Warren acted like he didn't hear Robert.

"So, what's the problem with this Auerbach chick? You think she's superhuman or something? Like a goddess? You drool all over her and get speechless like "Ayyy ahhh uhhhh, Sand-eeeeee!"'" He was making faces, his mouth all contorted like he was some sort of whacked out monster, like on the Friday night Creature Features.

"Come on, Robert, listen to me. She's just a G I R L, girl. That's all. Nothing to be afraid of. Talk to her for Godssakes."

"Ha, yeah, right, tell me about it, Warren. How many girls have you been out with besides Rachel in your life? What've you been going out with her since you were two or something?"

"Yeah, well, I don't know. Maybe I'm getting tired of that. Maybe I'm thinking of searching out new frontiers. You know how when those guys landed on the moon and said 'One small step for man, one great leap for mankind?' I think Rachel may just be the one small step for Warren Feingold. I think I'm ready to leap."

Robert put down his sandwich and looked at Warren. "Really? When did this all happen?"

"It happened about 11 o'clock on Saturday night when I was dropping Rachel off at her house. We were parked there like usual, necking and whatnot, and I slipped my hand under her blouse and she clapped her hand on mine, just like we haven't been dating like forever. Like it's 1955 or something. Jesus, what happened to the sexual revolution and all that? I mean, come on. It's 1975, and I can't even feel my girlfriend's bare breast."

"Shit," Robert said.

"Yeah, shit is right. I'm sick of it." Warren sat there, looking down at his hands. Then, without warning, he shifted gears, turned to Robert and said, "So, are you gonna talk to her, ask her out, or what?" Robert glanced in the direction of the table where she sat— the cheerleaders' table. She was talking to three of the other girls across the table, smiling and gesticulating, two blond-haired, letter-jacketed football players standing close behind her. The guys were Shawn Davis, the quarterback, who she was going out with, and Ted Harris, his star receiver. Robert turned back around to Warren and said, "Yeah, right. Talk to her. Like that's gonna happen, Warren.

She's beautiful and popular and, and ... look at me. Talking to her? I just don't see how that could ever happen."

At dinner that night, Robert was picking at his peas, while his older brother, Stuart, was kicking him under the table. "Knock it off," he whispered to Stuart, but Stuart just smiled and kicked him again, harder this time. Stuart the Tormenter. "What's the matter, Mr. Mope, don't like your peas?"

"Leave your brother alone, Stu," Mrs. Friedman said.

"Dora," his father said, "the boy is seventeen, he can fight his own battles."

Stu grinned.

"Did you boys hear the news?" Mr. Friedman said, folding his newspaper and setting it aside.

The two of them looked up. Their father was shaking his head.

"Seems somebody painted a swastika on the side of the Belmont Theatre. Some wise guy kids probably from Evanston or the city, who knows. Probably shvartzes."

Robert cringed inside at the use of that word: shvratzes.

"Do you have to say that, Dad?"

"Say what, what did I say?"

"God. Shvartzes. A little ironic...somebody's drawing swastikas and you're pointing fingers although you don't even know, and calling black people shvartzes. Do you see any irony there?"

"Irony, shmirony. I'm not a too-smart-for-his-own-good school boy like you with your hi-falutin vocabulary. Just telling you who I think might have done it."

Robert sighed and looked at his mother, who didn't say a word and was looking down at her plate, moving pieces of steak around but not eating any of them. Then he looked at Stu, who was shoveling it in like there was no tomorrow.

"It is pretty disturbing," Mr. Friedman said, a hunk of meat pushing out his cheek. "You live in a town where half of us are Jewish and you still have to deal with this crap. Will it ever end?"

"So, they don't know who did it?" Robert asked. "No, not really. It was there in the morning when the manager showed up. But someone said they might have seen somebody driving away from there last night. In an old Chevy with a bunch of shvartzes...excuse me..." he said, giving Robert a condescending look, "black boys in it, maybe."

"Maybe? Who saw them?"

"Not sure. It's all secondhand news. Herb down at the drugstore said he knew a guy who'd heard about it ... you know how that goes."

"Well, if nobody knows, nobody knows."

Stu dropped his fork on to his empty plate and said, "I don't know what the big deal is. It's just a bunch of lines on a wall. Big deal. They can paint over it."

No one said a word. The three of them just sat there, staring at Stu, who gazed back and forth between their faces and then said, "What?...What'd I say?"

There was talk of Nazis wanting to come march in the town that summer—American Nazis. Why, no one knew, except to stir things up. Quite a few Holocaust survivors had settled in this sleepy little village, this little suburb of Chicago, after World War II, most of them probably thinking that here they would be safe from all they had endured, safe in the heartland of America. But even though it annoyed Robert, he took little heed of all this, because his mind and heart were elsewhere, stuck on that image of beauty that he had formulated in his mind, who sat behind him in his Psych class, and whose name was stuck on his tongue: Sandy Sandy Sandy ... Sandy Auerbach.

"You're such a putz, you know what a putz is?" Warren said, as they walked to school the next day.

"Yeah, I know what a putz is. It's what your father calls you all the time."

"No shit. Hey, Robert, you got a cigarette? We could sneak a quick one before class. Come on. Oh, yeah, I forgot...you don't smoke. You're too square."

"Shit, Warren, you should hear how my dad coughs at the sink every night at dinner with his smoking. Everybody gets real quiet and he hacks away and it's enough to make me want to cough up my entire dinner. It's disgusting."

He looked at Robert and rolled his eyes. "God, Robert, one little smoke won't kill ya. You've got to loosen up a little. Maybe then Sandy what's-her-face would think you're cool, and you'd have the guts to say boo to her."

"Yeah, right."

"Come on, Rob. I know she's a smoker. She's out there in the parking lot every lunch period with her group puffing away like a pro. How'd you like to have those gorgeous succulent lips puffing away on you, huh?"

"Jesus, Warren, you're one perverted freak, you know that?"

"What's perverted about that? It's nature, dude. Loosen up, Robert, I'm telling you. It's for your own good." As they walked he took his cigarettes—a pack of Camels—out of his back pack, took one out and lit it up. "Come on, stud, one puff."

Warren stopped and stood by a tree, leaning against it.

"Okay, okay," Robert said, "if this'll make you shut up."

Warren passed him the cigarette and Robert put it between his lips. Then he took it out.

"No, genius, you've got to inhale, breathe in the smoke. Otherwise it doesn't count."

"Breathe it in. Okay, okay." Robert sucked the warm smoke into his lungs and immediately starting choking and coughing. Warren started laughing wildly and flailing his arms about like he'd just seen the funniest thing in his life, until Robert started to regain his breath and Warren said, "Well, that was great. God, are you a baby or what? Jesus, how are we ever gonna make you a man? Gimme the stick back anyway," Warren said, heading off to school. Robert stood there for a moment, then followed behind him.

She walked in a minute after he got to his seat. His head was down. He was pretending to read his book. He thought she looked at him for a second. At least it looked like that out of the corner of his eye. Or was he wrong? God, what the hell was wrong with him anyway? He knew she was in a league beyond his. Not that he was in any league at all if he thought about it too long. Better not to think about it, no don't even go there, he told himself. Shit.

"Robert," he heard someone say. A voice from behind. It was her. She was saying his name. He didn't know what to do.

"Hey, Robert!" she said. He turned around with a lump in his throat and tried to smile. She was looking at him.

"Could you get my pencil for me, Robert?" she said, pouting, staring at him with those big brown eyes of hers. "I dropped it." He didn't move. "On the floor," she said.

He bent down to pick it up, feeling his face turn hot, and handed it back to her. Her hand touched his for a second, and she said, "Thank you."

He turned around in his seat quickly. He heard girls laughing behind him. His face was red, his palms were sweaty, and his heart was racing. He was going to die. He was seventeen years old and he was going to die, keel right over in his Psych class. What would his parents say? He felt bad for them, but in other ways thought it would serve them right. Did they have even a clue of who he was? Did they care?

He sat through the class, not hearing a word Mr. Dewar said. The minutes ticked in slow motion on the clock over the teacher's head. Finally, years, decades later, it seemed, the bell finally rang. Robert scribbled down the assignment Mr. Dewar had written on the board and then closed his assignment book and shoved it and his psych book into his backpack. As he was doing so he saw a leg, an immobile bare leg standing next to him. He looked up. There, right beside him, stood Sandy Auerbach, holding her books close to her chest and smiling down at him. "Goodbye, Robert," she said. "I hope you have a pleasant rest of the day." He started to say something, but she'd already slipped on her shades and strolled out of the classroom, three other girls following close behind her like an entourage, chattering and giggling and glancing back at Robert with wide smiles on their faces.

"So, she said goodbye to you. Big fuckin' deal."

"Big fuckin' deal? That's all you can say?"

Warren pulled his Saran-wrapped sandwich out of his bag and opened it up. "Oh, God. Not pickle loaf again. The stuff makes me gag. My mom knows it, but she's mad at me, or she never pays attention to me, or something, either one, take your pick. I'll take anything over that shit. Whatta you got?"

"Peanut butter and jelly."

"Shit, I'll take it."

"Okay," Robert said, handing over his sandwich and making the exchange. There was nothing he hated more than PB and J. "So, about Sandy..."

Warren looked right at Robert then with a smug grin on his face. "Yeah, you heard me, Robert. Read my lips: Big ... fuckin' deal. She's playing with you, you know that, don't ya? Playing you for a fool cause she knows you're hot for her."

"Oh, Jesus, thanks a lot. That's all it could possibly be, Warren, right? She couldn't actually like me or anything. That would be too difficult to believe, wouldn't it? I guess I'm just not good enough for her, is that what you're telling me?"

Warren put the remainder of his sandwich back down on the plastic wrap, sighed, and looked over at Robert. "No, dumb fuck. God, you really are a dumb fuck sometimes. You're too good for her."

In the next few days something strange happened. Sandy Auerbach not only looked at Robert when she walked into class, but she actually starting saying "Hi" to him, and, after that, would stop to chat with him before class. Where did he live, she wanted to know, what did he like to do, she'd ask, always beaming at him with that brilliant smile of hers.

In the cafeteria the next day Robert and Warren were eating their sandwiches, not saying much, when a fracas broke out at the cheerleaders' table and the regular din of cafeteria suddenly died down. It was Sandy Auerbach and Shawn Davis going at it. She was screaming at him—it was kind of hard to hear too much from the distance—but he heard her tell him to go to hell and say that she never wanted to see him again. And there was something about a blonde bimbo. Then he was yelling back at her and storming off with his group of jacket jocks.

Warren didn't even look up. He just kept chewing his sandwich and taking slugs from his milk carton.

"What do you think that was all about?" Robert asked.

"Well," Warren said, "apparently there was this big party over the weekend and Davis got shit-faced and wound up with some blonde from South High and your love goddess found him with her. That's the Reader's Digest version."

"How the hell do you know that?"

Warren looked over at Robert, with a crooked grin. "I have my ways, pal, believe me. So, now's your big chance, stud...."

"My big chance?"

Just then a pudgy, pasty-faced girl with black-framed glasses, dressed in a pink dress and white bobby socks walked up behind them with her tray.

"Anyone sitting here?" she asked, pointing at the chair across from them.

Robert looked at Warren, who was looking at the table in front of him.

"No, Rach, sit down if you want," Warren said.

She moved around the table and sat across from Warren, getting herself settled, throwing quick nervous glances at him. Then she looked at Robert, trying to compose herself and smile. It didn't work too well. The smile quickly faded.

"So, how's it going, Robby? Who you have the hots for this week?"

Robert threw a glance at Warren, who rolled his eyes.

"Uh, not sure what you mean, Rachel. You know me," he said. "Stud of the universe." He laughed. "ha ... ha."

"Hmm. Yes." She smiled again and then turned sour, giving him the evil eye like ... like what? It was his fault that Warren was thinking of dumping her? Whatever.

"Well ... I really think I've got to be going. I forgot I've got some trig to finish up before next period. You both have a really wonderful lunch."

As he got up to leave Warren grabbed his arm. There was a pleading look on his face. Then he let go. "Talk to you later, man. Remember what I said."

"Huh?"

"You know."

"Oh. Yeah, that. You can't be serious. Later."

He didn't really know how it happened. He was just walking out of class and there she was strolling beside him, her books held against her chest, smiling at him, making small talk. It felt like he'd been thrust smack dab in the middle of an episode of The Twilight Zone. She was asking him about what he was taking and what he wanted to do and where he might go to college, with those big brown eyes, and that radiant smile. And then came the killer, the thing that really made him think he was dreaming. "There's a dance this Friday. Do you like dances?"

He blushed. He didn't know what to say. He'd never actually been to a dance.

"Ahh, sure, of course," he said. "Who doesn't?"

She moved closer to him then so he was almost pressed against the lockers. He could smell the sweet lilac scent of her perfume.

"I have a little favor to ask of you, Robert."

"You do," he said, and attempted to smile at her, though his heart felt like it was going to beat right through the walls of his chest.

"Yes," she said. "I do." She pouted and stared him right in the eyes. He didn't move. He didn't breathe. "I don't have a date for the dance and I'd really like to go."

"You would."

"Yes," she said, putting her hand on his shoulder, "I would." He was staring down at that hand, at her long fingers with the bright pink nails. "And..." she said, moving her hand toward his chin, and propping it up so that he was inches from her lips, her cheeks, her eyes. "I want you to take me."

"Me?" was all that came out of his mouth. He almost laughed but contained himself. "Me," he said again. "You want me to take you to the dance." He smiled at her, wondering what the joke was.

"Yes," she said, smiling wider, then moving closer to him, so he felt her breath on his ear. "And you know what? I won't take no for an answer. Because I always get my way." Then she pecked him on the cheek, scribbled her phone number on a piece of notebook paper, pressed it into his hand, then sauntered down the hall, waving over her shoulder and saying "Toodles. Call me."

Robert Friedman was left standing in the hallway, students moving hurriedly past him, rushing to their next classes. The bell rang but he didn't move. He just stared down at the numbers scribbled on that little scrap of paper.

"Okay, let me get this straight," Warren said, as they were walking out of the building. "She just came up to you in the hallway after class and asked you to take her to the dance. No way, Man. Have you been smoking some of that funny stuff that I don't know about? And if so, how come you've been keeping it all to yourself?"

"Honest to God. I swear on my mother's grave."

"Your mother's not dead, doofus."

"That's beside the point."

"Oh my God, this if fuckin' unbelievable. Between the two us."

"The two of us? Why's that?"

"Last night Rachel gave it up."

"Gave it up? What, you got to feel her up?"

"No, smartass, read my lips. She gave it up."

"Wow. She gave it up. Son now, I'm probably like the only virgin left in school, I guess, huh?

Suddenly Warren stopped, popped a cigarette into his mouth and stared off into the distance.

"So, you should be happy, right?" He gave Robert a look, took a drag of the cigarette, and exhaled slowly.

"I was, I should be. I don't know. Only one problem. It's like we're engaged or something now. I'm not exactly sure."

"You're not exactly sure?"

"I mean, I said things, during ... I don't know what the fuck I said. That's how it is, stud. Take it from me, Rob, remaining a virgin may not be the worst thing in the world that could ever happen to you." He was shaking his head looking up at the clouds. It looked like it might rain and it looked like Warren might start crying at any moment, too.

His parents were downstairs in the basement watching The Carol Burnett Show on the big color television. His brother was upstairs listening to his records and probably peeking at his Play-boys, stroking himself. Robert quietly picked up a chair from the kitchen table, and brought it to the stove, stood on the chair and opened the cupboard above it, where he knew his mother kept a bottle of cooking wine. He took the bottle out, got off the chair and carefully poured himself a glass of the red stuff. Manischevitz with the Star of David on the label. He put the cap on the bottle and started to drink the glass's contents. Awful, sour, syrupy stuff. But he needed it, he needed something to get the courage—he couldn't just call Sandy Auerbach. He drank the whole glass down, choking on the stuff. He stood still, listening for the sounds of his father and mother downstairs. He vaguely heard his mother's voice like a dull distant echo and heard his father coughing, so he figured he was still safe. At the sink, he turned the water on and filled the bottle back up with enough water that his mother wouldn't know that any was missing. Then he placed the bottle back in the cupboard, feeling a little light-headed as he stepped down off the chair.

He pulled the crumpled piece of paper out of the front pocket of his jeans, picked up the yellow wall phone, and dialed her number. The wine was beginning to do its magic—he didn't feel nervous anymore, only slightly sick to his stomach.

He dialed her number and listened to the metallic buzzing ring on the other end, until someone picked up and said, "Hullo?"

"Sandy?"

"No, just a minute," a man's voice said. "Who's this?"

"Uh...uh...just Robert, Rob. It's just Rob calling you can tell her...from school."

"Just Rob."

"Yes."

"Okay, hold on."

He heard the man—her father he imagined—yelling up to her: "Sandra, phone!" and her answering back, asking who it was, and his reply—"Some guy who says his name is Just Rob." Then, a moment later, she picked up.

"Hello, Just Rob."

"Uh...Hi...Sandy." He paused, caught his breath, didn't know what else to say. She laughed. He felt even more awkward.

"Are we just going to breathe at one another?" she asked.

"Sorry...I..."

"Relax, Rob. What are you so nervous about?"

What could he tell her? That she was so beautiful and popular and he was this inadequate little worm of a person, barely visible in high school. In fact, he had almost made a career in school of blending in with the walls, slipping by unnoticed in the halls. He was the guy who looked familiar but who no one could quite remember.

"So, how are you doing, Rob? Not going to chicken out on our date, Saturday night, are you?"

"Uh, no, no, I'm sorry. I'm such a..."

"Such a what?"

"Nothing, I'm sorry...I..."

"Would you do me a favor, Rob? Or do you like to be called Robert?"

"No, Rob is fine."

"Okay, Rob. Listen to me. You're a very nice guy and I find you very attractive and you don't have to feel so self-conscious."

"I'm sorry."

"And that's another thing. You're going to have to stop that."

"Stop what?"

"Stop saying you're sorry all the time!"

"Okay, okay...I'm...I mean I'm not..."

"So I'll see you on Saturday?" she asked. "At about eight? You know where I live? Do you have a pen and paper?"

He scrambled for pen and paper and scribbled down her address. Then he managed to get off the phone without saying anything else stupid, the butterflies in his stomach circling around, his heart racing like a revving engine. He stood there for a moment, staring at the phone, feeling somewhat optimistic, thinking, Maybe this is the start of something, the start of a life of some sort, for him, for Robert Friedman.

The night of the dance was hot, hotter than he remembered a day in May to be. He'd gotten the keys to his mom's car. His parents had been beaming when he'd told them that he was taking a girl to a dance. His mother had cried out "Our little boy is growing up!" and his father had slapped him on the back, full of fatherly pride, telling Rob stories of his boyhood, the old Why, when I was your age stories that Robert just barely avoided by telling them both what a lot of homework he had that night.

After his shower, he slid on a flowery purple shirt and some black bell bottoms, fixed his hair in the mirror with the blow dryer, getting the longish ends of his wavy, out of control, hair to curl under in back. Standing there primping in front of the mirror, pouting, practicing smiles, despite the overwhelming nervousness, the sickish feeling in his stomach. Just thinking about it. He was taking Sandra Auerbach to a school dance. What the fuck. What planet had he landed on?

His mother tried to kiss him as he left, then licked her fingers and pulled a strand of hair off his forehead.

"Jesus, Mom," he said. I just got it right, and now you're messing it up again!"

"Have fun, Son," his father said, looking up from the television in the living room for a second.

"I will, Dad," he said.

"And, one more thing..."

Oh, shit, Robert thought, he better not be wanting to give me some birds and the bees lecture here. I don't have time for that. But it wasn't that.

"Be careful with the damned car."

"Okay, Dad. I will. I promise."

He had the radio blasting. Creedence Clearwater Revival singing Fortunate Son. Following the directions he'd carefully written down to Sandra's house. A left on Bayview. All the way down to Lexington Avenue, then right onto her street, Fairview. Then driving slowly up to her house, 218 Fairview. It was a big two story with gothic white pillars out front, a huge lawn, and a two car garage. He was from the other side of town, where having a driveway and a small patch of grass was standard.

He parked the car in their long driveway and walked up the wide, winding steps. As he moved, the underground sprinklers started up and started swishing in circles on the green, weedless lawn. He stood in front of the door and took a deep breath before pushing the bell, thinking he'd done it now, there was no chance of backing out.

No one came to the door. In fact, there didn't appear to be any lights on in the house at all.

He pushed the bell again.

In a few minutes, the door swung open and an older man with an unshaven face, and wearing a white sleeveless T-shirt, pulled open the door. His eyes were half-closed like he'd been sleeping. "Who…what are you?" he asked.

"I'm here to see Sandy. We have a date."

The man scratched his head and laughed. "A date? I think you got your numbers or gals or dates mixed up, young fella. She went to a dance with her boyfriend, Shawn. You know Shawn, don't ya? The high school quarterback. Set all kind of records? Everybody knows Shawn."

Robert just stood there, the wind flown out of him.

"So, she's not here?" he said after a moment.

"No, they left about ten minutes ago."

"Oh," he said. Then he turned around and started walking back down the sidewalk.

"You're not one of us, are you?"

Robert stopped then and turned back around to look at the man.

"What? What do you mean?"

The man just stood there smiling, his teeth gleaming in the night, before he said, "Never mind," then closed the door and turned out the front light, leaving Robert standing there in the dark, wondering.

He would not come out of his room the rest of the weekend and dreaded the coming of Monday morning. It was hard enough facing his parents when he'd come home that night, but Monday was torturous. He avoided the lunch room, couldn't face Warren's inquisition. "So, how was the date, big guy?" He couldn't face anything, so he spent the hour in the back of the library, pretending to do his homework, hiding out.

And when the one o'clock bell rang, and he had to walk into that room, she was already there, sitting in the seat behind him, pretending he didn't exist again, just like it had been before. He didn't hear a word of the teacher's lecture. And, when the bell rang at the end of class he put his head down and stared down into his book bag until he knew she had passed. Then he followed her out of the classroom as she walked with two of her friends, the three of them strolling down the hallway like they owned it, their books held tight to their chests, the three of them laughing and fluttering about. He was conscious of the way they strutted, the way the boys watched them and smiled at them. Suddenly he was aware of everything as he walked behind them, following them, following her. And he noticed how he had somehow returned to the status of invisible person. Wondering what it was all about. Feeling the rage building up inside of him. Then she stopped at her locker, opened up the lock and her two friends said their goodbyes. And he stood behind her as she put her books on the shelf, waiting for her to face him.

She turned around and smiled at him with that phony smile of hers, and said "Excuse me," but he stood there in her way.

"No."

"No, what?" she said.

"Just ... no." She didn't say a word, a look of fear on her face for a moment.

"Why?" he said. "I need to know why."

The look of fear turned into a cold stare then, as she snarled at him, "You don't really think I would ever go out with you, do you? You don't think I would ever go out with a Jew?"

He stood there, staring at her, not saying a word, feeling the ice, the hatred in her eyes. Feeling it, letting it sink into his soul, but not backing off, not giving ground.

Just then there was a voice behind him. "This creep giving you trouble, Babe?"

He turned around. It was Shawn Davis. Robert didn't move then, but Shawn shoved him hard and Robert fell to the floor. Other students gathered around, pointing and talking. Robert saw him, he saw her then, the whole scene seeming to be in slow motion, the two of them laughing, the others circling around pointing at Robert on the floor, the way she closed her locker and Shawn threw his arm around her and the two of them walked off together. And that last thing Robert saw, that very final thing—the tattoo on his arm just below the sleeve of his T-shirt. The tattoo of the swastika wrapped around the shoulder of Sandra Auerbach.

Catching up with Cartucci

Q: You've mentioned that when you were a boy you liked to set animals on fire.

A: Yes. Animals and other things. Not that I was a pyro or anything. I just liked to watch them burn.

Q: What kind of animals were they?

A: Small things, mainly. A turtle, a couple of frogs. Once there was this mangy old alley cat roaming the neighborhood and—

Q: What was your method?

A: Oh, you know. Lighter fluid, gasoline, whatever was available. There was always some gasoline in the red gas can in the shed. The old man always made sure of that. He loved that little strip of lawn of his more than anything. Usually, it would take two guys—one would hold the animal, the other would douse the thing in fluid. Then we'd wait a minute or so to let the fluid soak in, just like it says on the charcoal bag, while the thing would try to clean itself off, then strike the match and VAR-OOM!! It was beautiful.

Q: Did the animals cry out as they burned?

A: Yeah. Sometimes the thing would shriek louder than hell, like EEEEEEEE!! Other times it would just make a soft little squeal, like somebody screaming down a tunnel.

Q: And this didn't bother you.

A: No, I didn't think about it much back then. I was pretty wild as a boy.

Q: Can you tell me a little about it?

A: I used to do all kinds of unbelievable things. One time a bunch of us went exploring at a construction site. This was on a Saturday afternoon. I drank a quart of beer and climbed up on the top beam of the structure—it was just the steel skeleton back then, but it was about four stories up.

Q: How old were you then?

A: Oh, I dunno. Let me see. About fifteen, sixteen. No, fifteen. I remember, I was working at the Landow Theatre because I couldn't get any other job and they were paying peanuts, I mean, it was under the minimum wage, even back then. It was a dollar twenty-five an hour.

Q: Did you ever kill anyone?

A: You mean, a person?

Q: Yes.

A: No. At least, not that I know of.

Q: Why are you grinning?

A: Am I? I didn't even notice.

Q: And you never had any trouble with the law?

A: No, nothing major. The usual—getting in fistfights and getting too drunk in my late teens, early twenties. That sort of thing. Yeah, I spent a couple nights in the drunk tank. It wasn't as bad as everyone makes out.

Q: Let me ask you this: Have you ever loved anyone?

A: Uhh, that's getting a little personal, don't you think?

Q: Yes, I'm sorry. You don't have to answer if you don't want.

A: Like I said it's personal.

Q: Okay then. We'll move on to the next one.

A: My mother.

Q: What's that?

A: My mother, I loved my mother. Doesn't everyone?

Q: I don't really know.

A: Well, you can put that down if you like. I loved my mother.

Q: When did she die?

A: Who said she died? She's living in Florida with my Uncle Joe. In Tampa.

Q: I see.

A: My old man, though, forget it.

Q: Yes?

A: He was one ripe asshole. Taught me about Jesus with the back of his belt. When he was really mad, sauced up, more times than not, he'd slip down on the leather, hit me with the buckle. It was a big old silver thing with steer horns on it. I still got the marks from it on my ass to prove it. You want to see?

Q: No, that won't be necessary.

A: It's kind of funny now. You can see the horns. I always get a laugh out of it with the ladies.

Q: And he died.

A: The old man? Yes, thank God. That he did. Drunk himself to death, or would've, if the guy who knocked him over the head with the tire iron hadn't got to him first.

Q: Hmmm. But, beside your dad, beside the beatings, would you say that you had a happy childhood overall?

A: Sure. Why not. It wasn't much different than other kids had. I didn't let none of it bother me.

Q: Let me get back to my original question. Was there anyone else, besides your mother, a girl, a woman, who you loved?

A: Sure. Lots of them. Some of them I don't even remember their names.

Q: You loved these women.

A: Sure. I've always had leanings that way. What do you take me for? A queer?

Q: And you've known love in other than physical terms?

A: Well, yeah. Once or twice.

Q: Do you want to elaborate on that?

A: Well, like I said, it is pretty personal. But, I guess that's what this is all about, right?

Q: Yes. You might say that.

A: Okay. I get ya. There was this one girl, Marina. I met her in high school. She was quite a girl. Took a lot of abuse from me, looking back. Too much, I guess. She finally got wise.

Q: So, it didn't work out in the end.

A: No.

Q: And you abused her physically.

A: Oh, yeah. Physically and mentally. All sorts of ways. Like I said, she put up with a lot of shit. But I thought she could take it. She was tough, like me. At least, that's what I thought. That's what drew me to her. We were living together, about a year or so. Tough, yeah, that's what I thought she was. Then one day I come home and she's crying on the living room floor. Just sitting there cross-legged, bawling her lungs out. I told her to get the hell out right then.

Q: You kicked her out?

A: Yeah. I didn't need that shit. I mean, I thought she was different.

Q: And that was it?

A: Yeah. She went back to her mother. We talked occasionally. But that was that, pretty much. I'd had it.

Q: And there was someone else?

A: Yeah. It was the same sort of thing. It turned out she misled me into thinking she was one thing, then she turned out to be another, nagging me all the time, asking, "When we gonna get married?" I told her "never" and "pack up" in the same breath. I thought we'd both wanted the same thing.

Q: Which was?

A: Oh, you know, companionship, sharing, but no heavy-duty commitments. We talked about it before she moved in. Then the marriage crap. It was more than I could take.

Q: Let me ask you this: Where were you when JFK was shot?

A: I was at home, sick from school that day. I think it was the mumps. No, measles.

Q: You weren't in Dallas that day?

A: No. I was sick in bed. I remember watching it all on TV. Why?

Q: Just one of those questions we throw in to make sure you're paying attention.

A: Oh. Okay.

Q: Here's another one. How did you feel when you threw Jake Fischbein down your basement stairs?

A: What?

Q: I believe it was during a Christmas party. You'd said he'd knocked down your Christmas tree.

A: Oh, yeah, the bastard. What was the question? How did I feel?

Q: Correct.

A: I don't really remember. Good, I guess.

Q: And he wasn't hurt, is that correct? Even though he rolled down twenty-two stairs?

A: I don't remember how many stairs there were.

Q: But he wasn't hurt.

A: No. At least nothing long-term. I'm sure it didn't feel good at the time.

Q: But he could have been hurt, isn't that true?

A: Yeah, I suppose.

Q: And you would do it again, today?

A: Of course. Well, not today. Like I said, I was kinda crazy back then. But if someone knocked over your Christmas tree, what would you do?

Q: I'm Jewish.

A: Well, whatever. Your menorah, I don't know.

Q: I'm the one asking the questions, if you don't mind.

A: Okay, sorry. You don't have to blow your top.

Q: Did it occur to you that he was drunk that night, that he didn't know what he was doing?

A: Who?

Q: Jake Fischbein.

A: Listen, it was nothing. He was nothing. It was a big mistake.

Q: Pushing him down the stairs?

A: No. Inviting him to the party. Dumb yid—oh, sorry, no offense. Didn't mean anything personal by that. It was just—well, you had to know the guy to know what I mean. He was a—how do you say it in your language? A putz. Did I get it right?

Q: Yes. You said it just right.

A: Anyways, that's what he was. A squirrel, a loser, a creep.

Q: You say he was a loser?

A: A pansy-faced, mother-lickin' fag, more or less.

Q: Are you through?

A: A slime-belching hook-nosed …

Q: Uhh uhh uhh.

A: Oh, yeah. Sorry. It's not that I have anything against them, against you people. It was just that Fischbein. He got on my ass. He smelled like his name.

Q: Then why did you invite him to your party?

A: Like I said, it was a mistake. His brother and me were pals. His brother was okay, cool, crazy like me. But that Jake, he was a cold fish.

Q: Fischbein.

A: Exactly.

Q: The night you threw him down the stairs, he was drinking straight out of that whiskey bottle you were passing around?

A: Oh, yeah. We all were. It was no biggie. He was a real wimp, couldn't handle his booze, not like a man, anyway.

Q: And you could.

A: Huh?

Q: Would you say you were inebriated when you threw Jake Fischbein down the stairs?

A: Yeah, I guess, but ...

Q: Now, if you will, for a moment, can you close your eyes?

A: What? What's this all about?

Q: Close your eyes, please. I do this with all my subjects. It's called creative imaging. Now, close your eyes, please.

A: Okay, okay. I'm doing it. Not that I like it much, but....

Q: Now, see if you can tell me what I'm touching you with. Here, on the arm.

A: It feels tickly, like a feather.

Q: And here.

A: Hard. Like a rock.

Q: And here, on your forehead.

A: It's cold, smooth. I dunno. Wait, I think I got it. A thirty-eight.

My Life of Crime

I'm working on the screen window with my box cutter. Once you make a big enough cut at the corner to grab onto a piece, the whole thing will strip off like the skin off a chicken. Then, just put one foot in, slowly, slowly. It's a job full of risks and excitement, but not one where you want any surprises. Usually it's just a fast in-and-out job. I scope the place out beforehand, so I know exactly what I want and where it is. I get in by saying I'm offering a free security system estimate. I've got the whole scam down—the ID card, the uniform, the clipboard with the company estimate sheet, everything. And on the way out I smile wide. "Thank you, ma'am. Hope to hear from you soon."

People ask me sometimes—the few I confide in—how I got started in the business. I've got no quick, easy answers.

I do remember the first time Bill Webber and I slipped the packaged fishing lures down our shorts. We were nine or ten. We had to wait until the rotating camera on the ceiling at E.J. Korvettes turned the other way, make sure no one else was around, then quick, no sudden motions, smoothly slip the packages off the pegs and down the front of our pants. Then we strolled to the next aisle to look at the baseball mitts and bats. We picked up the bats to test their heft, just like we were shopping. We left then, taking our time, joking with one another, our hands always at our sides to avoid suspicion. Once outside, on our bikes, we headed to Harms Woods and found our tree, the fallen one over the Des Plaines River. We dangled our legs over the sudsy flowing water and pulled up our booty. It was just like our very first Christmas.

"Did your dad smack ya?" Charlie asks as we're drinking beer at Syd's. He asks the same thing every night.

I put my beer mug down and look at him. "Now, why the hell would he do that?"

"He was a boozer, right? Left you and your mom with some floozy? Spent the mortgage on the horses?"

We stare at each other dumbly, then break out laughing.

Charlie's my best pal. We worked together for a while, but I broke it off. He knocked a lamp off a desk. It was the longest minute of my life. We got out of the place quick. Afterwards, we had a little talk, and I told him. We were sitting at a table in Syd's then, too. Charlie hadn't even touched his beer.

"Oh, Jake, come on. One little mistake. Anyone can make a mistake."

"A mistake, yes. Little, no. All it takes is one and you spend the next ten years in stir."

"But Jake," he said. He was so sorry looking. I thought he was going to wail. "How'm I gonna' manage without you? You're the best."

It was true. I figured my success on a little luck and lots of careful planning. Twenty-nine and I'd never been caught. Maybe that was the problem. All those years as a kid, slipping lures down the front of my pants, cassettes into my socks, watches in my inside jacket pocket, X-rated videotapes in my lunch box. And, when I graduated to house cracker, there were a few close calls, a German shepherd or two I hadn't counted on, a few quick escapes, but I was never collared.

But you can never be too careful, and with two guys you can never tell if the other guy's meeting your standards. You can't be responsible for him. That's why I went solo.

I remember my dad rocking me in his arms. I remember the smell of his pipe tobacco, the feel of his warm hands on my back, the deep, soothing hum of his voice. He didn't play the horses, drink or hit me or my mom. He sold advertising space for a local radio station. Never lost his temper. Never left us. We lived in the suburbs, had a vegetable garden and a nice patch of lawn.

"Puzzling, truly puzzling," Charlie says. Charlie never knew his dad. His mom worked as a waitress all her life. They lived on the west side, right under an El platform.

"He taught me to take pride in my work." We both laugh again. Charlie and I laugh a lot. We have a good time. But solo, outside of Syd's. He's doing okay, on his own, Charlie. I tell him to be careful. Not to get into something that's going to be more than he can manage on his own. He's like the little brother I never had.

Or was. I keep forgetting.

It was around Christmas time. He still hadn't gotten his girl, Crystal, anything yet.

"A nice easy little job," he said, smiling at me, over his beer. I grabbed his shoulder and looked into his eyes.

"Charlie, what do I always tell you? You've got to start a job with a clear mind. No booze. You're setting yourself up if you're lubed."

He laughed. "Lubed? Two beers, Jake, that's all I've had. Two lousy beers! What's that gonna do to me?"

"Charlie..."

He pulled my hand off his shoulder and stared at me, gritting his teeth, spitting the words out at me: "I don't work for you no more, Jake, remember that."

I'll always remember him that way, that anger in his eyes.

I read about it the next morning over a blueberry donut and a cup of coffee. On page seventeen it was. Just a little piece: "Burglar Shot by Homeowner on Addison Avenue." I knew right away.

It was one of the houses Charlie'd been scoping out.

I've got the other foot in now. There's nothing so exciting, even today, than that first step in.

I hear a sound. The bathroom door opens.

Missing Pieces

It was on an otherwise ordinary morning in July that Tom Morton woke up to find his left hand missing. He could still pinch it and feel it, but it was invisible. It had disappeared from sight.

This is how it happened. He opened his eyes, yawned, and reached to scratch an itch on his cheek with his left hand—he was left-handed—only to realize a moment after the scratch that he was scratching with an absent appendage. He was shaking like a blender set on pulverize, until he closed his eyes and said out loud, like some kind of mantra: "This is only a dream, this is only a dream, this is only a dream." Then he counted to ten and opened his eyes. The hand was still missing. He screamed out loud, lifting the arm which now seemed to end at the wrist. The funny thing about it, though, was that his hand was, somehow, still there. He could feel it. He just couldn't see it. But maybe, he thought, maybe there was a rational explanation for this. Maybe his eyesight had gone wacky. Or his brain. Or, or...he didn't know what. He hadn't had too much to drink last night after the job. It couldn't be that. He'd been bleary-eyed for sure, but it had never overlapped into morning, at least not to the extent of losing sight of a whole appendage.

He threw the covers off himself and started pacing, into the living room, into the kitchenette, trying to remember the details, every single event of the night before. He remembered driving to Rudy's—with both hands still visible—he remembered seeing them on the wheel—well, where else would they be? He remembered getting to Rudy's, getting the piece, loading it in the backseat, as they went to pick up Lou, then going to the job.

He stopped pacing. The job. Did it have something to do with that? He went to the living room and reached for the phone on the end table next to the couch. He reached at first with his left, out of habit, and grabbed the phone, but screamed and dropped it when it seemed to rise up in the air all by itself. Was he part ghost now or something? What the hell was going on? He bent down to the floor again, using his right hand this time, cradled the receiver between his head and shoulder and with the right again dialed Lou's number. After the third ring he heard the rough voice.

"Yeah?"

"Lou?"

"Huh."

"Tom."

"Yeah? What?"

"We did do that job last night, right, Lou?" There was a moment of silence at the other end.

"What's this, Tom, a gag? Been smokin' that funny herb, again? Little early for that, dontcha think?"

"No, no, Lou, you don't get it, I'm not smokin' nothin'. Something really weird has happened. You wouldn't believe it if ..."

"What is it, Tom? Cut to the chase, willya, cut to the chase. Got about three hours shut-eye last night. Botched jobs don't help me sleep none."

"It's..." He looked at his hand, or where his hand used to be, but still was, but ... he couldn't tell Lou. Lou'd think he was crazy. And the man would probably be right.

"Oh, it's nothing, Lou, nothing. Maybe I just drank too much last night. Feeling a little queasy, that's all."

"That's what you called to wake me up for? To tell me your li'l tummy aches?"

"No, no. Forget it. What time we gonna make the cut, eleven?"

"Yeah, eleven. At Rudy's. Be there. Now let me get back to sleep, asshole."

"Okay, okay, Lou, you're right." The line clicked off.

After sucking down a couple beers he relaxed some, raised his arm and wrist and missing hand and started laughing from the bottom of his belly, until he fell down on the floor. In a few minutes he got up, got himself back together (as much as possible, anyway) and went searching in his closet for his driving gloves. Then, finding one, he carefully pulled the thin brown leather over the invisible fingers, feeling for them with his visible hand as he went. And then, like new, it looked like there was a hand under there, like there was really nothing wrong with him at all.

Rudy was standing at his kitchen table counting the bills. "Guilt, what you got guilt about? And what's with that flaky glove? What are you, fuckin' Michael Jackson?"

"No, if you really wanna know I'm not fucking no one right now. And guilt, yeah, I got guilt after what happened last night."

"Christ, Tom. It's like this. We do a job. It don't always go the way we planned. We do the best we can, right, Lou?"

Lou sat at the table, pot belly forward, nodding, behind a bluish puff of cigar smoke that headed right in Tom's direction, made him choke and cough.

"Okay," he said, "we screwed up a little. Didn't think he'd have the nerve, that little weasel, that little shit, to go for the button."

"He twirled his cigar in his mouth and gave Tom a smile. "So things ain't going so hot with you and Gloria, huh?"

Rudy rubber banded some bills and tossed them across the table to Tom. "Here's your take."

Tom pulled the rubber band off the bills and counted. They were mostly singles. "Sixty-five fucking bucks? That's my take?"

"Hey, hey, Tommy boy. It was a convenience store, remember. You don't get much from them anymore, not with them goddamn drop boxes. Stay cool, relax. We'll try something more ambitious next time."

"A bank?"

Rudy scratched his balding dome. "What are you, crazy? With you? You're not ready for that yet. Is he, Lou?"

"No, not ready. We gotta start slow and easy. You gotta learn the trade, Tommy, work up to it. Me and Rudy been doin' this for a while, in between stays in them government hotels. You, you're just a baby. Ya need to learn to walk before you try to fly, ain't I right, Rudy?"

"Right, right, Lou. We gotta go slow, Tom, nice and easy. Especially after last night. Gunfire is not something we need. We got to keep our profiles low, if you know what I mean."

"I'm sorry about that guys. I just got jumpy."

"Jumpy is no good in this business," Lou said. "Cool is where it's at if you want to make it. Dig?"

"Yeah, sure. Cool."

"Okay, now go home and relax. And lose that faggy glove, too. We don't need none of that around us. Might rub off, y'know?"

He didn't say anything.

"All right, kid," he said, smiling a tired smile. "See you tomorrow, then. Two o'clock sharp here. Got it?"

"Yeah, Two sharp. Got it." Tom shoved the bills in his pocket and headed for the door.

Sixty-five lousy dollars. That's what he got for risking his neck, shooting a goddamned kid in the hand. What a fucking crock! He fit the key in the lock and heaved open the door. "Meowww!!" His cat, which he'd named "Cat", had been winged by the door. "Out of my fucking way, Cat," he said and, before he even thought about it, caught Cat with his left boot, near the back legs, and sent him flying against the wall. The feline lay there for a second, then got up on shaky legs. "Oh, baby, I'm sorry, my little Catty. Come to Papa. Papa's sorry." She arched her orange back and darted out of Tom Morton's reach, sliding into the dark, into the unreachable spaces of nothingness.

The alarm went off the next morning at eight. Tom couldn't open his eyes. He was groggy from the lack of sleep and the six-pack he'd wound up drinking the night before. Gloria was supposed to come by, but she'd made up some excuse before he'd accused of her of sleeping with her boss, she'd called him an asshole, he'd called her a bitch, and so it went. Another fucked up night in the life of Tom Morton, which he wound up spending in front of the tube, drinking too much (what else was new), switching from channel to channel, watching dumb TV game shows and sitcoms while making his mind go blank, and getting totally lubed.

He scratched his nose with his gloved, left hand, and yawned. Then he blinked, trying to keep his eyes open and stretched, looking at the brown glove rising above his head. Funny how you could get used to anything, the weirdest things, so fast.

He kicked off the covers, sat still at the edge of the bed, looking down at the floor for a second.

Oh no! This couldn't be happening again! This time it was his left foot. He felt it, but it wasn't there. He shook it, wiggled his toes, but it was no use. The leg ended at his ankle and just ... ended. What the hell was happening here? Was he in some sort of nightmare that he might never wake up from?

He reached down and grabbed it, felt the foot where it should have been, but couldn't see a thing. Maybe it was his eyes. Maybe they were going bad, playing tricks on him. He shut them, then opened them up again quick, but it was no use. The damned foot was still missing in action. AWOL. He pulled the glove off his left hand. Nothing. It was as absent as the foot. He sat there, at the edge of the bed, staring down at the place on the mattress where he should have been seeing the back of his hand and on the floor where he should have been seeing the top of his foot. Never a pretty foot, he would have to say that, but still, a foot.

Suddenly, he heard a noise in the bedroom and jumped. He'd never believed in ghosts, spirits, Ouija boards, that sort of thing, until he'd gone out with this waitress named Sheila, who'd spend hours in dazes talking to no one—dead people she'd told him later. He'd said, "Oh," at first, thinking, what kind of shit was this, until one time, this one time, she'd gotten out of one of her dazes to tell him stuff about his cousin, Freddie, the one who got run over by the train, that no one, no one in the world would know. (He'd never told her nothing about Freddie, not even his name.) And after that he'd thought about stuff he'd never even bothered thinking about. Heaven, hell, shadows of once living people flitting around behind window shades, sweeping around corners, in attics. Crazy, but there seemed to be something to it. And look at the shape he was in now. There was definitely something weird going on here, today, now.

He stood absolutely still, not even bothering to breathe. He heard it again, a sharp noise. He sat still for a second, then leaned forward carefully, putting his weight on the tips of his toes, then stood up. He moved slowly, not looking down at his left, mysteriously missing foot—they were demons maybe that had come and put a spell on him, or something like that—then moved carefully, slowly into the doorway, his heart thump thump thumping inside his chest. He paused at the doorway, hiding behind it when he heard a crash. He ran into the room only to find Cat streaking out, having flipped the dish of spaghetti and meatballs he'd left on the TV tray the night before onto the brown shag carpeting.

He was sitting in his mother's kitchen, sopping up runny eggs with a piece of burnt toast, and sweeping it all into his mouth.

"What's the matter with you, Tommy? You look like you haven't eaten in a week. Isn't your cousin Rudy looking after you? Feeding you at that warehouse of his?"

"Oh, yeah, Ma. Of course." The warehouse. She still thought Rudy ran a warehouse. She had seen it exactly once, about five years before, when Rudy had conned a friend of his, who owned a small magazine distribution operation, to let him use the warehouse for part of an afternoon to convince Tom's mother that he was the owner of the operation. It helped, too, that this friend of Rudy's owed Rudy a couple K for a gambling loan. All this Tom had learned soon after he'd started working jobs with his cousin and Lou.

Take your glove off, Tommy. Did I bring you up to wear gloves in the house? Or is that just sort of new deal or somethin' that all the kids are doin'?"

"Yeah, Mom, that's it, a new deal." He looked up from his plate and stared at his mother. She still thought of him as a kid.

"So, what's up with you and Gloria these days?"

"Huh?" he said, staring down at his plate, avoiding the eyes which he knew were trained on him—she always put the bead on him when she was asking about relationships. She wanted desperately to be a grandmother, she'd always said, before she was too old to be able to enjoy it. "Nothin'. Nothin's up with Gloria and me," he said, chewing on the piece of toast. "In fact, lately I've been thinkin' that maybe she ain't the one for me. She's too demanding or somethin'. Always wants her way."

"Ha," his mother said, and he looked up at her. She had a little, patronizing smile on her face. "You and her had another fight. Din't ya'?"

"Naw, naw. Why you say that?"

"Come on, Tommy. Give me the goods. I know these things."

He laughed a short burst of a laugh, then started mopping some more slippery yolk off his plate with the remaining piece of toast. "You know. How d'you know? You psychic or somethin'?"

"No, Tommy, I'm not psychic. I'm your mother. That's how I know."

He was chewing, his mouth open a little, staring at the refrigerator.

"So?" she said. "What's up?"

He looked at her for a second, feeling drained, tired all of the sudden, then looked away again. His mother. How did he live up to his mother? "Nothin's up. That's the problem. We ain't been gettin' along so good lately. I don't know what it is exactly." He was talking to himself more than his mother. "She don't like my chosen profession, I don't think."

"The warehouse? Hey, it's as good a job as any, right? It's not dishonest work, is it? What is she, the Queen of Sheba, that kind of work ain't good enough for her, when her father's chopping up slabs of steer all day long with blood on his apron? Where does she come off!"

He gazed back at his mother then with a feeling, a warm feeling, something like pride, love, whatever. She was actually fuming because of the way Gloria had been treating him for ... well, what she thought Gloria was treating him bad for. Warehouse job. Yeah, right. But seeing her face all scrunched up like that, her eyes tight, talking about Gloria made him think about what he hadn't thought about in a long time, had taken for granted, in fact. His mother loved him, she really loved him.

He'd had trouble sleeping that afternoon, thinking about the job that night, watched some soaps—they made him relax somehow, all these people, unlike any people he associated with, with their professions, their constant disasters, their money, their phony lives. What a laugh! It was all a game, life, with the fucking shit you had to deal with every day. It was all a game, a fucking game.

Twenty-two years old and sitting outside Rudy's house at ten to two in the morning, the motor off, freezing his ass off. For what? What kind of life was this? No education, sure, but he could still do better than this, couldn't he? Well, maybe not. The gig at the grocery hadn't worked out too well. He'd had a problem with the neatness thing, the making everything look just right. Pulling boxes and cans to the front of the shelf. And that thing about the customer was always right, that's what had really gotten him in trouble. Listening to old ladies complain about this or that all day. It got to him one time and he blew up. Mouthed off. That was the last he'd seen of that place, got his notice that very afternoon.

"Mrs. Fliegelhorn is one of our best customers," Mr. Flynn told him. "Been shopping here for twenty-five years. Do you know what that means? And you've been here, how long Tom? Two months. I can't have it. We just can't have it."

Then there'd been other jobs, of course. He'd been all sorts of things—delivery boy, bus boy, janitor, car hop, warehouse worker. None of them had panned out, had seemed to suit his skills and desires. And there was a thrill about the business he was in now that couldn't be beat. Like stock car racing must be to those drivers. Not that crime was the best way to go maybe. He didn't want to end up doing time like his uncle, like Lou, but maybe if he was extremely careful, if he was lucky....

There was a rapping on the glass of his window. Lou's big mug was in the glass. Tom rolled down the window.

"Come on, quit daydreamin', we gotta get goin'. Rudy's waitin'."

He stepped out of the car, and followed Lou into the back of Rudy's gray van. There the two of them put on their masks—lightweight black nylon masks—and checked their tools, after which Lou attached them to his belt.

The job went like a dream. The house was in an isolated location, next to a wooded area. They parked the van behind some trees, Lou cut through the screen window with his wire cutters, and with a heavy flashlight wrapped in a towel to muffle the sound, smashed the window, after which the two of them slid right into the house. Tom followed Lou in, while Rudy waited outside to keep watch. Lou had the job carefully cased, knew a guy who knew the owner (not that you wanted to know too many guys knowing too many things in this business, Lou had pointed out), had been over to his house socially and had told him, had gotten one drink too many into him and had started going on about how wonderful it was living in Longdale, how low the crime rate was in the area, how nobody ever got broken into there, had said in answer to the question about alarm systems, that he didn't believe in them, who needed them, the sign in the front of the house saying that he had one was enough, had even boasted about the fact that his wife kept her tiara in her top dresser drawer. Not that information like that was easy to buy. It had cost Lou a good bottle of bourbon. It paid to know the right guys, but you had to really know them. And even your best friends would turn you in if they were implicated. That was the way of thieves. There were damn few that could be trusted and even they couldn't be trusted. It was a game of survival, and the only one you could really trust was yourself.

So, they got into the house, walked right up to the bedroom by flashlight and snatched the tiara, then walked right out the back door and back to the van. It took all of ten minutes. And Lou with a ten thousand dollar tiara in his pocket, which would net three hot if he was lucky. Which meant one G each, but not bad for a night's work.

"The secret is awareness," Lou lectured as he pulled off his mask, and they drove home. "Be aware of all your surroundings. Take notes. Know as many people as you can, but don't let them know too much about you. Listen to conversations other people have. At the barbershop, at the deli. Pay attention. And then do your research."

There was much more to it then Tom had thought. It wasn't just smash a window, jump in and look for treasure. There could be an alarm, a dog, someone sleeping there that you didn't even know about. "That's why planning is the most important thing."

When he got back to his apartment, he fell into his bed, exhausted. Then he fell into a deep sleep of death.

He didn't wake up until about one o'clock in the afternoon, when the phone rang. It was Gloria. Apologizing about the night before, about not showing up. She didn't want to fight with him anymore. She loved him. Missed him. Wanted to see him. Asked if they could get together that night.

He picked her up at seven in front of her apartment building. After beeping his horn twice, he got out of the car and leaned against the front bumper. There was a swish of her curtains, a flash of her face, and in a moment she appeared through the glass door of the veranda, walking past the rows of copper-colored mailboxes, moving quickly toward him down the sidewalk. He stood with his arms spread like wings on the hood of his Camaro, a wide grin on his face as she walked to the door and stopped abruptly—stopped both walking and chewing the gum she incessantly chewed—and frowned at him.

"Aren't you gonna at least open the door for me?"

"What?"

"Tommy?"

He sighed and pulled his arms down. "The door, sure. No problem. What was I thinkin'?" Then he pushed himself up and walked around to the passenger side of the car to open the door for her.

She wanted to go out for a meal, but he was tired, he said, and wouldn't it be nice to have a nice meal there at his place, just the two of them, have a little wine, get cozy together? Truth was, he wanted her, needed her, it had been almost a week, way too long for him; he couldn't remember the last time he and Gloria had gone this long since he'd starting seeing her the summer before. He was a man, goddamnit, a man. She said it was all right, although she really wanted to go out, but being with him, she said, that was nice enough.

They ordered Chinese food—she loved, just adored Chinese food— "Chink" food, he called it, even though he got it for her, despite the fact that he really could have gone for a good steak, thought she might be able to cook one up for him, but went along with her because hey, where was the romance in that, and he would never get lucky like that, not against her will anyway.

They were sitting on the couch, in front of the TV, watching Jeopardy—Gloria was crazy about game shows, and that Alex Trebek—having just finished off their Moo Shu Gai Pan and him his Pork on a Stick, or whatever the hell the Chink name for it was, and he was pouring her more of the Chablis—not something foreign, but good old American-made, New York Chablis—in one of his actual wine glasses, one of the two he had, a piece that had caught his eye in a job about a month before. He held the glass out to her.

"Here you are my sweet lady." Her eyes moved away from the TV then toward him and she smiled, the dimples in the valleys of her cheeks appearing as if by magic. She was wearing a skirt tonight, something different, and those fishnet stockings that drove him absolutely out of his mind. He couldn't keep his eyes off those legs of hers. She definitely had the best legs in town. He lifted his beer bottle—he hated wine—to her glass, and clinked it.

"Here's to a long hard night tonight, baby," he said, and the smile on her face evaporated. She put the glass down on the coffee table—a rustic old relic that had probably been left in the apartment from the fifties. Not much had changed in the decor since then, not the curtains, the sink, even the refrigerator; it was like living in a time warp, in a time even before he was born. She looked at him sternly.

"So, that's all it is tonight, huh? About getting laid?"

"No, baby, not only about that. But that's nice, too, huh? Don't say you don't like it."

She looked down, played with the seam of her black skirt against the stockings.

"I never said that. It's just that sometimes a woman needs a little more. And, I don't see much progression in our relationship. I don't see any growth ..."

He burst out laughing. Her eyes narrowed even more.

"I'm sorry, baby. It's just, if you want to see some growth, let's go to the bedroom and I'll show you some growth."

Her back straightened, and she grabbed her purse.

"Come on, baby, what's the matter? We like to have fun, you like to have fun, don't ya'? What's wrong with that? Not everything has to be serious all the time."

She stood up now with her purse in hand, pretending he wasn't there, that he was invisible, it seemed.

"Come on, Gloria," he said, standing up and grabbing her from behind, spinning her around to face him, her face only inches from his now. He cupped her cheek with his right hand. She didn't look at him, looked past him, though her breath was hot on his right cheek and tears streamed down her own cheeks onto his hand.

"Do we have to be serious all the time, Glory?"

She turned her eyes to his then, an incredulous look on her face. "No, not all the time, Tommy, but some of the time. A girl needs it. A girl needs to know ..."

"I'll tell you what a girl needs and a girl needs to know," he said, grabbing her shoulder hard, and pulling her body against his.

"Oww, Tommy, stop. You're hurting me." But he didn't hear her now. His body heard only his need.

"A girl needs this," he said, kissing her hard on the lips, as she tried to say something, tried to pull away from him.

"Don't, Tommy," she said, managing to twist away from him for a second, but only a second, then he had her against him again, his mouth hot on hers, the urgency below his belt growing, pressing hard against her.

"Stop, Tommy, stop!" she said.

"No, baby, no, you know you want it, you know it."

"No, Tommy, not like this."

He had her down on the couch now, was pulling up the skirt, pulling down the fishnet stockings, rubbing his good hand up and down the warm smooth skin of her thighs, then pulling the blouse up, pulling the bra off of her ample breasts, as she pleaded with him and cried, his mind a blank, on automatic, his mouth working on its own, his lips, his tongue, traveling over her belly, her breasts and nipples, holding her arms down at her sides as she twisted from side to side, as he managed to pull his pants and underwear down and then her underwear, and then he was in her and pushing deeper and deeper, the difficulty of his penetration fueling his anger until his mouth was saying words he didn't even know, and he slapped her once across the face, her screams to no avail, her teeth not even hurting as they dug into the invisible flesh beneath the leather of the hand that once had been.

The next morning he woke up in a blur of alcoholic remembrance, his brain throbbing against the inside of his skull. What the hell had happened? He'd lost control, he'd remembered that much. Lost his temper. And then there was the little game with Gloria. Acting like she didn't want it. Fighting him, actually banging him with her fist (while he was banging her, of course). Then she'd stormed out and ... his head hurt too damned much to think about it.

He threw the covers off himself and tried to keep his eyes open. He sat on the edge of the bed and looked down at the floor between his legs. It was a funny view. Something was wrong. It was missing! His penis, his balls, the whole shebang, what the hell!! He stood up and howled to the ceiling, then ran to the door, pulled it open, and ran out into the courtyard, his brain a swirl of lava, screaming, raging to the black clouds in the sky above.

They were escorting him into the mental health center. He was wearing a robe they'd thrown on him and was talking like a ... well, lunatic, babbling on about Gloria, penis, and his arm and foot and God and Jesus Christ, himself. And there were other words, cancer, jewels, guns. It was all garbled together and he was the original batty babbling brook. Randall couldn't make hide nor hair of it.

Randall sighed as they got to the front desk. It was just another day in the life of an EMT. He had hold of the guy's left shoulder, and Bert had him by the right shoulder as they got him to the front desk.

"Hey, Martha, what's happening?" he said to the night nurse. "Long time no see."

"Yeah, like an hour and forty-five minutes. Yes, been a long time. What you got here?"

"This here is an unidentified white male, as they say in the biz. Caught him streaking through the streets with nothing on but a sock and this here glove. Don't know what the hell that's all about, but I'm sure he does."

The three of them looked at the incoming patient, halfway ex-pecting an answer. His eyes were glazed over and a thread of drool was dripping off his front lip. He was staring right at Randall. "My hand!" he said.

"What? What about your hand, fella? You want your glove off, is that what it is?"

The man backed away, his eyes widening with fear as Randall grabbed hold of the glove and ripped it off, after which the incom-ing screamed a scream of horror-show proportions.

"Goddamn it, man, it's just a goddamned glove. Here, you want it, take it back!" He slapped the glove in the man's hand. He had never quite gotten used to the wack route. Carving people out of cars, giving them CPR, hell that was nothing. It was the loony run that always gave him the willies. The man was hopping around like mad, staring at the glove in his hand, then put his other hand over it, and screamed again.

Just then, two orderlies showed up, one big black man named Darrell, who didn't put up with any guff, and a shorter white guy that Randall didn't know.

"Just in time, Captain Darrell. This one's just flipped out totally. Caught him running through the streets stark naked. Mumbled in the truck about missing body parts and shit. Don't know what the hell happened to him. Then he just started screaming like a hawk. Real frightened looking. A sorry case, I'd say. Better check him in, before you gotta check me in."

"No problem, Randall," Darrell said, smiling, a toothpick in the corner of his grin. "We'll take it from here. Send you back on your way to save the rest of the world."

"Much obliged, pardner. You take it easy now, Slim, y'hear?" he said, patting the patient on his shoulder very lightly, afraid anything more would set him off again.

Bad Neighborhood

We live in a rough neighborhood.

I see the evidence every morning—the walls spray-painted with the names of rival gangs, the drunks curled up fetally in the doorways, wrapped up in their tattered pea coats and wearing the stench of alcohol and death. I walk past the broken glass on the walk, the burned-out, boarded buildings, the dried blood and, occasionally, the chalked outline of a victim, a ghostly figure on the cold cement.

In the deadest hours of the night, I've been jarred awake by a single piercing cry, a scream for help so real that it couldn't have been a part of a dream. I've stood naked in the dark, shivering by the cold glass of the bedroom window, looking out and wondering where the sound came from, but seeing only blackness, and hearing nothing but the stillness of the night. There's nothing you can do then, you're helpless. You light up a cigarette with wavering hands, turn on the hall light, the bathroom light, any light you can find, check the locks on your doors, on your windows, listen at the door of your daughter's room for the sound of her light steady breath, then slip back, shivering still, into bed, press up against your woman's back, listen to her sigh, listen to the silence of the night, stare at the black sea of the ceiling, and wonder when the night's going to end.

The nightmares are supposed to confine themselves to the night, not spill over into the days. But something goes wrong one day, something goes very wrong.

I'm standing in line at the grocery checkout. My four-year-old, Laurie's riding in the cart. The place is buzzing like usual, the monotone of voices mixing with the Muzak and the ringing of cash registers. Laurie's whining, "Daddy, Daddy, can I have some gum, please, please Daddy?" So I reach over and pick out a pack of Juicy Fruit, tear it open, and hand it to her just to keep her quiet.

There's only one guy in front of us in line. He puts a pack of Oreos down on the conveyer, and that's all. I get busy pulling stuff out of the cart and placing it on the black conveyer. Behind me these crazy old ladies are standing with a cart filled with nothing but cans of cat food, and they're talking about the scandal sheet headlines like they're real. They're talking about three-headed babies and a girl who supposedly gave birth to a half-dog, half-person, and a man who's predicted that the world will end sometime on October 11th when the moon ascends to the house of Virgo, or something like that. I'm not listening to any of it; it's garbage, even if today is the 11th. I'm just shoveling my stuff onto the conveyer when Laurie starts laughing and tugging on my sleeve, saying, "Look, Daddy, look!"

"What? I'm trying to put these groceries up, can't ya see that?" But then I see something funny's goin' on. The cashier —this skinny blonde-haired girl who looks like she ought to be in school some-where—is standing in front of the opened cash drawer, rubbing her hands together real slow, and she's looking at the guy in front of us with these wide, unblinking eyes.

"Daaad, look!" Laurie says, pointing. "That man's got a gun!" Suddenly, the people behind me shut up, and the man twists around toward us.

"Isn't it funny, Daddy? Just like TV!"

All I can see at first is the tip of the gun sticking out of the pocket of his battered black leather jacket. The gun's pointed right at me. My feet and legs are ice. I don't know what to do.

The man's skin is pale, like raw dough with little beads of sweat running down his cheeks, leaving little wet tracks, and he's got a couple days' growth of stubble, grease in his hair, and these hollow, scared-looking eyes. He's looking right at me like he knows me, like we were classmates at prep school or something.

Then he looks at Laurie with those wild eyes, the gun pointed at her now, its dull tip quivering as he says in a low shaky voice, "Shut up, little girl. Just shut up." She starts crying. I should do something, but I don't. The ice has reached up to my throat, choking; it's worked its way up to my tongue, my lips, my eyes.

The guy turns back around.

I'm just standing there trying to control it, keep myself from shaking. I wonder what kind of man I am, standing there helpless while this is going on in front of my eyes? But I'm no hero, never wanted to die young. I've got my girl to think about, my wife.

I close my eyes and think about the day before, leaning out the window and seeing Laurie playing stick guns with her friends in the courtyard, how they all went "bang bang" at one another and how, when one of the girls fell down and stayed down too long, Laurie got annoyed and shook the girl with her foot, saying, "C'mon, Allie, you can wake up now."

I open my eyes, need to pay attention, protect my child. The man's teetering from one foot to the other like he has to use the john. "C'mon now," he says to the cashier, I mean business, don't give me no trouble." She doesn't move from where she's standing, just opens a brown paper bag and slowly starts moving handfuls of bills from the till to the bag, but her hands are shaking so bad she has trouble finding the opening. The guy looks behind us real quick, like he's expecting trouble, then reaches over just as quick with his free hand and grabs some bills out of the till and stuffs them into the bag. Then he grabs the bag and runs out of the store with stiff legs.

Laurie's still crying, and the cashier starts crying now too, and rips off her blue smock, throws it on the counter, and runs away somewhere. I leave the groceries on the conveyer and push the cart and Laurie quickly out of the store.

Outside there's a light drizzle. Laurie's still crying, protesting: "But Dad, how come we left all our groceries in the store?"

And I just say, "Be quiet for a little while, baby, okay?"

When we're in the car and all buckled in with the locks down, she finally sniffs up the tears and stops. Then she's laughing again, just like that. "Daddy, wasn't that funny?" she says.

"What?"

"You know. The man with the gun. Wasn't it, wasn't it funny, Daddy?"

"Yeah. Funny." I drive the car out of the lot, onto the rain-slicked street, and there he is, walking across the street in his black leather jacket, right in front of us. I push down hard on the gas.

"Daddy, watch out!" Laurie yells. It unnerves me. I can't do it. I slow down just enough so that he can scurry out of the way. But for a moment I almost did it, right in front of my own daughter. What has this town turned me into?

I drive past the factory where I used to work before I got laid off, where Mary, my woman, works, where just about everyone I know works or used to work. We go past the service station on the corner with it's broken sign, past the burned out Tastee-Freeze, which I can never remember being open, past the place where I'm supposed to turn—past our building, past our block.

"Where ya going, Dad?" Laurie squeals.

I don't say anything. I just keep on driving, headed for the Interstate, the way out of town. When I get onto the ramp, I step on the gas to build up steam, then take my foot off and brake, coast to the shoulder and stop. I don't know what comes over me then. I just start to cry, start blubbering like I haven't done since I was a kid. And Laurie is saying over and over again, "What's the matter, Daddy, what's the matter?" But I can't stop. I'm thirty-five years old, and I can't make anything stop. Laurie pats my shoulder and says, "Don't cry, Daddy, it'll be all right," just like her mother would, even though she doesn't even know what happened. But her face, her little patting hand, make the tears stop. I get hold of myself, tell her, "You're right, baby, everything'll be just fine."

I look at the kid, smiling at me with her motherly concern. So young, so innocent. I pat her lightly on the head. Then I back the car off the ramp and head back home, thinking, desperately wondering how I'm going to get my family out of this place. And where would we go? Is there any place safe to go?

Glass Slippers

I

Something keeps you going, keeps you moving after that first push out the door. I don't know exactly what it is. It's like you're on one of those playground merry-go-rounds and then whee! You fly ... you scream and close your eyes real tight until the tears start flowing down your cheeks, and you're clinging tight to the bar, got to hold on. And the longer you ride the faster it whips (it's gravity, centrifugal force or something). It whips until everything's spinning too fast, the faces, the landscapes, the highway signs—it's all a blur, all a fog.

You wake up in a room, you look at the ceiling, at the walls and, for a second, you're afraid, there's no recognition, and you don't know where you are or how you got there. Then it all comes back to you, reality washing back into your skull, wiping away the stain of night, the tortured, twisted figures that come at you in the dark.

My name is Martin Tyler. I'm in Austin, Texas. United States of America. The planet Earth. More specifically, I'm in Room 209, the Del Rio Motel, Austin, Texas, United States, Earth. It's February 21st, 1979. I'm the owner of a '67 peach-colored Mustang and a very nasty hangover.

I repeated these things to myself until finally the walls and the ceiling stopped spinning and I could get up safely from the rickety motel bed.

And then I remembered something else.

I was twenty-eight years old and in need of a job.

Again.

II

I was twenty-eight years old and badly in need of a beer after an interview for a photo-processing order taker conducted by a balding man with beady little eyes and a rodent wide grin.

I was hot, feeling small as I drove to a local bar, thinking that I hadn't really wanted to work in one of those instamatic-sized boxes, taking people's film, stuffing it into envelopes, tearing off stubs and saying "Have a good day," chimpanzee-style for eight hours a day anyway. It was work for high school kids and aging housewives who'd never worked a day in their lives.

I saw the HELP WANTED sign out of the corner of my eye as I walked into Rudy's Stop On Inn for a beer or three to calm myself down. After a couple I was still fuming about all the interviews I'd gone through in the last couple of weeks. They were usually conducted by mindless sadists. And there'd been the polygraphs. There'd been three of those tests in three little white rooms. Apparently the only persons qualified to administer them were well-trained ex-Nazis whose teeth all glowed metallic as they smiled and strapped you up to the machines that each of them secretly wished would produce searing currents of electricity rather than merely a bunch of jagged lines evidencing physiological responses to various yes-no questions.

Do you take illicit drugs of any kind?

What do you consider illicit?

Anything illegal. Just answer the question, please, or we'll have to start all over again.

That would be a shame.

Now, I'll repeat the question one more time. Just answer yes or no. Do you now or have you ever taken illicit drugs of any kind?

No. (The tracing needle would jump a little on this one but not enough to worry about.)

Do you drink more than two six-packs of beer a week?

No. (The needle would jump a little more on this one, but I'd still be safe.)

Did you ever steal anything other than the pencil you told me about that you accidentally put in your pocket on the way home from work in the drugstore in 1973?

No. (The tracing needle would go crazy and I'd be out of a job.)

I'd stolen quite a few things as a kid but wasn't about to admit it all now. It hadn't ever been anything big. Just candy, cassette tapes, beer, one of every kind of rubber made, which I'd never used ... it was the stuff of adolescence in the suburbs of Chicago.

And there were the fishing lures.

As a kid it was a challenge to go into the E.J. Korvettes store, a place that was hooked up with these revolving video cameras that hung from the ceiling at strategically calculated intervals, and stick three or four fishing lures in my pocket when the camera wasn't looking, then turn around and walk right out of the store. It made me feel like I'd beaten the system. I'd beaten the guys who'd stared at me Big Brother-style while I roamed through their store.

It made a kid proud.

But I'd outgrown those days and it was pretty humiliating to have to list everything I'd ever stolen as a brat just to get a crummy two-bit job. And, even if I did make a list, there'd always be something I'd forget and then remember as they'd ask the question again and the machine would go wild, the Nazi's metal glowing in his canine smile and I'd be out of a job, simple as that. What employer in his right mind would hire a guy who'd admitted stealing as much as I had, anyway?

So, I didn't tell them and saved a little pride while losing a job. I'd lost some pretty good paying jobs for pride's sake. But, after a while, I just figured if they wouldn't judge me for what I was now and not for the mistakes I'd made as a kid then they didn't really deserve me.

It was a couple of beers later and I was feeling pretty good again. Back to my old self. I remembered the HELP WANTED sign in the window and thought, what the hell, I'd give it one more try. What did I have to lose?

I went right up to a guy who looked like the manager. They're easy to spot—they're the ones who always stand around doing nothing.

"You Rudy?" I asked. "I'm looking for a job."

"Nice to meet you. I'm William Rodgers."

"Sorry, I was looking for Rudy." I took a long slug from the beer bottle and, after looking at the deadpan, bespectacled face before me for a few moments, feeling for all the children whose parents imposed tragedies on them, said, "Will Rodgers. Your parents sure had some sense of humor."

He stared at me sadly, tired of the jokes I imagine, gazing out at the restaurant where John Joneses and Sam Smiths quietly drank their beers in peace. "There is no Rudy. That's just the name of the place."

"Some gimmick."

"So you need a job, huh?"

I felt like I was talking to a mirror.

"What can you do?"

"Drink beer. Maybe do a little song and dance; for an extra buck or two I get up on the tables, but absolutely, positively, no windows."

The man reached under the counter and produced an application. His expression had not changed. "Fill this out," he said, shoving a pencil, the name of the bar inscribed on it, toward me. Then William disappeared in the back somewhere.

The pencil had no point. I asked a waitress to get me a pencil or Mr. Rodgers. She produced neither. I sat down at a table and polished off a couple more beers. When Rodgers came out I was bleary-eyed.

"All set?" he asked.

"I haven't filled out the application yet. No point to this Rudy's Stop On Inn writing utensil."

"That's okay. Can you start tonight?"

"Start what?"

"Working at the door, checking ID's, keeping the kids out, that sort of thing. It's real simple. Most of the time you just stand there against the wall, watching the band play."

"How much do I make?"

"Well, only minimum, but if you're interested in getting into our management program, it's an excellent place to start. Let me tell you a little about...."

"Not interested. What time tonight?"

III

Thus, my career as a bouncer began.

It didn't last long.

When people came, they came en masse. If the girls were pretty but underage I'd let them in. If they were homely but forty I'd card them. The guys all got carded. Most of the night I just stood there twiddling my thumbs while the crowd got progressively drunker.

It was a new phenomenon, watching people get drunk while I remained on the sidelines, calm, cool, and sober. It wasn't much fun.

After a couple of nights I thought I'd go crazy. There was only so much thumb twiddling you could do. Occasionally a customer or a waitress would hang around my wall and chat. I was thinking very seriously about quitting, but one of the managers beat me to it.

I'd let in a blonde-haired seventeen-year-old (she'd had the cutest smile) on a brown-haired, buck-toothed friend's ID. Sure, she could have dyed her hair and had her teeth fixed since the picture, but if you could have seen the picture and the girl you would have known. There could be no mistake.

Roseanne—the assistant manager on duty—looked at the confiscated ID and glared at me. She got a guy from the kitchen to take my place and pulled me into the hallway.

"What the hell is this all about? What are we paying you for, anyway?"

I didn't know what to tell her. It was all pretty much a mystery to me, too. The woman's acne-scarred face turned bright red. I expected to see smoke start coming out of her ears at any moment. Just as her mouth opened to spout the fatal words, Will Rodgers came to my rescue, snatching me from the woman's fiendish hold. He led me down the hallway to his office.

"Have a seat, Martin." I did. Will closed the door, and sat behind his desk. "Looks like you're just not cut out for working the door, huh?"

I shrugged.

"Look, if Roseanne had her way you'd be out of here in a minute. But I'm the manager around here and I get the feeling that you want to work. And I need another man in the kitchen. It's hard work. It gets real crazy back there sometimes. But I think you're up to it."

"How much does it pay?"

He squirmed a little and looked away from me. "Well, that pays minimum too, I'm afraid. But if you're interested in getting into management, it's a good place ..."

"You're kidding me, aren't you? I'm supposed to bust my ass for that kind of money?"

Will's look turned fatherly. "It's up to you. There are a lot of people out there looking for jobs who'd be happy to take what we're offering ... what I'm offering you right now. It's your decision."

I thought about the two weeks I'd already spent in this town, staying at a run down motel, looking for a job, being interviewed by moley-looking men, while my wallet had grown thinner and thinner. I took the wallet out of my back pocket and looked at the faded cowhide, the strands of fabric that barely held it together. I didn't have much choice. I thought about the polygraphs and squinted hard as thoughts of electricity sparked through my brain.

"Yes, yes, I'll take it!" I said, succumbing, giving in to the pain. And then quietly, "When do I begin?"

IV

I began the next morning.

It wasn't much of a job. There were a couple of younger guys in the kitchen making sandwiches on these big steel trays, cutting up different types of processed meats with an electric slicer. I was issued a white apron and a little white paper hat. Then they gave me the broom. I had to go through the whole bar and sweep up all the crap the drunks had dropped on the floor the night before. I'd do my sweeping, occasionally finding a quarter, a dime, a nickel. I kept my eyes open for tens and twenties but they never showed up. Sometimes a pretty girl would walk by the windows and I'd take a break to watch. Even if I'd given up being with women, they were still nice to look at.

After a quick mop job and after checking out the johns to see what atrocities had been left on the floors there from the night before, I was back in the kitchen, helping out with the sandwiches, and setting things up for the lunch rush.

There were these little scales you weighed the meat on. They looked like cheap postage scales, the kind you buy in the drugstore. You were to put only four ounces of meat on a sandwich. Sometimes, I was told, the bosses would come back and double check the weights. They'd have tantrums if there were over four ounces of meat on a bun. Against company policy, you know.

The bosses didn't know it, but while their eyes were focused on profits and promotions, they were probably doing their customers a favor. Some of the meat had a distinct iodine smell to it, the natural smell of decay. I seriously doubted that anyone could eat more than four ounces of some of that meat and leave the restaurant without a stretcher. Not to say that anyone would be able to tell the stuff was rotten when they ate it with all the lettuce and tomato and fresh dressing plopped on top of it.

The lettuce was also camouflaged. Or transformed. I was told to rinse the brown stuff with potato starch. Three or four soakings and voila, the stuff almost looked fresh again. It was green but tasted like hell. Occasionally salads would come back with the customers' complaints that the lettuce just didn't taste right. If that happened, we'd give them some of the new lettuce that was kept in the back of the cooler. Otherwise we'd stick a few slices of old meat on the hill of lettuce, shove a couple of overripe cherry tomatoes into its side and then smother the whole thing with croutons and dressing to hide the bitter taste of potato starch.

Besides the quality of the food and the low pay, the job wasn't so bad. I saved money on food due to a loss of appetite from all the bad food and by stuffing myself on the good stuff, the safe stuff, while the manager wasn't around. All the guys did it.

Once Roseanne walked into the kitchen just as I was shoving a corn chip into my mouth. She blew up at me and wrote something down on a pad of paper, then tore off the slip and handed it to me.

"I'm giving you a written warning. One more time and you're automatically terminated." It sounded serious. She stared at me with those cold marble eyes of hers, then walked out of the kitchen with a small, sadistic smile on her face.

At the lunch rush, each of us got our own stations. There were four of us. One guy would make nachos all afternoon, scooping chips out, throwing a few jalapeno slices on them and ladling some artificial cheese sauce over them. Another guy would just make salads and usually there'd be a couple of guys making sandwiches, taking them off the tin trays, dressing them and popping them into the microwave for thirty seconds.

Lunch was the only busy time. The tickets would come flying back to the kitchen, and all of us would make our mechanical motions which were never quite quick enough for Roseanne. Occasionally the whole machine-like order would fall apart when a waitress came back to bitch about getting a wrong order or getting only one pickle spear instead of two. It got on my nerves real fast, all these college girls whining about everything because even though their tips depended to a great extent on how we sent out the orders, we didn't get any part of those tips, so why should we care?

The only one who really did care was Tom, a nineteen-year-old high school dropout who aspired to be a rock guitarist but would never make it—he was too clean. Tom had been working in the sweatshop for two years. He'd been rewarded for his loyalty with 25 cents in raises and the honorary title of Kitchen Manager, which just meant he had to work harder and longer for under four dollars an hour.

When the waitresses came back to the kitchen crying, Tom would talk to them softly and see what had happened. He'd calm them down, fix their orders, get them fresh lettuce, whatever it took. While he worked at being nice to the waitresses, he didn't seem to see that they all looked down their noses at the kitchen crew. Most of them were sorority girls making a little extra cash. Why did they want to mess around with dishwashers and pot scrubbers? After a couple of weeks I got the feeling that each of them considered her job only temporary until her prince arrived and sat at one of the tables in her section and pulled this slipper, this magnificent glass slipper, out of his alligator-skin briefcase.

There were exceptions though.

V

One of the exceptions was a woman named Jackie. She was older, about thirty-five or so. She had alluring green eyes, platinum blonde hair, and she always left the front of her blouse open one button too far. Good for business, I guess.

The moment I saw Jackie it was bang like old times, like the time I first saw my first love, Blair Thomson. One look and I turned to jelly inside and my knees got shaky. In short time I was stuttering in her presence and thinking crazy thoughts. Seeing her as I was trying to fall asleep at night. Imagining long passionate kisses under waterfalls, lusty naked embraces by a peaceful stream, that sort of romantic crap. I'd try out her name, see how it fit with mine. Jackie Tyler. Hmmm. I'd imagine how we'd own a little shop in a peaceful little town somewhere and live a pleasant, uncomplicated life together.

Okay, I get carried away. I mean, I don't even believe in love at first sight. Hell, it didn't do me any good back when I was nineteen, that first time I saw Blair. First sight love could only lead to one thing. Heartbreak. I was no fool. I knew this. Still, I couldn't help myself after that first look at Jackie.

All this stuff was spinning around in my head and I'd barely spoken to the woman.

When I asked about her the other guys told me to forget it. She was married. They were guessing.

After a while she noticed how I looked at her and would stop by in the kitchen once in a while for a little chat and a wink when things got slow.

When I finally worked up the nerve to ask her out for a drink she didn't flinch, said "Sure, why not?" with a broad smile on her face. We went to a place not too far from Rudy's where they were having two-for-one Margaritas. It was there that I learned the truth. Jackie wasn't married but lived with a construction worker named Clem. I pictured him as one of these big musclebound types carrying bundles of two-by-fours over each shoulder. Jackie and I sat close together, sipping our drinks. She'd bought them. I liked that. I didn't like Clem.

"Oh, he's all right really. He makes a good living. It pays for the groceries. I don't really have to work. I'd just go crazy if I didn't have something to do. I'm just not ready to play housewife again, you know? You got a light, Marty?"

I lit her up and she stared into my eyes. Too long. I looked down at my drink. After the second Margarita my id was creeping out from under a bush, but my ego kept it in check, reminding it of Clem with the two-by-four biceps. As I drank quicker his image started to blur considerably.

She told me about her ex-husband. He'd beaten her up good a couple of times. By the time he'd put her in the hospital, she'd decided to leave the lout. She'd left Boston, Mass. for Austin, Texas.

She put her hand on my shoulder and looked at me in a vague sort of way, evidence that she was already getting sloshed, which was further evidenced by the way she tried not to slur her words as she told me, "You know what's funny about the whole thing? I still miss the guy sometimes. I don't even know why. I guess some of us are just suckers when it comes to love." She took another sip of her Margarita, then seemed to reconsider it, said "What the hell," and finished it all in one gulp.

I told her about Blair, the girl I'd loved but lost. The moment I'd seen her, my world had changed. Nothing else had seemed to matter than her, being with her. She was my love at first sight girl although she hadn't been the same way with me. But after a couple of months the feeling was mutual. We couldn't stand to be without each other. After six months we were talking about getting married. There was just one problem—Blair's family had money, big money, old money. Her mother couldn't see her hanging around with a bum like me. So, on a gloomy autumn night, she kissed me one last time, tears running down her cheeks, and told me she couldn't see me anymore, that she couldn't go against her family. I brought up true love, Romeo and Juliet ("Yeah," she said, "and look how that turned out"), everything I could think of, but she wouldn't go against her family's wishes. How could she? She was just a proper eighteen-year-old girl. Raised and bred on the golden nipple. A week later I was packing my bags, checking out of my dorm, and hitting the road.

I'd been on it ever since.

"Did you ever wonder what happened to her?"

"Oh yeah, I found out from a friend of mine. She got married about a year after I left. To a construction worker," I said, raising my eyebrows at her.

"No," she said.

"Yes," I said.

"Maybe if you'd stayed a while instead of running away, things would have worked out with you two," Jackie said and sipped her Margarita. "Maybe..." she said, but trailed off, and looked at me warily. "I'm sorry, Marty. Who am I to judge, after I've screwed up my own life so bad."

I waved at the bartender for another drink. Jackie was silent again, staring down at her napkin. I put my hand over hers. Then with the other hand I took my new drink and took a long swallow. I wasn't very good at this, but the alcohol helped. I was definitely feeling the effects, so in the "what-the hell" spirit, set forth. "Jackie, I have to tell you something now. You know that first time I saw you was a lot like that first time I saw Blair. I don't know what it is about you, but when I saw you I felt ..."

"Hold it right there, Marty," she said, staring right at me and giving my hand a bone-crunching squeeze. "You don't even know me, so don't even think about telling me about what you think you feel for me."

She loosened her grip and patted my hand.

"Poor soft-hearted Marty. You're like a lost little puppy dog. Looking for someone to love. And in all the wrong places, I might add." She lit herself another cigarette with the lighter I'd left on the bar, then took a deep drag and exhaled with a sigh. "I can't explain it all, Marty, life, the weird zig zags and curves it throws at you. Who can? All I know's this. Sometimes you've got to do what you've got to do. Love is for pups. You'll learn that some day. When you're out of your puphood."

She got up with a little difficulty from the stool and threw some bills on the counter. "It's on me, Marty. Now I've got to get going. Clem's probably home by now. Probably steaming mad, too, that I'm not there, that his dinner's not waiting for him on the table. Nothing like a steaming gorilla. Maybe I'll make some steaming bananas for his supper." She smiled at me sadly. "Don't get me wrong, Marty. I like you a lot. Just don't go falling right away for women, for the wrong women, for women you don't even know. You might just get what you wish for. And then where are ya'?" She put her hand on my shoulder and winked at me. "Look, I'll see you tomorrow. Okay?"

I forced it out: "Okay."

I was twenty-eight years old and I'd never been with a woman longer than a month or two since Blair. It had just been one lie after another. To them, to myself.

As Jackie headed for the door I had a sinking feeling. I was dog-paddling in a foggy pool of strangers, flapping my hands like mad to stay up. Within inches of my hand was a rope, a tow line. As Jackie closed the door behind her I saw the tow line slide down into the murky depths. Out of reach.

VI

Roseanne liked to play games with the guys. She could be a supreme bitch when she wanted to, but if you played along with her she'd let up some. She'd come up to you at the end of the day and wrap her arms around you, with a little moony smile, telling you she wanted to be friends, and you knew what that meant, and knew also that no job in the world was worth that, as she crooned in her uncharacteristically soft voice, "How 'bout taking Rosie for a little drinkee poo?"

Roseanne, being a lonely sort, did this to every male employee she could get her hands on. Amazingly, some of them went along with her ... for the drink at least. They didn't like to work their asses to the bone for a lousy $3.25 an hour.

Roseanne was not an attractive woman. She had a baggy, saggy backside, a face that was badly scarred from adolescence and long stringy black hair. Nobody would have been surprised to find a witch's supply of bats' wings and cats' tails in her purse.

She'd make me do things twice or three times that needed to be done only once. She'd make me wash the ceiling and the windows Any little dirty job she could conjure up I'd get stuck with.

She must have really been mad for me.

And I, I had it real bad for Jackie. After that night of almost-confessions and Margaritas, she'd been very nice to me, coming back to chat with me whenever she could, carefully avoiding any of the things we'd talked about that night. Roseanne saw the two of us chatting in the back and started to push Jackie extra hard. After a while Jackie's visits were not so much to exchange a few pleasant words as to escape Roseanne's wrath and blow off some steam.

In short time Roseanne had ruled the kitchen off limits to the waitresses when they weren't getting orders. This didn't go over very well with the guys in the back. Seeing the girls every now and then made for a much happier ship.

I went up to Tom.

"Tom, we gotta do something about that bitch."

Tom put his finger to his lip. "Shh! Not so loud. Are you crazy? She could be coming back here any second!"

"I don't give a shit when she comes back here! Now listen, Tom ..."

"What do you want me to do?"

"Well, you are the kitchen manager. Go to Rodgers about it. What are you afraid of? You afraid you'll miss a nickel raise five years down the road?"

Tom was staring at his Hush Puppies.

"Why do you guys put up with it? I don't get it. Do you know she made me wash the same dishes three times this morning just because she found a hair on one of the glasses? A black hair, too. If I was you, man, I'd go out and find real jobs, where they don't push you around like you're a little speck of dirt."

Tom looked close to tears. He was too soft for his own good. A buddy of his, Shawn, who had just started working there, came to his aid.

"What the hell do you know about it, Tyler? You're a big talker, but you're working here, too, aren't you? You know how tough it is to get a job in a college town like this when you haven't even graduated high school? When everybody at college is looking for bread and the locals pay the wetbacks a dollar an hour for sixty hours a week and they still keep smiling? Sure, it's easy for you. You been to college. But you're just gonna wind up an old bum like my old man was. But not us, Tyler, not me."

I looked into Shawn's raging eyes. I felt calm. I didn't feel sorry for him. I'd worked at more jobs than he had years. Bad jobs too. Like the twelve hour days at the cat food factory, packing little boxes into cartons, never being able to slow down or the chutes would overflow, and you'd have cat food all over the floor. Twelve hours of being a piece of a machine and not one English voice to talk with.

But even that wasn't bad compared to what could really happen to you. I had gone to one or two interviews dressed in my brother's gray three piece. I'd played the role of energetic young go-getter but then after two days on the job I'd stripped off the tie. I wasn't ready to donate my soul to the Corporation; I wasn't fool enough to rip my heart out and send it special delivery to the CEO of the Corp., all the while singing a continuous Muzak drone to myself while I smiled and blinked.

I was a different kind of fool. Creditors didn't own me, mortgage people didn't own me. They could kick me around a bit, and they had, but I didn't have to stand there and take it. My life wasn't neatly filed and sewn up in their banks or computer files.

I wasn't that kind of fool. But what kind of fool was I?

"You're gonna be a bum just like my old man, lying in the gutter by the time you're forty, begging for a quarter, for another bottle. Wait and see. But I'm gonna be something."

I looked back at the boy, nodding at him and smiling. "You're right, Shawn. You've got your head on straight. Grab on to what you got and don't let 'em take it away from you. Hang on tight to it and squeeze. But it'll be your own neck you're squeezing and you won't even know it till there's hardly any air left to get through."

He looked at me like I was nuts. He didn't understand, but he had an excuse. He was only nineteen.

After work I knocked on Rodgers' door. He seemed to be in good spirits as he counted the afternoon's take.

"What can I do for you, Martin? How're things doing in the kitchen?"

"Well, that's what I wanted to talk to you about. It's Roseanne."

"What about her?"

"She's a hard ass bitch, that's what. You're going to lose some good people because of her." I stared at the bills as he counted. They were hundreds.

"There's nothing I can do about it, Martin. It's out of my hands."

"What do you mean, out of your hands? You're the manager here, right?"

"Not after tonight."

"What?"

"Didn't you hear? They're transferring me to Corpus. Tonight's my last night. They're sending a new assistant out here, but Roseanne will be your new manager." Rodgers didn't look up, but continued to count the money. I stuck out my hand. "Congratulations, Will." I didn't dislike him that much. After all, he'd gotten me the job there and he'd saved my job once, whatever that was worth. He looked up at me and smiled.

"You know something, Martin? I'm going to miss this place. God knows why. I guess a place just grows on you." Sort of like sores on your privates, I thought. He looked about ready to cry. Then he snapped out of it and walked back to the green metal cabinet behind him. "Here, I know they're in here somewhere ..."

I didn't know why but suddenly I was sick to my stomach with the smell of nine years of dirty dishes, the thought of all the authoritarian little nothings playing soldiers in their dirty little jobs, kicking people below them to make their lives seem a little more important, to make the company its profits. I was heartsick for Jackie and for all the women I'd had and had let slip away. For all the women I knew I'd never have. I was tired of the cheap, roach-ridden apartments, the paper thin walls, the loud music pounding through those walls at all hours of the night, the treeless streets where I always wound up living in cities full of trees. And there were the cracks. It always seemed funny to me that whenever the paper reported that the city crews were out fixing the cracks in the streets somehow they never got to my street, where the real cracks were and where the real cracks remained.

It made you real mad.

I stared at the stack of hundreds, just sitting there waiting to be grabbed, to be stuffed in my pocket—how many cracks would that fill?—just as Will Rodgers turned back around.

"Here they are." He was smiling again. He was reaching toward me, holding a cigar in his pudgy hand. I wondered if it was loaded. I imagined him drawling, "I never met a man I didn't like." And, I imagined it was probably true.

I grabbed the cigar, gave my thanks, and closed the door on William Rodgers.

VII

The next day I was peeking through the hole—there was a little hole in the wall through which all the orders came back to us in the kitchen. From that hole you could see most of the restaurant. When things got slow and all our work was caught up I'd stand there for a while looking for pretty girls or whatever, killing time.

For some reason Roseanne hadn't come back to the kitchen more than once or twice to bitch that day. She seemed to be in a good mood for once, bathing in her new role as Manager of Rudy's. MANAGER. A couple more years of hard work and she might make it up there into the executive ranks, right up there with the gods.

She wasn't the only one who'd been promoted. Earlier that morning Tom had come up to me excitedly to show off his new badge. He'd decided to join the Rudy's management training program. It saddened me some. Tom was young, but I'd always thought of him as a bright kid. He'd had his job in the kitchen for a long time and didn't have to put up with too much shit. When you were paid that kind of money and were that low on the totem pole no one really expected too much out of you. Now he'd be getting shit from both ends, the top and the bottom. Being a nice guy I figured it would take him a little longer than average to become a hard ass, feeding and training us like we were nothing more than animals in a cage while he flexed his almighty whip and snapped it for sport. I gave him six months tops.

I had to put up with another speech from his buddy, Shawn, the punk, who was also considering joining the program. I figured management would be right up his alley. He was already a first grade asshole.

"Hey, what about you, Tyler? You're not getting any younger. You know what kind of money those guys make? You want to wash dishes, push a broom for the rest of your life? You like drivin that old clunker of a car you got? Do the girls flock around it in awe as you start 'er up? Hell, I've heard you crank her before. Sounds like an old lady farting. Now me, I'm gonna get me something sleek and fast. Trans Am with a sunroof and racing stripes. A powerful machine. Then I'll watch all the pussy flock my way. You ever get any pussy, Tyler? I'll bet you haven't seen a bit of tail in quit some time, huh, Tyler?"

Tom was pulling at the kid's arm from behind. "C'mon, Shawn, that's enough." The kid shrugged him off. He had a crooked smile on his face. He was enjoying himself.

"Let's see, I'm just curious, Tyler. How long has it been? Two years? Three? Am I getting close, Tyler? Or maybe you don't like women at all. Yeah, maybe you're just an old fag ..." He started laughing now as Tom yanked harder on Shawn's arm and yelled, "Stop it, Shawn!" The kid slashed his arm back around, catching Tom with an elbow and knocking him down. Then Shawn was on the ground, helping Tom up, examining his cut lip. "Hey man, I'm sorry. I didn't mean it. I was kidding around with Tyler a little. I didn't mean to hurt you, pal...."

The two of them sat there on the floor staring at me. I hadn't moved throughout the whole thing. A couple of years before I would have swung at the punk right away. Now I more or less felt sorry for him.

When Shawn got up and went to the back, Tom came up to me, trying to apologize for his friend. I told him it was all right and went back to my hole.

I saw my girl, Jackie. Only she wasn't a girl. And she wasn't mine.

Jackie was walking past Roseanne with a full tray of orders. Roseanne was watching over her new kingdom. As Jackie walked just past the spot where Roseanne stood, the back tip of her tray flipped over and the dishes went crashing to the floor.

Jackie was in a rage, crying, swearing. Roseanne tied into her, calling her clumsy and useless and ended it all with the magic words, "You're fired!" as Jackie ripped off her little brown apron with the company logo printed neatly in front and tossed it at Roseanne with all her might, sending nickels, dimes and quarters that had been in the pockets flying all over the restaurant.

Jackie was headed for the door.

I ran out of the kitchen in my dirty white apron, past Roseanne who yelled after me, "If you step out that door, Tyler, don't bother coming back in!" At the door I pulled the apron off and balled it up in my fist, a fist that would gladly have made contact with those sneering little eyes of Roseanne's. I tossed the apron at her. It unfurled like a flag and floated down on a customer.

When I got out to the parking lot, Jackie had the T-Bird started up and was shutting the door. I ran in front of the car as her wheels squealed. She slammed on the brakes.

"What the hell are you doing, Marty, trying to get yourself killed? Get out of my way!" I pulled open the passenger side door and jumped in. She stepped on the gas, and the T-Bird squealed out of the lot.

"Jackie, I love you." She was starting to cry. I took her hand at a red light. "We could run away together, find a new town, make a new start together. You don't really love that lumberjack you're living with. Do you?" She shook her head and broke down, falling into my arms.

Someone honked. The light had turned green.

We went to the same bar we'd gone to before. As I helped her with her door, she stood up and kissed me passionately, the tears still in her eyes. I held her tight. Then we walked arm in arm into the bar.

I was excited. I could barely stay seated at our booth as I drank my beer. I was overflowing with plans, with ideas of where we would go, how we would work it. We'd get jobs for a while and save up enough for our own business. Maybe a little bookstore. It had never occurred to me that something like this could really happen. It was the first time I'd ever stated my simple dreams out loud.

Jackie didn't say anything. She let me blabber on about how wonderful it was going to be, how we would find a place neither of us had been before, we could just take an atlas and pick blindly. It would be an adventure. I felt like I was sixteen again.

The drinks only seemed to sober Jackie up. The tears had all dried up. She was staring at the wall.

"We should probably leave as soon as possible, don't you think? Of course we'll have to think of something for Clem but that'll be no problem...."

"I can't go with you, Marty," she said, still staring at the wall.

"What? But I thought ... I thought there was no question. Of course, if you need more time I understand. If you need a few days..."

"I can't go with you now or ever, Marty." She turned toward me and looked deeply into my eyes. I put the beer mug down. I didn't understand, suddenly felt that life line slipping away again.

She cupped my face tenderly in her hands and kissed me lightly on the lips. "It's not you. You're precious. I could easily fall in love with you. But I've got people here, commitments. Clem ... I can't just take off and leave him. He needs someone to take care of him."

"But you don't love him. You said..."

She looked down at the palms of her hands. "You don't understand. There's more to life ... I'm too old ... getting old ... I'm afraid. I can't just run off! He's good to me. Wants me to marry him. If I go with you what kind of life am I going to have? What kind of life are we going to have? You working in some lousy kitchen, me waiting tables for the rest of my life? There'll never be any bookstore, any pie in the sky dream. We'll be struggling, always struggling. I don't want to have to live like that anymore. I want to live."

I felt broken. I couldn't say anything. I wanted to live too. I was tired of all the crummy jobs, the highway signs that never stopped coming.

She grabbed my hand and squeezed it hard.

"You can't just run away when things get bad, Marty, because you can't run away from yourself. You can't win at every game you play. You've got to compromise and take as much of the pot as you can."

I looked at her sadly, feeling like I'd been personally betrayed by her, just as I'd been betrayed by Tom at the restaurant. They'd sold out their dreams for pennies. But what good were dreams? Where were we all going, where were we all headed in the end anyway? I didn't know what I believed anymore.

But that was bullshit, copping out. We all have to live and make the best of it, whatever time we have.

Suddenly I was hot, feeling like I should put my hands on her shoulders and shake her real good. I stared hard at her across the table. She wasn't looking at me.

"Jackie, do you really believe you can compromise your life like that and still retain any of your happiness? By giving up, giving in to what others want for you? Is that what you really want? To marry that dumb construction worker and have a bed that smells like pine and wake up every morning picking splinters out of your side?"

Her palm felt like cold steel as it struck my face. After that we both sat frozen, like two strangers, two statues in the park waiting for the pigeons to circle round and hit their mark.

Then she spoke. "Why can't you just let me live my own life, have some respect and let me live it the way I want to? We're different, Marty. We have different needs."

Leave, I thought. Just leave.

"Your answers aren't answers at all for me, can't you see that?"

I'd lost again. I had to realize that.

I turned away from Jackie, got up, and walked to the door. She yelled from behind, "Don't you understand, don't you understand anything?"

No, I thought. Nothing at all.

Her voice died as the heavy wooden door shut behind me. I walked toward the road, hitched a ride back to the restaurant and drove back to my apartment.

After packing my things up in the car and settling my bill with the desk clerk, I took out a road atlas, placed it on the hood of my car, closed my eyes and with great solitary ceremony leafed through the atlas and speared one finger between the turning pages.

I didn't bother to open my eyes just yet. I imagined a small, sleepy town. A shop. TYLER BOOKS. A woman. A fireplace.

I wondered how much longer I would run.

Life Rafts and Lies

I met Jenny at my brother Hal's wedding rehearsal. To be there, I'd driven twenty-two hours straight from Austin—where I lived, where I no longer belonged—to Chicago.

Jenny was the bride-to-be's sister. As the best man and maid of honor, we walked down the aisle together, our arms interlocked. And, afterward, at the dinner for the rehearsal participants, we sat next to each other.

She smiled and leaned toward me. "Martin," she whispered, "do you think you could ... you know ... order me a beer? They won't serve me." Her smile was soft enough to sink into.

"Really? You look at least twenty-one." (I, myself, was just a shade over twenty-two.)

"Shhh," she said, leaning closer to me. "You don't want everyone to hear."

"How old are you?" I whispered back. Our cheeks were almost touching.

"Nineteen," she said. "Boy, I really could go for a beer."

"I know what you mean. Don't worry. I'll take care of it." Her eyes glistened and her smile widened. The way she was looking at me, I thought, maybe she could be my life raft for a little while. God knew I needed one.

Those were bad days for me. It had been nearly six months since I'd lost my girlfriend, Laura. We'd met in Austin, where I'd gone to graduate school in advertising for a semester before dropping out. I didn't know where I was going, but I knew that road was the wrong one. I wanted to do something useful with my life.

The day after I'd arrived in Austin I'd met Laura at a bar I'd gone to alone. She'd come up to my table after I was already half-crocked, kicked off her shoes, and pulled me on to the dance floor. She was only seventeen and there was a simple brightness in her eyes, in her smile, that lifted me up. But she had a darker side, too. She'd experienced too much already in her short life—drugs, sex—there'd been lots of boys already—and a nervous breakdown about a year before; and she would fall under clouds of desperate depression that wouldn't lift for days, obliterating the sun. But I wouldn't learn about all this until later.

It was her light that drew me to her on that first night. And from the moment we kissed that night on the dance floor, we were inseparable.

Then, however, she'd gone to England for the summer with her parents to visit relatives. It was there that she'd had a second nervous breakdown. She heard voices, couldn't think straight, wrote me letters and cards in a funny, shaky hand, telling me she was getting better every day. Weeks turned into months, and dates I locked onto for Laura's imminent return to Austin with her parents were constantly changed. Still I held on. Time dragged, and almost a year passed.

Then, at the beginning of April, I received a perfumed card from her saying how much she was looking forward to seeing me, how we would soon be back together again. She'd drawn a large red heart, with a tear falling off of it, and inside it had scribbled "I Love You!!!" Her writing was more coherent and less shaky than it had been. She'd written the date on inside of the card—March 26th. I didn't know then, as I read it, as I put the card to my nose to inhale her perfume, my hopes momentarily soaring at the thought of her return, that she was already dead.

I didn't find out anything about it until days later, when I read a note dated April 1st, written in her mother's now shaky hand. At first, reading the date, I thought it was some sort of sick joke. Laura had a relapse, her mother said. She'd been tired and frustrated with her situation, with being away from her friends, and from me.

It had happened in the middle of the afternoon. Her parents were out shopping. There were some sleeping pills on the table beside her bed. She swallowed the whole bottle. After finding her lifeless on her bed, her parents had called the ambulance and they'd rushed her to the hospital. There they'd pumped her stomach out and everyone thought she was all right. But something happened, something in the night. A stroke, maybe. They wouldn't know for sure until after the autopsy. Not that the cause of her death or anything else in the world seem to matter after hearing that word, the word that made the harsh truth stick in my gut, between my ears like a hard, jagged rock. Autopsy. There it was. Was there any other word so cold sounding, so cruel?

And now I was back in Illinois for my brother's wedding, still walking around, but feeling this dead spot inside. I knew I would never get over her. But there I was, three days after the rehearsal, strolling down the aisle, arm in arm with this girl I'd just met, who I'd ordered a beer for, who, with her long face and curly dark hair, could have been Laura. But her name was Jenny.

After making it down the aisle, there was still the reception to deal with. I bypassed the handshaking bit and headed straight for the bar. I got a gin and tonic and made my way back through the crowd in the hall—mostly strangers, my brother's clients—and put my back against a wall, trying to melt into it. My Uncle Jake, the ex-hippie businessman, spotted me and headed, in his bouncing, jangling manner, right to me.

"How's it going, Martin?" I shrugged. He put his hand on my shoulder.

"I heard you had some bad news." I nodded, held my breath for a second, then, in a tumble of words, told the story once again. It was funny how, at first, I'd thought I needed to get it all out, but it never gave me any relief, only seemed to cheapen things, trying to put it into words. You couldn't describe the hammer shot, the sudden void that filled you inside. And now I didn't want to talk about it anymore, just wanted to put it behind me. But it was nice knowing that someone cared, especially on a day like this. I mean, in another year or so it could've been our wedding.

I stood back against the wall and closed my eyes, nursing my drink.

"Look alive," Hal said, walking past me. "This is a wedding, not a funeral."

People filtered into the big party room. I was to sit at the table in front. I found my name card and sat down. Then I saw Jenny come into the room. She was breathtaking in her frilly pink best gal dress. And then, like an angel sent to tide me over, she sat down beside me, turned and smiled. "We meet again," she said.

"Yes, we do," was all I managed to say.

As the best man, I was obligated to make the toast. It was about the last thing in the world I wanted to do. It would have been impossible without the gin, without Jenny's warm smile to encourage me.

So, already half-crocked when all the happy guests starting clinking their glasses, I stood up on shaky legs, and recited the gobbledygook I'd written and memorized the night before: "I hear a lot of people say that you lose your freedom when you get married, but I, I think that it's just the opposite, that when two people come together in marriage it's something very special, the start of a new life, and when two people come together in marriage they eventually find their freedom together." I knew they were all lies, but the kind of lies people wanted, they expected to hear at a wedding. I toasted Hal and Dena then for their newfound freedom. "Here,

here!" someone shouted from the back of the hall. Then, for just a moment, there was an eerie silence in the room as if it had turned into a house of prayer. I closed my eyes, wondering after Laura's freedom. Then, the mix of mumbling voices and laughter returned. I opened my eyes and sat back down.

I looked over at Jenny for reassurance. Could she give me just a little of that? We were both already tipsy from beer, gin, and champagne. She put her hand lightly on my shoulder, leaned toward me. "That was beautiful," she said, her smile wide.

"Thanks." I took a sip of champagne. It was very sweet, but had a bitter aftertaste.

We danced closely that night, between trips to the bar. We were both young and we were both free, although I didn't really want to be. I clung to her and closed my eyes, feeling her body against mine, wanting the night, the fog in my brain to last. Wanting it desperately, though knowing it was impossible, everything in life was impossible now.

She caught the bouquet and I the garter belt. People joked with us, said maybe we'd be next. We laughed and looked at each other. We'd just met. Besides, I no longer believed in luck or faith or any other goddamned thing.

Drunk on booze, on holding her, I told her about Laura. She told me about the guy she'd just broken up with.

Later, we walked to the motel, across the way, where she was staying. We sat on her bed, necking.

"I don't usually do this with guys I've just met," she said once, coming up for air.

"Me neither," I said.

She had Laura's curly brown hair and large brown eyes. If I closed my eyes and squinted hard enough she might just become Laura. But, that ... I was supposed to forget all that, remember?

"You're not at all like your brother," she said, staring into my eyes.

"How are we different?" Her statement was obviously true, but I wasn't sure why.

She smiled and considered for a moment, looking at the ceiling.

"I don't know," she said. "You're just so much more ... laid back than him." Funny how they always thought that about me, although I didn't really think of myself like that at all. Disoriented, a mess, yes.

"He has plans, big plans," I said. "Marrying your sister is just part of it. He planned that even before he met her, on getting married, and"—I glanced at my watch—"looks like he was right on schedule with that."

"How about you? Do you have any plans?"

"Nothing solid. I'm just going day by day right now. I'm working on getting back with the living."

"Do I pass?"

"Stand up," I said. She did. "Turn around." She turned. "Once more." She did a pirouette, then stood glaring at me, her hands on her hips.

"Well?"

I put my hands behind my head and lay back down on the bed. "You pass with flying colors."

"What a relief," she said. She was smiling again.

"Come here," I said.

She lay next to me, on her side.

"How about you?" I asked.

"How about me what?"

"Plans. You gonna be a bank teller the rest of your life?"

"No. That's just temporary. I'm going to start taking classes again. Finish my degree."

"In what?"

"I don't know. Business, accounting maybe."

"Like my brother."

"You really don't like him much, do you?"

"You know he married your sister because she was a virgin, don't you? I mean, that's not the only reason. He told me once though that he had to marry a virgin. At first I thought he was joking. But, no, not Hal. I still can't believe it. I mean, even that there is such a thing as a twenty-five year old virgin anymore. But ... I'm sorry. She is your sister...."

"No, it's okay. I don't understand them either. I know all about it. They made a pact, I don't know if it was written or anything, that they wouldn't do anything until they were married. Can you imagine? Going a year and a half like that?"

"They must've done something. I'd go out of my mind."

"Yeah. something. What if they find out that they're no good together in bed?"

"They could get a quicky divorce."

"I don't know," Jenny said, reaching for the pack of cigarettes on the night stand. She took one out and lit it, then flopped down on the bed again. "I never could understand Dena either. She was always Miss Perfect in our family. Too perfect if you ask me. I always thought that being so good, going to church every Sunday, taking care of my parents, never drinking and ... well, what you said, someday she'd crack up. But she hasn't. I guess I was wrong."

"No, you weren't. You were right on target. She married my brother, didn't she?"

I left her room that night, promising her that I would see her again, that I was moving back home from Texas. I didn't know it until that night, until meeting her.

The next morning I left for Austin to collect my things—not that there was much to collect—a small television, my stereo, an odd assortment of clothes and possessions—and to tie up loose ends, mostly things that didn't really matter much at all. A two-bit job in a restaurant. A couple of friends, more like acquaintances, to say goodbye to, and the efficiency apartment I was renting on a month-to-month lease. There was nothing much more than that.

I landed back at my parents' doorstep a week later, all my possessions jammed inside my aging blue Mustang. It had been a grueling drive from Austin with a pit stop in Nowhere, Missouri. I was back home, or something approximating home, twenty-two years old and feeling like there was no place in the world for me after Laura—I'd pinned my hopes on that girl, unrealistic as it might have been. But she'd loved me without question, without judgment, made me feel like I had worth in the world, that I was someone. It had been a first for me, to be loved so unconditionally, and to be able to let my guard down. Maybe there really wasn't anything wrong with me. Maybe my life meant something. And I'd loved her just as unconditionally, loved her like I never thought I'd love anyone. And then, just like that, she was gone. And I was right back where I'd started: in my parents' house, alone.

I set out looking for a job, for anything I could get. I needed the money and had no idea what I wanted to do with my life. I interviewed for jobs in publishing houses, offices, supermarkets, warehouses, and was turned down everywhere I went. Finding that my B.S. in psychology wasn't worth much in the real world.

I had called Jenny the day after I got back into town, not really knowing if I wanted to, and wondering what else I would do by myself. I couldn't do that, couldn't be by myself anymore.

We started seeing each other regularly. I'd drive from the north side of Chicago—Skokie, where I'd grown up, where my parents still lived—through downtown, past its impossibly tall buildings—the John Hancock, the Sears Tower—to Cicero, where she lived with her parents. It was a long drive. The first couple of times we went out, I'd make the hour and a half drive home, weaving my way through the lanes of never-ending traffic on the Eisenhower, the Kennedy, and the Edens Expressways. But, after that, we followed my brother and sister-in-law's example. After Hal had started seeing Dena, he'd slept over in the Kzinskis' spare bedroom. It was a small house, but with all the children gone except for Jenny, there were two empty bedrooms.

There was a sadness to it. I wasn't really ready for it. Maybe she wasn't either. On nights when I didn't stay over, I'd lay in bed in my own room, my bed of childhood, and stare at the ceiling, trying to conjure Laura's face out of the darkness. I'd had a dream about her one night about a month before, back in Austin. I'd been struggling, in agony, since the night I'd found out, asking "Why?" to a different ceiling but to the same darkness, with no response.

I never could really communicate with Jenny's parents. Her father was about eighty, her mother about twenty years younger, and neither of them knew English too well. They'd come from Czechoslovakia before World War Two had started. Actually, they'd gone to Argentina first. Dena had been born there. Mr. K had been a farmer—Jenny told me all this—but things had started going bad with the government, so he'd moved his family here. Two years later, Jenny was born. They'd given her that name because it was popular, it was American.

He couldn't really speak to me, but he seemed to like me. He kept busy. He was, among other things, a writer—he'd been writing his memoirs for years. All in all it was about twelve hundred pages, Jenny said. The book was being serialized in a Czech newspaper. It told of his adventures in World War One, how the family had fled the Nazis to South America before the Second World War, his days there as a potato farmer, and, finally, the move to America, his life there in Cicero, where many other Czech families lived. She showed me some of the newspapers with his serialized story in it, but, besides his name, it didn't mean anything to me—I couldn't even see how some of the words could be pronounced. In places there were as many as five consonants crammed together without a vowel. It was a very strange language.

He couldn't talk to me, although he'd try to, saying something I didn't understand, then smiling and shaking his head. On my first visit he brought me down to the basement. I expected he had a bar or a still down there. What did I know? But when he turned on the light, dozens of glowing faces were staring at me. Marionettes! Another little secret. He was a closet puppet maker. But these weren't just crude puppets. They were lifelike, each one different, each with its own human expression. A gypsy with a red scarf and a single wooden earring, smiling seductively at me, her dark eyebrows raised, a tall faceless man in a green suit, staring out into nowhere, as if he'd lost his heart and soul, and many smaller marionettes, children with exuberant, untarnished looks of joy on their faces. I put a finger out to touch the marionettes, but hesitated. I looked at Mister Kzinski. He smiled and muttered something, gesturing with his hands to let me know it was all right. I put my fingers on the wood of one small girl's face. I'd expected it to be rough and cold, but it was smooth and strangely warm. Then, suddenly, I was startled as she jumped and came to life, dancing and leaning closer to me. Behind me, Mr. K laughed loudly. His left hand was up high on the wooden cross controlling the marionette. He made her sing a Czech song that sounded like Mary Had a Little Lamb. "Eh?" he said, "You like?" He was beaming at me.

"Yes," I said, smiling back. "I like."

Her parents thought we were just like Hal and Dena. We didn't do anything to make them think otherwise, so they gave us their implicit trust. On the first night I was to stay over, I didn't even put my arm around Jenny as we sat on the couch watching television with her mother, while her father, feet propped up in his Lazy Boy, studied his Czech newspaper. Still, Jenny and I both knew what was ahead, and looked forward to the evening with contained excitement. I could see it in her eyes, the way she held my gaze from time to time and squeezed my hand.

I was to sleep in the guest bedroom, right off the front door. The house reminded me of a railroad car. It was very long and narrow, with the doors to all the bedrooms on the left. All the main rooms—the living room in the front, followed by the dining room, with a bathroom in between, and the kitchen, in the back of the house—were on the right side of the little house.

At about nine o'clock, Mr. and Mrs. Kzinski got up and said "Goodnight"—it was one of the few English words they'd both learned—Mr. Kzinski, in his sleeveless white T-shirt, saying it before yawning in an exaggerated manner and giving his belly a firm slap, Mrs. Kzinski smiling shyly behind her husband, saying it quietly, before disappearing down the hall behind him.

Jenny looked at me, her eyes sparkling. I moved toward her, gave her a long, lingering kiss. When it was over, she pulled back a little and smiled.

"I think I'll get ready for bed now," she said.

"What should I do?" I was sitting there, my bare arm lying upon the arm of the couch, beer in hand.

"You get ready, too."

I'd brought the necessities—toothpaste, toothbrush, and a change of clothes—my job interview suit—in my back pack, along with my robe. I never wore pajamas, but usually just slept in my underwear. In the guest bedroom, I slipped everything off, except my underwear, and wrapped the robe around me, then returned to the couch. My half-drunk beer sat on the table beside the couch, next to two empties. Johnny Carson was on TV. He was doing one of his things, making fun, deadpan, of some bleached blonde actress on his right, while the audience, in expected response, roared with laughter at every gesture, every eyeroll Johnny made. I could have done without it, but it was welcome noise given the circumstances.

Then Jenny came out, wrapped up tight in a pink terrycloth robe. She cozied up next to me. I took a last gulp of beer and put my arm around her.

"Sexy outfit," I said. "What've you got under there?" I tried to take a peek.

"Shhh. My mom and dad." She slapped my hand lightly, but smiled at me. She turned her face up. We kissed for a long time, before, finally, she took my hand and said, "Come on."

"Do you think it's safe?" I whispered.

She led me onward into the darkness of my room.

I turned the light on. She had taken her robe off. She was wearing a short white nightie.

"Could you get the light?" she said. "I like it off."

We couldn't move much. The bed creaked. It was awkward. So we stayed locked together, barely moving. At one point, I started moving down her body, each movement making the bed creak, until I got to where I wanted to be. I tried kissing her between her legs, but she put her hand on the top of my head and said, "Don't."

I stopped. "Why?"

"I don't know," she said. "I don't like it." So I slowly worked my way back up, bed creaking as I went. What followed, followed, but it was over much too soon. She lay in my arms for only a few minutes before getting up, saying she was afraid that she would fall asleep. She gave me a peck on the lips and slipped out, leaving me alone in the room.

In the early morning I missed her. I crept carefully down to her room and got in bed with her. She woke with a start, rolled into my arms, and we were at it again.

"What time is it?" she asked.

"Does it matter?"

"It must be early. It's still dark out."

I kissed her. I wanted her again. Only her bed creaked more than the other, and her parents were sleeping on the other side of the wall.

"Stop," she whispered. I did. She pushed me away gently, pulled the covers off the bed and put them on the floor. Then she lay on her back, opened her arms to me, and smiled.

I woke up beside her on that pallet she'd made us on the floor. I was thinking about her parents, wondering if her father had a shotgun down in the basement along with all his wood, carving tools, and puppets. But, there wasn't a sound in the house. Jenny was still asleep, her bare back pressed against me. I turned over and shook her lightly. She yawned, stretched her arms, and curled up against me, smiling, her eyes still closed.

"Jenny," I said.

"I'm tired," she said.

"Your parents," I whispered.

"Oh, they don't get up till late. They sleep like logs. What time is it, anyway?" I checked the clock on her dresser.

"It's six o'clock." I said. She opened her eyes, then kissed me.

With her parents on the other side of the wall, hopefully asleep, she started getting dressed. Through her window, behind the shade, the sky was starting to turn from black to dull gray. I sat on the floor, in my underwear, watching her, her nearly perfect body. Feeling something like pride in ownership, some male feeling like that, though I knew it was stupid, no one owned anyone or anything. What we'd done might mean nothing at all to her, for all I knew. Maybe she did this all the time. Who could tell? We got along all right together, but we hardly knew each other. Still, I needed to fill the void that had been Laura. So what was wrong with Jenny? Nothing that I could see. But it's always like that when you just meet someone, isn't it?

Jenny slipped her bra on first, then her panties, and then her black nylons. She smiled at me, thinking me silly probably, sitting there, holding my breath, in awe really, watching her dress for work, like she did every other day of her life. She went to her closet, pulled out a black skirt and a white blouse. First she pulled the skirt over her legs, zipped it up, then slipped on the blouse.

"Will you help me with this?" she asked, and turned around. I tried to put the little hooks together behind her neck, her fine, delicate neck. Just to touch her, to touch....

"Oooh, your hand's cold," she whispered, pulling away, but turned back around and smiled. We kissed once slowly, sleepily. Then she patted my ass and pulled away from me. She reached down beneath her bed, scooped up her heels, and slipped them on.

By the time I was dressed, butter was sizzling in the kitchen. I walked out, and tentatively moved toward the sound. I was afraid what I might see on her parents' faces. Afraid what I might see in her father's hand—he'd carved all those marionettes himself. Jenny, coming out of the bathroom, met me in the hall, and said, "How do I look?"

"Luscious," I said, wanting to grab her, but stopping myself. "Come have some breakfast," she said, and pulled me into the kitchen.

Her mother, in a frumpy old dress, was working the frypan. She smiled as we walked in, said something in Czech to Jenny, who sat down, looked at me and smiled for an instant. Then she unzipped her small black purse and pulled out a pack of Winstons. I could hear her father, gargling in the bathroom.

"What'd your mom say?"

"She said you look nice in your suit."

"Tell her she looks nice, too."

She did. Her mother laughed and pulled her robe tightly around her, saying something that sounded like "Hoch jemny ihar."

Jenny lit her cigarette, inhaled with relish and let it out in a cloud of white smoke. Then she smiled at me. "She says the nice boy is a liar."

After breakfast I dropped her off at the bank where she worked. I watched her walk to the door, enticing in the way she moved in her tight black skirt. She waved, yelled, "Call me," and disappeared behind the door. I wanted to shout out after her, tell her to stop, but it was too late. I imagined being one of the lucky men who came in to make a deposit at her window, watching her bright smile unfold. I was jealous, wished I could be one of them. Maybe I would surprise her, come in later and open up an account. But that was stupid, she would think I was spying on her, even though it wouldn't be like that at all. I just wanted to get another look at her, before I forgot.

I drove over to her house a couple times a week. One night she told me about the abortions. She'd had two of them. We were drinking Amaretto before we left—it had become our little ritual, sitting around her kitchen table, drinking, after I arrived—and she told me about them.

"Don't ever tell anyone, you promise?"

"Sure, okay, I promise. It'll be our little secret." I couldn't keep myself from smiling. She'd told me a secret.

"Now, you tell me one," she said, leaning across the table, smiling, putting her cheek next to mine.

"Tell you one?"

"A secret."

"Oh, okay. I don't know if I have any."

She pulled back, and took another slurp from her glass.

"You must have. Everyone does."

"Well, I probably do. Let's see." I closed my eyes, trying to remember something that might match her display of intimacy.

"Think of something you never told anyone before."

"Okay. Here goes. When I was about thirteen, I threw rocks at cars on the expressway."

"You did?" Her face lit up. She put her hand on my arm, squeezed tightly. "Did anyone get hurt?"

"No. Just me."

One day when I went over, after a long day of job interviews, we sat in the kitchen drinking, as usual. We were confiding in each other again. I was telling her how I'd flown Laura up to Minnesota when I was visiting my uncle up there, last summer, how she'd sneak into my room, late at night.

"You really loved her, didn't you? You miss her a lot."

I looked down at my drink.

"What would you have done with her today, if she were still alive?"

"I don't know. Maybe go to the Armadillo beer garden. Sit out there and listen to music. But, I forgot—they tore down the Armadillo."

Her eyes shone. "Let's go." She got up and grabbed my hand.

"Where?"

"I dunno. For a walk."

"In the rain?"

"Yeah."

"Why?"

"Why not?"

We walked across the street hand in hand. It wasn't a downpour, but a steady rain. She took me to a park, where she stopped, trying to light her cigarette. Finally, I took the lighter from her and lit it while she cupped her hands around the tip. Her hair was hanging down now, all the curls flattened out, dripping wet.

I pushed her on the swing, pushed her higher as she laughed, as she screamed "Wheee!" It was just like having fun. I kept pushing her, until, suddenly, all the air came out of me, and I stopped.

She twisted around to look at me. "What's the matter?"

"I don't know." I shoved my hands in my pockets. I was shivering. It was Laura, remembering a day with her like this.

Jenny got up off the swing and came toward me. I kissed her softly and said, "Let's go back."

That Sunday she invited me over for dinner. Her parents seemed to like me, though I couldn't imagine why. I assumed it was because they thought I was like my brother, Hal. They knew nothing about the midnight rendezvous between Jenny and me in their front bedroom, twice a week. Mr. Kzinski stood at the head of the table, a white napkin tucked into his collar to cover his clean white shirt. I'd worn my suit pants and a white shirt at Jenny's request. It was like some sort of occasion, but I didn't know what. Mr. Kzinksi said something to me, and laughed. I looked at Jenny, but she just patted my hand and smiled.

Mr. Kzinski put on a Czech record, a polka of some sort. He started clapping and laughing. He tried to get his wife to get up and dance with him, but she just looked down at her lap, her face turning red. "Jenny?" he asked, looking at her. She shook her head at him, and said, "No, Papa," then looked at me. I reached for her hand and squeezed.

I knew there was no malice in them. How could there be? They were such gentle people. Still, when they talked it was in Czech and Jenny didn't bother to interpret. I couldn't help feeling a little paranoid when someone said something I couldn't understand and they all looked at me and smiled or laughed.

"I'll have to teach you Czech, that's all," Jenny said later.

Things went smoothly for a couple of months, then something happened. I was to take Jenny and her nine-year old nephew, Timmy—the son of Jenny's other older sister, Rita—to an amusement park for the day. When I showed up at nine o'clock sharp on Saturday morning, as I'd been instructed, Jenny was not there. Where was she?

Her mother looked at me with worried eyes and, in her best broken English, told me, "She no come home last night."

I was stunned. I'd thought things had been going so well between us. And now this.

"Sit, sit," she said, impatient, almost angry with me, it seemed, as if I had something to do with it, as if I'd failed in my job of keeping her youngest daughter in line.

I planted myself on the couch and waited, wordlessly, watching the Coyote chase the Roadrunner. I felt for the guy. He'd never get that pesky bird.

About half an hour later she showed up. Her mother met her at the door and scowled at her in Czech. "Momma, please," she said, and walked to her room without looking at me. I was wondering why I was still there.

She came out ten minutes later in clean clothes and with a fresh layer of makeup on her face.

"Hi," she said, standing before me. "Ready to go? Timmy'll be waiting for us." There were dark circles under her eyes.

"Okay," I said.

It wasn't until we were in the car, driving to her sister's house that I asked, "So, where were you?"

"I was with my friend, Marla. At another friend's house."

I took a deep breath, then asked, "Was this other friend a guy?"

She didn't look at me. She lit her cigarette and gazed out the window. "Yeah," she said. "He's a fireman, an older guy."

What was that supposed to mean? I was an older guy too. I looked at her, but she was still staring out the window. She sighed.

"He's just a friend, Martin. We were drinking and it was late, so we stayed over." It was all she said to explain why she'd spent the night at another guy's house. And, she'd never mentioned her friend Marla before.

We didn't talk much the rest of the way. Still, I went along with it, if not for her, for her nephew. He'd been looking forward to this all week. He came out to the car, a pudgy little blonde-haired boy, all smiles and bright eyes.

With Timmy in tow, Jenny and I somehow managed to make it through the whole day, roller coasters and bumper cars, hot dogs and snow cones, without saying more than the necessary words to one another.

Afterwards, I didn't call her and she didn't call me.

I kept looking for a job, going on interviews. By necessity I had to continue lowering my aspirations. A month later, I was still unemployed, wondering if I'd ever find a job. One day I saw an ad for an ice cream vendor route. I couldn't exactly see myself being one of those guys in the broken down trucks wearing a little white ice cream suit, but what else could I do? I decided to check it out.

The place of the interview was right near Jenny's house. It was a Saturday, so I decided to drive by and see if she was home.

When I drove up it felt just like it always had driving up to her house, not like we hadn't talked in a month.

I knocked on the door and her mother came. She wasn't smiling at me like she used to, but she let me in.

She disappeared and, in a moment, Jenny came to meet me.

"Hi," she said, a blank expression on her face.

"I was just in the neighborhood, I have an interview, so I thought I'd drop by."

"I'm glad you did," she said, and gave me a tired smile.

She led me into the kitchen and poured me some of the Amaretto we always drank. We both started getting drunk and talking about our families, about her job and my prospects, about everything but what was on our minds. We sat there, pretending for a little while that nothing had happened, nothing had come between us.

She walked me to my car an hour later, and leaned toward me through the open window, just like she used to in our first days together, when she'd come out to the car with me and we'd have trouble telling each other goodnight. It was an impulse. I didn't know how she felt about it, if she thought we would just be friends now, but didn't wait to ask. I kissed her through that window, as the spring breeze swirled around us, and the cars swished by. She was hesitant at first, but then started to respond. And, about a minute later, she pulled back into the street and stared at me, looking angry at first, then just sort of confused.

She looked nothing like Laura. She was Jenny.

"So what do you think?" I asked.

She was still gazing at me with that befuddled look. But, suddenly, like a bud unfolding, there was a little smile, and she said " I'm sorry about what happened."

I looked at her for a moment, not knowing what to say. "Okay," I finally said.

"No, I mean it. I'm really sorry. I like you. I really like you."

Neither of us said anything, but we didn't have to. There was something stated in the way our eyes were locked on one another's that didn't require further explanation.

We kissed through the window one more time, and she stood back.

"Call me," she said.

"I will."

I started the car up then and pulled away slowly. In my rear view mirror I could see her standing by the curb, waving. As I drove she got smaller and smaller, only it wasn't her standing there waving anymore, but Laura, and if I listened hard enough I could hear her whispering in my ear: "It's okay Martin, it's okay."

A Ghost in Manhattan

The first time Andrew saw her was in front of the New York City Library. They were walking in opposite directions. When he saw hers in the blur of faces, he stopped, his eye the shutter clicking: the hazel, almond-shaped eyes, the thin, arching eyebrows, the broad nose which he'd thought a masterpiece, which he'd traced one night with his fingertips to memorize its perfect proportions, and those lips, how could he forget those lips? The whole snapshot—for that's what it was, quick as she passed—overlapped with the photograph he'd been carrying in his mind and in his wallet for the last ten years.

He saw the two of them floating in a canoe on Town Lake in Austin, the lake a sheet of glass, the hills ahead of them green and inviting. Glowing, that's how he'd felt then. There was a lightness in his chest and in his head. He loved her so much, watching her as she lay back in the boat, her face behind green lenses turned up to the sky, her reddish-brown hair gleaming with streaks of gold in the sunshine. The two of them drifting, just drifting.

He was standing in a time warp, staring at the place she'd been, but by the time he jerked around to find where she'd gone, it was too late, she was lost in the sea of the crowd.

In the days to come he took long lunches, walking from the office on Madison along the perimeter of Central Park down to the library. There, on the steps beside one of the huge seated lions, he would eat his hot dog and pretzel, sip his coffee, timing it so that he would be there at just the time he'd seen her that other day. He told himself he enjoyed the air and the good brisk walk. Besides, he liked to avoid the elaborate lunches which the agency regulars held for important or prospective clients, to get them lubed and well-fed, to ease them into the afternoon presentation. There was so much ass-kissing going on in those lunches that he was always surprised on returning to the office to find that anyone still had their pants on. Who needed it? He was sick of this life. A hot dog and a cup of coffee—the Spartan life, like he'd lived once, long ago, when ... but he stopped himself from thinking about it. Still, he kept his eye on the crowd as the people passed by. I've always been a people-watcher, he told himself.

She did not pass by.

Could it really have been her? As the days passed, he doubted himself more and more. Maybe something he'd seen or heard had brought up a memory of Laura and then, at that moment, he'd seen someone who looked like her. That's all it was. His mind was playing tricks on him. His imagination had been working overtime. That's what he thought.

Until he saw her again.

He was out on a lunch time stroll. She was walking into Macy's. His red tie loosened, his navy blue jacket folded over his arm, he pushed his way past the other pedestrians and hurried into the store after her. Once inside, he spotted her instantly. She was wearing tight, faded jeans, and an orange blouse with a print of a large tiger that seemed to be strolling down her back. He slowed down and followed her at a careful distance. She walked at a leisurely pace, one hand on the black handbag that hung from her shoulder. The walk was so familiar to him, one he had studied a hundred times before and studied again now, as she sashayed down the aisle, stopping at the perfume case. How could he forget that walk? He had died a little inside every time he'd watched her walk away. And she'd always been walking away. He remembered that time at the airport when, right before she'd gone down the ramp, she'd tried to cheer him up, saying, "It's not like we'll never see each other again." She was there, smiling at him, and then she'd disappeared down that long white vinyl tunnel without even looking back. Who could have known that it would, in fact, be their last moment together?

He pretended to be interested in a display of watches across the aisle from her, as she stood at the jewelry counter, trying on a bracelet, and slowly—it was like he was watching her in a dream— lifted her arm in front of her to examine how it looked on her. But this was crazy. She was dead. He hadn't been to the funeral—it had taken place in Britain. But why would anyone lie about that, about someone dying?

There certainly were possibilities. What if she'd gotten pregnant and the trip to England had just been a way to get him out of her life, or to take care of the baby? And when he hadn't relented in his telephone calls and letters, her parents had invented the second breakdown. Easy enough to believe. She'd already had one before. And, after that, when he'd suggested that he go over to England to be with her, her mother had written him a letter trying to discourage him, saying the economy in England was so bad it was hard enough for Brits to find a job, let alone foreigners. He'd be lucky to even get a work permit. But he hadn't given up. And what better way to get rid of him than to invent the circumstances—her death from an overdose of sleeping pills. But could it really have happened that way? Could it really be her?

He was mesmerized, staring at her. Suddenly, she glanced in his direction. He looked away quickly, then counted to ten, and looked back, but by then all he could see was a glimpse of the lion moving away fast. He hurried after her. She wasn't running, but walking quickly, quicker than she'd been before, that was for sure. Could she have recognized him after all these years? His heart started beating wildly. If she was trying to get away from him, it could only mean it was her, and he wasn't going crazy. Now that he'd found her, he couldn't lose her again! He sped up, desperate to catch her. She seemed to be moving even faster now. But there was a crowd ahead of her at the door, slowing her down. And, in a moment, he easily caught up with her. She didn't look back at him, or even acknowledge his presence. At the exit's bottleneck, he was only inches away from her, could smell her perfume. He would recognize that scent anywhere. It was the scent she had sprayed on the last card she'd sent him. Even after he'd heard she was dead, the scent had lingered for months. At first he had taken the card out every day and held it to his nose, breathing it in deep, as if by doing so he could breathe the last scents of her very life in. But after a while, he'd stacked it, and all her other correspondences, in a shoe box, organizing the letters by date, and stowing them in the back of his bedroom closet. It was his own personal museum of memories, his own dead letter file, the only remaining evidence he had of her, of their relationship.

The clot at the door loosened, and through the revolving doors they went, the tiger just ahead of him. She went to the left and he followed close behind. Not once did she turn around to look at him. You couldn't really, if you wanted to live in New York. In New York you always felt like you were being followed, but if you turned around every time you thought you were, you'd spend your day walking in circles.

She walked up the steps of a well-maintained brownstone. He watched her from across the street, as she put the key into the lock, opened the door and disappeared inside.

He leaned against the side of a building, pulled out a cigarette and lit it, wondering what to do next. A light went on upstairs in the brownstone. The curtains were closed, but suddenly she appeared through the crack in the middle, and Andrew ducked behind the side of the building. When, after a few moments, he looked back, she was no longer there, but the curtains were still fluttering as if she were.

Now was the nervy part. He had to do something. He had to confront this person. But what if she wasn't Laura? What if she wasn't even the same woman he'd seen the last time he'd thought he'd seen Laura? What if the entire female population suddenly started to look like his memory of Laura?

Making a fool of himself wasn't really the problem—hell, that was practically part of his job description. No, the problem was, what if it was her? Then what would he, what would she do?

He finished the cigarette, then threw it on the sidewalk, and stamped on it with the toe of his black oxford. He slipped back into his jacket, buttoned his shirt, and tightened his tie so that, once again, the silk pressed firmly against his neck. Then he stepped out from behind the building and walked slowly, but without hesitation, toward her building, wondering if she would recognize him. After all, it had been, how many, ten years? And he'd never even worn a suit when he'd known her, at least not when she was around.

He stopped at the front door and surveyed the names by the buzzers. There were two buzzers, one marked "Rodriguez," and the other "Durham." No "Mailer," but, hell, there could have been a lot of reasons for that—divorced, married ...but he hadn't considered that. What if by now—it certainly didn't take a lot of imagination to consider—she was married? Then what? But what if she wasn't? What then, anyway?

What the hell. He was going to drive himself nuts with all this thinking. Just go ahead and do it. He took a breath, then firmly pressed the bell for "Durham." (She certainly couldn't be "Rodriguez," or could she?)

After the second ring, a voice came over the speaker. "Yes?"

"Umm ... Ms. Durham? I know this is going to sound strange, but, I think I might know you, or ... used to know you. I was wondering if I could come up, just for a moment."

"Who is this?"

"I'd rather not say right now. I know this is unusual, but, if you'd just give me a moment...."

"I usually don't let just anybody up, you know. This is New York. How is it I know you, anyway? And how come you won't tell me who you are? What's your name?"

He took a breath. It was the only way. "Andrew. Andrew Dwyer."

He let go of the speaker button. The voice came over the speaker quickly, too quickly: "Andrew ..." she said, then the intercom cut off. In a few seconds later, though, the voice came back on. "I'm sorry. I'm afraid I don't know anyone by that name."

He put his finger back on the speaker button again. "Please, please, I know this is very strange, but if I could just see you for a minute. That's all I'm asking."

"Well, I must be crazy, but ... okay. Only for a minute, though. I've got a lot to do. Hold on. I'll buzz you in."

When she opened the door he was sure, for a moment. It was the way she smiled. Her hair was a little shorter maybe, but still the same reddish-brown. She even had the right eyes—they were green and wide. She had to be Laura, didn't she?

"Ms. Durham. I'm really sorry to intrude like this. I'm Andrew Dwyer." He extended his hand to her, let him take her hand in his and loosely shake it. Then she quickly pulled away from him. "Oh," she said, looking flustered, throwing both her hands up in the air, "It's all right. Come on in."

She led him down a narrow hallway into her living room. "Sit," she said, motioning to a plush, sky blue sofa. He sank down into it with the weight he'd been carrying around for ten years. She sat in one of the chairs across the room from him. He'd never thought he would be here, seeing her alive again. Life was nothing if not strange.

He looked around the room, wanting to look just at her, but not wanting to make her feel uncomfortable. There were pictures on the walls, abstracts with splashes of bright colors—pinks, and greens and yellows. In the dining room, through the hallway, there was a solid looking oblong table made of dark wood, and six chairs placed around it. Here, in the living room, there was a spinet piano to his left, too modern to fit in with the antique decor. Across the room where his hostess sat were two cherry wood chairs, with high carved backs and claw feet. Then he saw the photographs. They were on top of the piano. He stood up and moved across the room toward them.

"Do you mind?" he asked, as he reached for the framed pictures.

"No," she said, waving her assent. "It's all right." She tried to smile, but looked nervous, and watched him very closely.

There was a picture of her, this woman he was standing in front of, who might or might not be Laura, and a man, a thin sort of man in a blue suit. And, on the other side of the frame, a picture of a young boy of about five or six, he guessed.

"A good looking boy. Your ... son?"

"Yes" she said. He was trying to understand the look he saw in her eyes at that moment, something cold and distant. Resentment, perhaps? For the intrusion? Or maybe it was for another reason. The mention of her son, perhaps their son ....

He carefully placed the picture back on top of the piano, and turned to the woman. Looking at her now, he didn't know what to think.

"I've got a picture, too," he said. He pulled out his wallet, removed the little photo booth picture of Laura he'd kept under his license forever, and handed it to the woman. She examined it.

"A pretty girl," she said.

"She was," he said, then, looking right at her, "and still is."

He was expecting a reaction, something that would give her away, but her look was a blank. "I don't know what you mean," she said, stiffly handing him back the photo. "I've never seen her before in my life."

"You haven't." But what if he was wrong? What if she really didn't know who the girl in the picture was? What if, obsessed, he'd merely convinced himself of something that wasn't true?

"Listen, I'm really sorry to intrude like this. It's just ... I'm very confused and ... I don't know where to begin. Your name's not Laura by any chance, is it?"

"No, it's not. I'm Lana. Lana Durham." Lana. Not far from Laura. It wouldn't take much of a stretch of the imagination to change her name to that, but what about the last name?

"Durham. You're married, that's your married name, right?"

"Hey! What is all this, anyway? I don't even know you! Why should I answer any of your questions? How do I know you're not some kind of psycho killer or something?"

"Because ... I'm not."

She stood with her arms crossed in front of her, a skeptical look on her face. "Oh, well, now that's very reassuring." She sighed and the guarded look on her face seemed to soften some. Maybe she was beginning to realize that he was harmless. Now her look was more one of curiosity that anything. She ventured a small smile.

"What are you, anyway, a detective? Looking for some girl?"

"No, I'm not a detective. But I am looking for ... someone. Laura. It's a long story. I'm sorry. I guess I can see why you might think I'm some sort of psycho. Who knows, maybe I am."

"Hey now, Mister, if you're going to start anything funny, I think you better just leave right now."

He raised his hands, palms forwards. "I'm sorry. I guess that wasn't the right thing, what I really meant to say. It's just ... I really need to know if you are ... who you are."

She was still standing there, several feet from him, her arms crossed in front of her. Now it was his turn to sigh. He felt like the tears were going to start to run. All the memories, the years of wondering hit him at once.

She took a step closer to him. "Are you all right?" she asked. "You look pale all of the sudden. Can I get you something to drink, maybe?"

"No, no, it's all right. It's just, I'm just ..." Try as he might, he couldn't get the words out.

"I'm sorry about being this way, about being so suspicious and all."

"Oh, don't worry about it. I know. I don't blame you at all. Maybe," he said, "maybe what I really need to do is explain this all to you."

"That would be a good idea," she said, coming even closer to him, putting her hand lightly on his shoulder. "Would you like to sit down?"

"Yes, that would be nice," he said, looking into her eyes, and wiping the moisture from his eyes.

He sat, and tried to smile. She sat, also, on the other side of the couch. Then he started his story, staring down at his hands. "Where should I start? From the beginning, I guess. Where else to start? Okay, here's how it was. There was this girl I met when I was in college, back in Austin, Texas. Her name was Laura Mailer. I met her one night at a bar. She asked me to dance. She saved me. I was bombed good, pretty lost in those days, and she saved me. We started seeing each other every day and ... but you don't want to hear all this."

"No, go on. It's all right."

He looked at her, tentatively. She smiled. "I'm listening," she said.

"Okay, well ... she was only seventeen, I was twenty-two. Then one day she went away to England for the summer. She never came back. I got a letter from her mother saying she'd had a breakdown, and three months later another letter saying she'd taken an overdose of sedatives and died in the night after suffering a stroke."

He stopped for a moment, watching her. She didn't move a muscle. "Flash ahead, ten years or so. I'm working in New York, in Manhattan, for an ad agency. One day I'm walking by the New York Public Library and I see this woman. It's her, it's Laura. But before I know it, she's gone, lost in the crowd. It was like seeing a ghost. Then I start going back every day, eating my lunch on the library steps, waiting to see her pass by. But nothing happens. I don't see her again. I tell myself I've just been a fool, driving myself crazy. After a while everything starts getting back to normal. But then, then I see her again. It's her, I know it from the way she walks, the way she smiles. I get close enough to her that I can even smell her perfume. And you know what?"

He watched her, waited for her to respond.

"What?" she finally said.

"It's the same scent Laura wore. I don't know the name of it, but that smell is programmed in my brain. You see, I cling to what I can remember, and there's so little left of her. If I forget, who'll remember? So, that perfume, I'll never forget it. I saw this woman at Macy's. Today."

"So, that was you. You were following me."

"And now, here I am, here you are, sitting across from the biggest fool in New York. Unless ... unless ..." He looked at her closely, wanting it to be true.

She stood up suddenly, avoiding his gaze, and meshing her hands together.

"And now," Andrew said, "I guess you're just going to tell me you're sorry, but you're just not her."

"I'm sorry, Mr. Dwyer, but what can I say? Maybe this girl really did have a breakdown, or maybe there were circumstances beyond her control or ... or maybe she did die, just as you were told."

"Yes, that's what I was told."

"So why would you doubt it? Or did you think I—I was that ghost you saw that day?"

He laughed suddenly. He couldn't help himself. Then he told her, "Yes, that's exactly what I thought for a while, after I started to doubt myself. But then I started thinking. There could have been any number of reasons why I was told Laura died, all of them revolving around the fact that her parents may not have wanted me around her anymore. Maybe they found out that our relationship was more ... involved than they'd thought. Or maybe there was more to it than that."

"Like what?"

He looked over at the photograph on the piano. "A baby?"

The woman stood frozen for a moment.

"Are you crazy? Who would go to such lengths to pretend such a horrible thing? Why not just write him a Dear John letter?"

"That's a good question. Maybe her parents thought it wouldn't work with me. I was persistent. In the over twelve months that she was over there, I wrote her religiously, every week. I even called her every month, at what? A dollar a minute? They must've thought I was nuts. But I never stopped." He paused for a moment, then looked her directly in the eyes. "You see, you don't stop if you really love someone, if it's someone you'll never stop loving...."

He stood up and moved toward her. Her face flushed and her eyes widened in what looked like fear. He stopped less than a foot from her, staring in to the sea of her green eyes, searching for something there. He reached into his pocket and pulled out the necklace.

"Here," he said, placing it in her hands. "This is what they sent me of yours after they told me you were dead." It was the butterfly necklace he'd given her just before she'd left for England, the last time he'd seen her. She held it loosely in her hands, her look now seeming more one of sympathy than of fear.

"Mr. Dwyer, I—"

There was a sound at the door, the scratching of a key in the lock. In a moment, a young boy was in the room, apparently the boy in the picture, but older now. He stopped in the doorway, books held up against his chest, looking at two of them.

"Allan," Lana said brightly. "You're home!" She moved away from Andrew, and walked toward the boy. Then she led him by the arm across the room to Andrew.

"Allan, I want you to meet Mr. Dwyer." The boy had brown hair and brown eyes, just like Andrew, just like about seventy-five per cent of the general population, for that matter. He shook Andrew's hand and said, "Very nice to meet you, Mr. Dwyer."

Andrew smiled widely at him. "Well, young man it sure is nice to meet you. You look just like your mother." Then he turned to Lana, and asked, "How old did you say he was now, Lana?"

She stared at him, a flash of anger in her eyes. "Ten," she said, finally. He studied her look, tried to figure out if it meant what he thought. Then he turned back to the boy.

"You're such a big boy. And with such good manners. Your mother and father must be very proud of you."

"You know my dad? He doesn't live here anymore. He moved to Seattle."

"I'm sorry to hear that."

The boy shrugged. "He's not my real dad, anyway."

Andrew glanced back at Lana. Her stare had turned icy.

"His father died in a plane crash. About ten years ago, before he was born. Allan didn't even know him."

She put her hand on the boy's back and led him away from Andrew. "Well, let's put our books away, and I'll make you a nice snack, okay? Mr. Dwyer was just leaving."

The boy looked back at Andrew uncertainly. "It was nice meeting you, Mr. Dwyer."

When she came back, she said, "I suppose you believe he's your son, too. What kind of man are you? You must spend half your life chasing women who look like your ex-girlfriend." It was like a blow to the chest and it must have showed.

"I'm—I'm sorry, but somebody's got to tell you. Get on with your life. Don't spend it searching for ghosts who aren't there."

He sighed deeply. She was right. He was a fool, had been deluding himself on and off for what, ten years? Why?

"Mrs. Durham. I don't know what to say. I'm sorry, I'm really, really sorry. You must think I'm some kind of nut case." He tried to smile. "I guess you're right. It doesn't make any sense. When someone's dead, they're dead. You can't bring them back again. I'm sorry for disturbing you. I better just go. Thanks for humoring me."

He headed for the door. He had just gotten it open when her voice came from behind: "Mr. Dwyer?"

He stopped and turned around.

She walked over to him. The two of them were facing each other in the threshold.

"I know what I said may have been a little harsh. I'm sorry." She kissed him on the cheek. "Take care of yourself," she said.

He looked her in the eyes.

"Thanks," he said. "You too."

Then he closed the door gently behind him.

On the other side of the door, she still held the butterfly necklace in the cup of her hand, having meant to give it back to him. But now she felt weak, fell against the hard wood of the door between them, and opened her clenched hand to look once again at the little butterfly on the chain, touching it with her fingertip, remembering, remembering it all, and crying the first tears she'd cried in a very long time.

Sacrificial Rites

The trouble started with the columnist. Where the hell did he come from, and why was he messing with the lives of Carol and her daughter? It was none of his business, not at all.

She should have known better than to trust him. He was a columnist, and she'd read some of his other moralizing columns. Like he was so damn good, better than all the people he was writing about. She should have expected it. It was funny really that she'd been so naive, considering what she'd been doing for the last three years. And when the column came out, she was afraid to walk out of the apartment. He didn't use her name, but put down enough identifying information—the name of the school, the hospital, her position, even the class her daughter was in. God, there were only twelve kids in Patty's class. Did he really think he was doing anyone any good? Enlightening mankind by victimizing others? Or was it just to sell papers, sensationalism, like the talk shows on TV? Was that all it was? And now she was disgraced. Even her job was in jeopardy.

She could see him now with his innocent, youthful smile, the little bow tie that made him look about fifteen years old.

They'd met for coffee in a little restaurant near the hospital when she got off from her job at the hospital at 3:00. He was already sitting at a booth in front of a coffee cup, waving her over.

"Mrs. Reynolds. Thanks for coming. I hope you don't mind I ordered ahead. I was afraid they'd kick me out if I just sat down here. They seem to get their share of vagrant types."

She stood there, trying to smile at him, wondering what he meant by that. She'd suggested the place, after all.

"Well, sit, sit. Please."

She sat.

"What'll you have? Coffee, tea? A piece of pie, maybe?"

"Just coffee. I'm trying to watch my weight."

"Why? You look just fine. C'mon. I'll have one too. The paper doesn't give me much, but a piece of pie I don't think they would mind."

"No, really. Coffee's fine."

He smiled, a sincere sort of smile, at least it seemed that way then. "You're a woman who knows what she wants, huh? Maybe I'll use that as my angle."

"Angle?"

"Well, you know. You write a column, you've gotta have an angle. You could write any piece twelve different ways and wind up with twelve different stories. Surely you know that. The news is only more deceptive for trying to sound objective. Take a murder. You can write it from the viewpoint of victim's family—the blood-thirsty, justice-to-be done, hang the son-of-a-bitch angle—or you can play it from the neighbors' viewpoint—you know, the old, he seemed like a nice guy, watered his lawn, cut his grass, kept to himself, we never would have dreamed that he would be capable of such a thing bit. Or you can play it another way, say the poor guy, he couldn't help himself murdering the old lady, he had so much rage from his childhood, beaten by one mother's lover after another, locked in a closet by another without food for three days, that sort of bit, he's society's fault, ya know? Anyway you play it, they're the facts. But objective? It's just a matter of how you marshal the facts. Know what I mean?"

He was stirring his coffee in quick little circles, the spoon grating as it scraped against the inside of the cup.

"Now, me, writing a column, I don't have to even pretend that I'm objective. I just write it the way I feel. What seems right, the truth, you know?"

The truth. He'd actually said that, just after he'd said basically that there is no capital T truth.

"So, why don't we begin." He whipped a little note pad out of his shirt pocket and clicked his fifty-cent pen.

"Where do you want me to start?"

"Wait a minute. Where are my manners? I never did get you that tea."

"Coffee."

"Yeah, sorry, Carol. You don't mind if I call you Carol, do ya'?"

"Not if you don't mind me calling you Bob."

"Yeah, sure." He grinned wide, staring at her with his brown, unblinking eyes. "Why not." Then he turned his head sharply and called the waitress by name: "Hey, Jill, how about some more java over here for my friend?"

A woman with bright red hair and a big backside came over, snapping her gum, smiling at the columnist. Everybody loved him. He was a local celebrity.

"Sure, Bob. What'll it be, gorgeous?" she said, still looking at him, a little awestruck maybe. Carol thought maybe she was a little, too, sitting with this guy whose face was in the paper everyday.

"Coffee, Carol? Is that what you want? No pie, the paper, like I told ya ..."

"Coffee," Carol said. The waitress gave her a cup and poured some of the steaming fluid from a brown pitcher. Then she stood, mooning at Bob.

"You sure are cute. More handsome than that picture of you in the paper. Truthfully, you should get a new one. It doesn't do you justice."

"Hey, thanks, Jill. You're not bad yourself."

"So, when you gonna do a column about me? I'll give you the lowdown on why a woman of my many talents puts up with serving a bunch of thankless low-lives—yourselves excluded, of course—everyday, with no thanks. Why do I put up with it, you wonder? When I've got a degree in English Lit? I'll let you in on a little secret. I've got a dynamite novel nearly completed, that's going to make a great movie. You'll be able to say you interviewed me when I was just a waitress at this greasy spoon. What do you say, Bob?" she asked, a hand on her hip. "I'll give you the inside story, an exclusive."

Bob seemed to be taking it all in with enthusiasm. Or was it just that she had a body to go with her mouth? "Hey, Jill," he said, "it sounds great. I'll tell you what. Right now I'm full up with stuff for a while, but here's my card." He pulled one out of his shirt pocket and handed it to her. "Call me in a couple weeks. Then maybe we'll see what you've got. Okay?"

"You mean it? Yeah, yeah, sure. Thanks."

The moment she was gone the columnist leaned over confidentially toward Carol. "They've all got novels, every third waitress from here to Albany. But they don't have anything. Now you, you've got a real story. Speaking of which ..."

"What's it like to be so famous?"

He laughed a staccato laugh—it sounded a little like machine gun fire. "It's not all it's cracked up to be, believe me. You work ten hours a day—I get to work at eight every morning and leave at seven, sometimes eight at night. It's a lot of hard work, a little glory, and even littler pay. What can I say?

"So, where were we?" he asked, staring at his blank pad. "Start wherever you like. Start with what you told me over the phone. Refresh my memory."

"About my daughter, about Patty, you mean?"

"Sure. Why not."

So she told him about Patty, a sweet kid, a smart kid with big things ahead of her. "I'd do anything for that girl," she said. "To give her the best, a better life than mine. That's your angle, if you want."

"Hmmm?" he said, looking up. "Oh, yeah, sure, sure. Not bad. The mother who'd do anything for her daughter. Even sell herself to strange men."

Carol's pulse quickened, her face reddened. "It's not exactly like that."

"Oh, no, no, so tell me what it is like."

"Well, after I was divorced, I started seeing a lot of men. That's all. Most of them weren't all that pleasant to be around but I still, you know, had my needs."

"Can't live with 'em, can't live without them."

"Right. So, I had my needs, but wasn't really finding anyone I could really go for, and then there was the school, the city school, kids getting knifed in the hallways, I didn't want that to happen to my girl. But where else could I send her?"

"There are lots of private schools in the city."

"Sure. Catholic schools. No thanks. I went to one of them my-self back in Philly when I was a girl. Thanks, but no thanks. I told ya. I only want the best for my girl."

"So it had to be Springdale."

"Yes. The best."

"And that costs a pretty penny, doesn't it?"

"They have financial aid, but even with that, I couldn't afford it on my salary. Nurses' aides don't exactly make a killing in Rochester."

"I see. So, you had your needs, and you had your daughter's needs to think about, and you were seeing all these guys...."

"So, I thought, what the hell. Kill two birds with one stone. Meet my needs and her needs at the same time. It's not as bad as it sounds. I'm not strutting around on street corners in a leather mini, poking my head in strangers' windows."

"What exactly are you doing?"

"I told you on the phone. I've got three or four friends, it varies some times. We have an understanding between us, an arrangement, that's all. It helps us all out. Everyone benefits from the situation. What could be simpler?"

He looked up from his notebook then and smiled at Carol with a bloodthirsty look that made her shiver, made her sorry for everything she'd said.

And two days later, when the paper came out ... how could he have done that to her? Made her seem so depraved, so ugly. She thought she'd made her position, her angle clear. But he had his own angle, going on, as he did, about how we lived in a time when nothing was sacred, when money was king, when people would do anything to get ahead, to help their children get ahead, no matter how ugly and degrading the act was. What ever happened to old-fashioned morality? That sort of sermonizing. His angle.

But as if that weren't enough, he'd put in those little details. He'd promised her before she'd left the restaurant that day that she would be totally unidentifiable, unrecognizable. He'd lied to her, the moralizing son of a bitch.

She'd seen the paper during her regular 2:00 lunch break in the hospital cafeteria. She'd spilled coffee all over herself when she'd opened to the second section, where his somber face appeared above his column, and she read the words. She managed to keep down the half of the tuna sandwich she'd eaten, although the taste of bile burned in her throat. She tried to regain her composure. She cleaned up her trash, looking at no one, not daring to, then headed for the door and the nearest pay phone.

She dialed the number, reading off the ripped piece of envelope she still had in her purse.

"Bob Shepherd, please."

"I'm sorry, Mr. Shepherd's on another line right now. Let me take your name and number and have him call you back."

He didn't call back that afternoon, or the next, despite the many times she'd called for him. He'd used her, chewed her up and spat her out. It was worse than what she did, what he thought the guys that visited her did to her. It was much worse.

For two days she didn't leave the house. Patty took care of her, started to worry about her. She even called Stan and Mark to call off her meetings with them. Stan knew what it was about. He'd seen the paper, sent her a dozen roses. What did that Shepherd know about anything? Stan was the most decent guy she knew. He cared, he truly cared about her. What was wrong with that? He'd even said he'd leave his wife for Carol, if she didn't have all that goddamned money. It was Rhonda's money that had financed his beer distributorship. He'd cut his own neck if he left her. And what was the need? Why couldn't people just leave things, leave other people alone.

She spent the two days lying in bed, eating tuna sandwiches, eating one row of Oreos after another, watching television. It was mindless noise, but it was needed right now.

When, after two days, she decided to venture out, she felt as if everyone, Mr. Marx at the deli on the corner, the pharmacist at the drugstore, and her landlady, old Mrs. Griggs, knew about it. Not even a hello amongst them. And what about the kids, what about the Springdale parents, or even Patty's own classmates? But, never mind them. Nurse Crawford, the head nurse from the hospital, had called. She said not to bother to come in to work, and that she wanted to speak with Carol at ten o'clock the next morning in her office about what she said was a very serious matter that had come to her attention. So, she could probably kiss her job goodbye. And what about Patty? While Carol had made sure the paper was not around for Patty to see the day the column came out, she could not be sure Patty hadn't heard about it from the kids at school, could she?

"You want me to take care of this guy, this Shepherd guy? I've got some friends who can do it for me." Mark Niccio was a friend. After two years of meeting twice a week, they were comfortable with each another, they were good friends. So much for Bob Shepherd's morality. Little he knew about it. Narrow-minded bastard.

"So, whattaya say? I could make a couple of phone calls...some of the guys from the old neighborhood ..."

"No, Mark. Thank you. It's not what I want."

"Then maybe I'll do something myself. You know where the guy lives?"

"Now Mark, honey, please."

"I wanna do it, Carol. I need to do it for what he did to you and your little girl. I want to see this guy hurt."

"You won't Mark. You'd blacken his eye and what do you think you'd read about in the paper the next day? You want that? You know how complicated that could get?"

"No, no. You're right. We don't need that. I got enough trouble with Marcia, already, I don't need any more. I don't need you getting messed up with her. She's one tough broad when she wants to be. A real mean one. You've seen some of the marks she's left on me."

"Thank you, but ... no. It's not what I want."

The next morning it wasn't Carol, but Patty who didn't get out of bed. Carol padded softly into her daughter's room. Patty was snuggling with her teddy bear—thirteen and still hugging bears, maybe that was good—when Carol came into the room.

"You okay, honey?"

"I'm not feeling well enough for school today."

"You sick? Here, let me feel your head." Patty pushed Carol's hand away as she moved it toward her daughter's forehead. Patty was staring at her mother. "Go away. Get out of my room."

"Is something wrong, darling? Is there something you want to talk about?"

"I said get out of my room you whore!"

Carol was shaking as she left the room. She sat down at the kitchen table and tried to light a cigarette, but her hands were trembling too much. So this is what it had come to, what Shepherd's words had done.

It was in her nightstand in a hollowed out Bible. After the break-in two years ago, Mark had given it to her as a gift. "No charge," he'd said, then stripped off his shirt. "We gotta look out for our little girl," he said, standing there in his jockey shorts, the little black revolver lying like a baby in his soft pink palm.

She took it now and stashed it in her purse. Maybe I need to calm down, think about this first, she thought. But Patty's words reverberated in her memory. Things had been going so well for them. What right, what right did that man have to destroy it all?

She rode down the elevator to the garage, walked slowly to her car. No need to draw any suspicion. Then she pulled out of the garage, even waving to the garage operator, Julio, as she headed out into the light.

The traffic was light for this time of day. It wasn't seven-thirty yet. He wouldn't be in yet. I get to work at eight every morning....

It had the feel of a dream. She didn't have to think. She felt light-headed and knew exactly what would happen, as if it had already happened a hundred times before—she would park her Celica at the lot across the street, wait by the door to the Herald Building, act like she was waiting to meet someone for coffee. She'd smile at him and say, "Bob, how good to see you again. Why didn't you return my call? Oh, that's alright. I know you're a very busy man, you've got the city's moral upkeeping to think about. I just wanted to let you know I was leaving town, and to thank you for all you've done. What, you're in a hurry? I'm sorry, I know. Just one more thing, please. I have something for you in my purse, a message." She would smile, snap open her purse and reach inside for the dull black moral to his story.

The Widow Across the Way

Sylvia, the eighty-two-year-old widow across the hall, wants my girlfriend, I mean wants her. But maybe I'm wrong. She's lonely. Her husband's been dead for twelve years. She drinks. But, still, she leaves the door to her apartment propped open, telling Lily she does it when she's taking a bath, for Lily, just in case.... And she's constantly telling Lily how beautiful she is, grabbing her, and trying to kiss her on the lips. Lily deflects the lips with a quick turn of the cheek, and later comes back to tell me "God, she really grosses me out sometimes." And she tells me how Sylvia said if something happens then Lily can come home and tell me "It wasn't that bad at all."

In the morning I kiss Lily goodbye and she puts her finger to her lips to shoosh me as I creep out of the apartment, giving her a quick wave, and closing the door carefully, slowly, behind me. Sylvia's door is cracked open. I ease open the outside door and close it until it locks with a click. Before I'm two steps away from the door I hear a distinct rat-tat-tat behind me. Like machine gun fire, but it's not. It's her—Sylvia—who was waiting for me to leave. I envision her standing there, hiding behind the door, like a lioness waiting for its prey to enter the field from the brush. I stand still and hear it again: "Rat-tat-tat." And in my mind's eye I see Lily standing behind the door, her hand on her cheek, holding her breath, trying not to make a sound. Waiting for Sylvia to go away.

When I get to work Lily calls me: "You're not going to believe what she did this time." Then she proceeds to tell me. "She was vacuuming the hallway in her underwear—bra and panties—saying 'Don't I look sexy? Isn't my bra pretty? Do you want to touch it?' And afterwards talking about how she was going to take a bath and her pussy would be nice and clean.'"

"She said that?"

"What?"

I look around me at work. I can't really say it here in the corporate cubicle world.

I whisper: "You know. The P word."

"Oh, yeah. She definitely said it. And she asked me if I wanted to come in and scrub her back."

"She didn't."

"She did."

"God."

"We've got to do something about this, Jack. This is how my day goes. It's crazy. Right after you left she knocked on the door, like she was waiting for you to leave."

"I know, I know, I heard her."

"You heard her?"

"I heard her knocking, I mean. Just after I got outside."

"And when I didn't answer, she walked around to the kitchen window and knocked on it, yelling my name. I tell you I feel like a prisoner in this apartment. I'm afraid to even play the stereo because she might hear it and knock. And at four o'clock I just know she's going to want to have a cigarette in the hall and cocktail hour."

"She's bored, she's alone. She has nothing to do. And you do."

"Yes, that's the point—I do. I've got deadlines to meet and an eighty-two-year-old neighbor who wants me to watch soap operas with her and wash her back and whatever else she has in mind. I mean I feel sorry for her because she's all alone, and I like her, I love her, don't get me wrong, but she's driving me crazzzzzzzzzzzy."

"We have to do something," I say.

"Yes, we do."

Lily sighs on the other end of the line.

"Well, you better get back to work. We'll figure something out."

"Yes, we have to," I say.

This much we're agreed on. We have to do something before we both go crazy.

We're both just settling into this happy life together after serving long sentences in our prior marriages. Somehow we found each other. It seems like a miracle to each of us, to find happiness after so much misery before. And we selfishly hoard our time alone together now.

So the question is Sylvia. What are we going to do about Sylvia?

It's Friday night and the three of us are sitting in the hallway as has become our ritual. "Having a little party," Sylvia calls it. I'm on my folding chair between Lily and Sylvia as they sit in their white plastic patio chairs in front of the square modular plastic table with the ashtray on it. We're sitting next to the door and occasionally Lily will prop the door open a little even though it's twelve degrees outside because I don't smoke and she doesn't want me to be breathing in all these fumes. They're both smoking, a drink in each of their hands. Sylvia has her Bloody Mary, Lily her scotch on the rocks. I'm drinking an ale out of the bottle, listening to them talk for the most part. Occasionally they'll bring me into the conversation. One time Lily gives me a great big smile, turns to Sylvia and says "Isn't he great?" Sylvia smiles at me with that narrow skeletal face of hers, leans over and rubs my arm. "Oh, yes, and soooo good looking. Maybe when you're out of commission you can lend him to me."

Lily laughs and I smile, pretending this kind of talk doesn't bother me, doesn't bother Lily. Did she really say what I think she said? Out of commission?

"Or maybe," she says, "if you leave your door open, I can sneak in in the middle of the night for a threesome."

Lily and I look at each other again, searching in each other's eyes. Did this eighty-two-year-old woman really say this just now? Does she have no limits? My God, she's eighty two years old! Together, we look back at Sylvia. She's smiling.

I take a swallow of ale and laugh, gazing at Lily. "I think we're going to keep the door locked tonight, Hon, what do you think?"

"Oh, that doesn't matter, because I have the key."

It's true. She does. She has the keys since the apartment manager doesn't live on premises and Sylvia's been here for forty-five years.

"Well, uhhh, we'll have the latch on, right, Hon?" I'm looking at Lily for help.

She smiles at me and winks, pats my knee.

She needs a man. A Cassanovic octogenarian.

Thursdays Sylvia plays cards at her club so Lily gets to breathe some, at least for a while. Sylvia's "club" is a country club she and her husband used to play golf at and to which she now goes every Thursday morning to play euchre with her lady friends. They play for nickels, dimes, and quarters. It's Sylvia's only day out, except for the weekends when she drives up to the suburbs to take care of her ninety-six-year-old friend, Doris, for the weekend.

Doris is in a wheel chair, has a hard time getting around, but still hangs on fiercely to her independence.

On Saturdays Sylvia goes shopping for Doris, prepares her meals for the week—dishing them into carefully labeled Tupperware containers and placing them in the freezer—cleans up, does laundry and whatever else needs to be done.

"'If it weren't for Sylvia, I don't know what I'd do.' That's what she tells people," says Sylvia, "and it's true."

"Why don't you move in with her?" Lily asks, "instead of doing all that?"

Sylvia takes a drag on her cigarette, the orange tip glowing in the darkness, and exhales into the gathering cloud of smoky fog that was beginning to fill the narrow hallway. Then she scowls and stares at Lily.

"There's no way in hell I could actually live with that woman. She can be as mean as all get up if you give her half a chance. Last week she told me that I was just spoiled by my husband, spoiled, that I never had to do a thing. Imagine that. I may not have had to work outside the home but I worked—I took care of him, had his meals on the table the moment he got home, ironed his shirts, his underwear, kept the place clean, did laundry. It wasn't like I never lifted a finger! Talk about gratitude! After all I do for her. And this is someone who's supposed to be my friend?"

There are tears gleaming in Sylvia's eyes now. I sit there still, as Lily gets up quickly, walks around my chair and puts her arms around Sylvia from behind, saying, "Oh, Sylvia, she didn't mean anything! She's probably just frustrated with her situation, afraid that she's losing her independence. I'm sure she didn't mean a thing. She didn't mean it to come out the way it did."

Sylvia sniffles a little and wipes her eyes with a tissue, then turns her face toward Lily, puts her hands on the sides of Lily's head and says, "You are the dearest, sweetest girl. I don't know what I would do without you." Then she purses her lips and tries to pull her lips towards her, which Lily avoids by a quick turn of the head so that all that Sylvia gets is a sharp smack on Lily's right cheek.

And now Lily's staring at me with a befuddled look on her face.

"Hon," she says, "would you mind …" and I read her mind, reach for her glass, just as she says, "getting me another drink, please."

"Do you think she's serious?" Lily asks me later as we're sitting on the couch staring at the television.

"Serious?" I ask.

"You know what I mean. The way she always seems to be … you know … hitting on me."

I scratch my beard. "I don't know," I say. It honestly baffles me, this whole Sylvia situation.

"Well she's creeping me out. Did I tell you that she grabbed my butt when I was walking out of her apartment this afternoon?"

"Grabbed it?"

"Yes, I mean tight. A couple good squeezes and she wouldn't let go."

"And what did you do?"

"I didn't know what to do. She caught me off guard. I laughed it off, pretended it was nothing."

"God, who knew we'd be living across the hall from an over-sexed eighty-year-old. Maybe we should look on one of those online dating services for a friend for her."

"How many eighty-year-old guys are on the Internet?"

"Well … you have a good point, but it's probably worth a try, isn't it?"

To our surprise, Lily finds a couple of guys on an online dating service. One's named Chuck. He's seventy-eight, weighs three hundred pounds, has a liver-spotted cue-ball of a head and is looking for women from the age range of—could it be?—forty to sixty years old.

I'm looking over her shoulder as she types. "That's got to be a mistake."

"Nooooo, I don't think so," Lily says. "God, some men are bastards no matter how old they get."

"They're just older bastards."

"Exactly."

She clicks on a second man's profile. His name is Edgar. He's seventy-eight, smiling, has little fringes of white hair over his ears and is wearing a bow tie.

"He's cute," Lily says, and turns half around in her chair to face me. "What do you think?"

"He doesn't do all that much for me, but then again, I am a guy."

"Oh, yeah, I forgot that," she says, smiling wide.

"Smart ass," I say.

"He likes to golf and play cards. Just like Sylvia! And have the occasional cocktail."

"God, we've heard enough of Sylvia's cock tales to last us a lifetime."

"You haven't heard half of them."

"Really."

"She's always trying to get info on our sex life. Like hinting around, asking me if we like this, if we do that."

"And what do you say?"

"I don't say anything. Just that everyone has their own preferences, you know?"

"Yeah."

"Like Sylvia doesn't like giving oral sex, thinks it's disgusting. Only she calls it oil sex."

"Oil?"

"Yeah. She has trouble with the r's. So what do you think of Edgar?"

"His ears are a little big, but hell what can you do."

"Their ears are all big at that age."

"Really?"

"Yeah, it's a well known fact. The cartilage of the ear continues to grow as you get older."

"I'll take your word for it."

"So what should we do? Answer her ad like we're Sylvia? Or just send him a note saying we have someone he might like to meet? She doesn't really want to meet anyone, she says."

"That's what she says. But maybe if the right guy came along ..."

"That's what I think."

"If the right guy came along she might not be trying to grab my honey's ass every time she walks by."

We answer the guy's ad, tell him the scoop, figure if he likes we'll invite him to dinner, tell Sylvia he's a friend of the family (one of our's family—the details we have to work out yet). And in a couple of days he answers us, sends an e-mail saying he'd be delighted to meet our "little lady."

"Well, she might be little. I don't know about the lady part," I say.

"Jack. Be nice."

"I mean ... oil sex."

So, we set things up. Lily gets his phone number and tells him Friday would be good. "He sounds cute, nice. He's got the nicest laugh," she says. Then we invite Sylvia over for dinner. We don't tell her about Edgar, though. Figure she might not like it if we did that, but once she was there what was she going to do, leave?

The big night comes.

Sylvia knocks on the door at six forty-five. She's standing there with a bottle of wine and a big smile, her arms outstretched to hug Lily. Lily accepts her arms for an instant and pats Sylvia on the back, then takes her wine into the kitchen and tells her to make herself at home.

"It was so nice of the two of you to invite me over like this," she says, sitting on the couch and crossing her legs. "We're just like one big happy family, aren't we?"

Lily frowns at me from the kitchen. She's holding the bottle and motioning for me to come in. "I can't get this bottle, Jack. Can you do it for me?"

I walk into the kitchen, take the bottle as Lily walks behind me and closes the kitchen door behind us.

"I can't do this," she says. "I feel like I'm betraying her."

I work at the bottle with the wine opener on my pocket knife, snaking the endlessly looping piece of metal into the cork.

"What do you mean? She needs someone. We've talked about this," I say, trying to remain calm, one hand on the neck of the bottle as I start to yank my pocket knife and the cork straight up, inching it out until it comes free with a little popping sound.

"You don't understand. She told me she doesn't want to be with anyone, that she had a good man and he's gone now, that she can live with his memory."

"His memory and lunging for you and making lewd comments to both of us every chance she gets."

She puts her hand on my shoulder, as I pour her a glass of Chablis.

"Wine?" I ask, offering the glass to her.

"Sure," she says. "Why not?"

Five minutes later I'm sitting in a chair opposite Sylvia, who's sitting on the couch with her glass of wine. Sylvia's asking me about my job, general chit-chat type stuff, when there's a knock at the door.

"Oh my," Sylvia says. "You two weren't expecting someone, were you?"

"Not that I know of," I say, as Lily rounds the corner and answers the door. I get only a glimpse of the man—Edgar—with his bow tie and his large bunch of flowers—before Lily closes the door behind her.

I glance at Sylvia. She's sipping her drink, looking at me with a worried expression. "Jack," she says.

"Hmmm?" I say, sipping my beer.

"You might want to go out there and help Lily, Jack. Maybe she's in some kind of trouble."

I smile and let out a quick burst of nervous laughter, then clear my throat and get up. "Maybe you're right, Sylvia. Maybe I should see what's going on out there."

I get up off the couch and head to the door, open and shut it behind me. Lily is telling the man, "No, no, the flowers were not a good idea. I told you, you were just supposed to be a friend of my mother's who was stopping by unannounced. The flowers are a dead giveaway that's not true."

The man's eyes are two large sad eggs. "But they're so beautiful," he says." He looks over at me for help. "Aren't they?"

"Oh, yes, yes, they really are."

Lily shoots me a look and rolls her eyes. I'm obviously being of no help in this situation.

"Look, Edgar, we really appreciate the gesture, but if you want to do this, we're going to have to nix the flowers or say you brought them for me. Okay?"

"Sure. Okay," he says in one breath, then hands Lily the bouquet, rubs his hands together and says, "So, where's the hot babe?" Lily and I look at each other.

Lily introduces Edgar to Sylvia, telling him of the fictitious relationship and circumstances that brought him here. Sylvia takes an immediate shine to him.

"I don't mean to be interrupting you here," he even says, having regained the spin of his role fairly quickly.

"Oh, no, no bother at all," Sylvia says.

And Lily jumps in: "You know, Edgar, have you had dinner yet? Why don't you stay for dinner. We have more than enough."

"Yes, that's a wonderful idea," Sylvia says, putting her hand on Edgar's shoulder. "Why don't you?"

Edgar's face turns red like he's just had quick flash of too much sun.

"Well, if you really want me to."

Lily and Sylvia join in, "Sure, yeah."

Lily looks at me. "Yes, yeah, we'd love to have you stay, Edgar. Please. We insist."

He smiles and sits on the couch.

"Let me get you something to drink," I volunteer. "Some wine, a beer?"

Half an hour later we're at the table. Sylvia's put away three or four glasses of wine and it's clear she's feeling fine. She's talking only to Edgar. I drop my fork and catch a glimpse of her bare foot inching it's way up Edgar's leg. I sit back up and see him turning red again, sitting upright in a stiff posture.

After dinner the two of them are sitting back on the couch. Sylvia's inches from Edgar's face, her wine glass in one hand, her other hand playing with Edgar's yellow and black polka-dotted tie.

I'm helping Lily wash the dishes. She washes and hands each dish for me to dry.

"This is great, Hon, isn't it? Our plan seems to be working."

"Shhhh, not too loud," she says

"How many beers have you had? They'll hear you?"

"The way it looks, I don't think they're hearing anything right now, but the beating of their own hearts. Look at them," I say, pausing with my wiping.

Lily pauses, too. "They look so cute together, don't they?"

"Yes, sweetie, they do," I say. "They were made for each other."

"No," she says, "that would be me and you." She reaches up and gives me a quick peck on the cheek.

Then she laughs. "God," she says, "you and Edgar are a pair."

"What do you mean?"

"You're blushing!"

Two hours later, Sylvia's leading Edgar by the hand across the hall for "a night cap," she says, and Edgar's not fighting. He's got a great big smile on his face.

After they leave, Lily falls against me, leaning her head against my chest. I hold her loosely, rubbing her back. "This was something, wasn't it? Really something."

"You're really something," she says, smiling up at me, giving me that look, then leading me, without a word, by the hand, into the bedroom.

Sylvia is crying. She's been crying all day, Lily tells me.

"He tried to kiss me, and I couldn't ... I just couldn't ... I looked at Don's picture and I just knew I could never kiss him. I could never kiss anyone but Don." She's sobbing and Lily has her arm around Lily, patting her back.

"I know, I know," she says.

I'm sitting in my usual spot, beer between my legs, watching the scene, swigging from the bottle once in a while.

"He was my one true love. No one could ever take his place. Why did I try to fool myself? And Edgar seems like such a nice man. I feel bad about it. He asked for my phone number but I didn't give it to him. I said we could be friends but that was all. I'm a one-man woman. And what does a one-man woman do when her man's been gone for ten years? Live on the memories?" She turned her head toward Lily, her eyes red, a lost look on her face. "Tell me, Lily, what does a woman do?"

Lily is sitting in the hallway with Sylvia as I pack the last of the boxes up in the truck. We've found a house of our own. It's what we need. A place of our own.

Sylvia is crying and Lily's patting her back. I pull the back door down on the van and slide the ramp back into place, then head back into the building where the two of them are sitting.

"Well," I say, "looks like we're all set to go."

Sylvia stands up.

"Are you sure you couldn't use a tenant? I don't cost a lot to feed and I can cook a thing or two." There's a pleading look in her eyes.

I don't answer.

"Oh, I don't know why you two have to leave. You're the best neighbors I've had in forty-two years." Then she glares at me. "Why do you have to take her away from me?"

I'm stunned. But then she breaks down again, holds her arms out, says "Come here," and hugs Lily in one arm and me in the other. "I love you guys," she says, weeping. Then Lily's crying and I'm crying, we're all crying. We stand there for about five minutes, then I break loose, stick my hands in my pockets looking at the two of them.

Lily breaks away, too.

"We'll have you over for dinner," she says. "We'll come visit often. It's not like we're going to the moon."

Sylvia looks like she's about to fall over.

"I'll be fine," she says and works her mouth into a smile.

Then Lily pats Sylvia on the back and follows me out the door. I help her into the passenger side of the truck, then jump in on the other side and start up the engine. We begin inching away from the building. I take a look in the side mirror. Sylvia's standing there, hands by her sides, as I continue out of the parking lot onto the street. She's getting smaller and smaller until she's out of sight. She vanishes completely.

Chestnut Street

On the street where I grew up people didn't live so much as they died. Big deaths, little deaths. Nate Wasserman—father of Bobby, Joe and Arnold, who I babysat once, who jumped me, stole my glasses, and hid them from me—he was the first to go. A jeweler, he was ambushed on a trip to Jamaica, gunned down in an alleyway behind his hotel. When they found his body, the jewels he'd been carrying were long gone. He was the man who lit fireworks in his backyard every Fourth of July. My parents didn't approve. They shook their heads and said it wasn't safe, kids lost their hands doing stuff like that. To us kids, though, he was a folk hero. He'd brought fireworks to Chestnut Street. His death was one of our most dramatic.

It was a small inconspicuous street, with a cul-de-sac at the end so you could turn around, but the death and cancer rates on it were spectacular. People said there used to be a swamp where the street is, and they'd filled it in with something, made it livable. Now people are saying there might have been dioxin in the fill, that they're going to have to shut the whole area down, make it something like a ghost town.

It was a peaceful little suburban street, not a lot of noise on it, unless we were playing football, complete with passing patterns behind parked cars.

Our football games were orchestrated by an older kid, Jack Baylor, who went just by "Baylor" and had an authentic, professional NFL football that he'd caught in the stands during one of the Bears games. He always played quarterback and his team always won. He could really whip a football. The question was whether any of us could catch it.

He had short legs, but could outrun any of us. With his index finger, he would map out each of our passing patterns on another boy's back. "Okay, Sam," he would say, "go straight out about five steps, then hook back, like this, behind that blue Impala and then out again." We'd watch, careful students, as he diagrammed our paths.

Baylor's father got lung cancer when Baylor was eighteen, when we were all too big to play football on the street anymore. And, by then, he was already in college, studying to be whatever he would become.

We usually played our games strictly on the straight part of the street, never venturing into the cul-de-sac, where the Reisers lived. They were sort of an odd bunch, I don't really remember why now, maybe just because they were quiet. Nobody really knew them, none of the three boys played football in the fall, or baseball in the summer, or basketball in the spring, just after the thaw, like the rest of us. They kept to themselves. Andrew was in my sister Dana's grade. He was always bringing bugs to school, threatening to throw them down girls' backs. His older brother, Jeremiah, was a studious sort, into science and blowing things up.

Andrew was the wild one. One day he was playing with three other boys by the railroad tracks, about a half mile from Chestnut Street. He was only thirteen. They were down by the tracks, drinking whiskey from a flask one of the boys had snuck from his father's bar. It started like that, only then Andrew made his dare. At least, that's how one of the other boys, Mark McConnell, told it afterwards. They didn't have the guts, Andrew said, to lay right down on the tracks while the train was approaching. "Oh yeah!" the others had replied vehemently. Boys in our neighborhood always took dares seriously, although with this one, Mark McConnell admitted, he was a little shaky. Even so, they'd waited together for the 4:45 freight. It was right on time. At 4:43 they heard its whistle, felt the tracks' vibrations. It was then that Andrew had calmly laid down. The other boys, looking at one another, followed his example. "Now, the one of us who stays down the longest is the real man. The rest of you are all pussy shits. Right?"

"Right," the others replied, less vehemently this time.

As it turned out, Andrew won the dare, hands down. His body was so mangled the coroner had to examine his molars to make a positive ID.

We had neighbors we didn't get along with, the Forrests. They didn't die or even get cancer, although sometimes we wished they would. There was a strip of bushes between our houses which our fathers had planted together.

They had two girls and we had two boys and a girl. The Forrest girls were fairly homely, all knee bones and elbows, with not much else on them. For years our parents wouldn't talk to their parents. I think it all started when the younger Forrest girl, Becky, who was in my sister's grade, pushed Dana off her bike and then wouldn't apologize. Some nonsense like that. And, from there, things just started to escalate. It got so ridiculous that one day we came out of the house amazed, my brother, Will, and me, to find the bushes between our houses half cut. Not just one half of the bushes cut, but all of them cut, but only halfway in. That didn't make Will or me particularly happy. We had other things to do with our Saturdays— bicycle trips to take with the guys to the lagoons, where we would pretend to fish (we never caught anything), trips to the Magic Castle Miniature Golf Course, where on one of the holes an elevator actually took your ball all the way up a small model of the Empire State Building and then spit it out again. But seeing those hedges halfway cut like that, even though they looked sort of wacky, looked okay to us, we knew our dad would blow a gasket and have us out there all day with his electric hedge trimmer to level them off, fuming behind us, supervising as Will and I took turns on the ladder with the instant digit remover. But that was the sort of thing the Forrests did. They wouldn't have thought to ask us for help. No, Mr. Forrest would just get out there himself and start hacking halfway in. I guess the feud was too well under way by then.

For the rest of our years of growing up and, as far as I know, for the next twenty years, my parents and the Forrests didn't talk to each other. Their houses no more than twenty feet apart, driveways side by side.

But a couple of years after I left for college, Mr. Forrest started talking to me. I'm not sure why exactly, but he did. I'd pull in the driveway with my sky blue Mustang and he'd look up from his front yard gardening, smile, walk over to me, and ask me how I was doing. The first time it shocked the hell out of me, this guy that never said boo to us, never even looked at us, all of the sudden being friendly.

I went into the house with my vinyl suitcase and asked my mom and dad if they and the Forrests had started talking to each other again. "No," my mom said, wiping her hands on her apron, "Why?"

"Because he just shook my hand and asked me how I've been."

My mom gaped at me for a moment. Then she regained her composure and smiled at my dad, who was sitting at the kitchen table, reading his newspaper. "Well, how's about that, Bernie?"

"How's about what?" he said, looking up from behind his thick glasses, which magnified his eyeballs, made his stare seem even twice as large.

"So Sam, did he ask you if you want to take Becky out on the town?"

"Oh, Bernard, stop. He was just trying to be friendly to our little Sammy. Now that he's all grown up." She came over to me and hugged me too tight, for too long. I let her though, knowing I only had to put up with it for breaks and summer vacations. I could see the top of her head as she squeezed. It seemed that the taller I got, the more she shrunk. That's how life goes, I guess. We all shrink in the end.

There was another family next to the Reisers, down at the end of the block, that we didn't know too well. Their kids had grown up before we all had, so the parents were a little older. She had the big C though, the mother. I don't know what kind it was, but she didn't last long.

Marty Hoffman lived across the street and down two houses from us. He was Will's friend more than mine. They were in the same grade, a year ahead of me. Will, Marty, and David Bender from down the street were like a team back then. They were always together. Bender was the guy whose front tooth I knocked out, tagging him too hard during a pickup game of football in the driveway by our bus stop. He was a thin little guy and I was big for my age. I gave him a little shove and he went flying, face first into the garage door. After that he was running home, hand over his face, blood running through his fingers. But I figure it was all for the better, destiny maybe. If it wasn't for me, Bender might never have become a dentist.

Marty Hoffman became a lawyer. As a kid, he was straight-laced, and slightly overweight. I was shocked when I saw him years later at college. We both went to the same school out in the middle of the cornfields of central Illinois. On a bad day, when the wind was blowing just right, the perfume of cow manure pervaded the campus. When I saw him, Hoffman was on the Quad. He was more than thin—he looked like one of those Holocaust victims you see in all the old pictures from World War II. His hair was a frizzy black mess, little curls springing out here and there, a two days growth of stubble on his face. But it was the eyes that gave him away, the glassy stare—he was an obvious pothead.

He went on to become a very successful lawyer, down in Miami, specializing in real estate, I believe.

It wasn't until Hoffman and I had both grown up and gone away that Mr. Hoffman got the big C back on Chestnut Street. Nobody really thought about it much, that it might have had something to do with our street. It was just what was happening to people nowadays.

My mom got it, too. And my brother, Will, even though he no longer lived there at the time. They both got it within a year of each other, varying forms of lymphoma.

"Keep in touch, promise me that," Will said. This was something that the Will I knew as an adult would not ordinarily have said. He was an accountant, very much into making money. He and I had grown apart long before, and gone our separate ways. He'd never had time for the family. But, now he was lying in a hospital bed, undergoing daily radiation treatments. He could die. I'd come home, all the way from Austin, Texas, where I was going to Graduate School, to see him. (I rarely came home anymore—it was too damned far; it was one of the reasons I'd chosen Austin.)

"Please, please, keep in touch."

"I will," I said, choking on my words.

"Lying in this hospital here, like this, you realize what's really important. I had a wild dream. Let me tell you about it. I saw God, Sam, even though you know I never really bought into that much. And the funny thing was he didn't come as this old wise, white-bearded Santa-Claus type. He looked just like an ordinary guy. Actually, he looked a little like Mr. Forrest—you know, tall, big nose, losing his hair some. You know what he told me?"

I shook my head.

"Take care of your family. Those were his very words."

I didn't know what to say. At that time, before Will married Patsy, we—Dad, Mom, Dana and me—were his family.

In a year's time, though, Will would be cured, happily back, immersed in his booming business of deductions and debit sheets, a regular money-making machine, ignoring the rest of us, once again. It was almost a relief.

By then Mom had gotten it. I'd come home (from Dallas, or I think it was Dallas then) to find my mom and brother sitting on the couch in our old living room (the living room which, as kids, we were never allowed to sit in) talking in some secret sort of code. They were having a regular conversation, one listing off the names of various medications, the other answering with the names of two or three others.

Very bizarre.

My mom came through it all right, too, although she lost most of her hair, went around for a time with a wig. When she decided to hang that up, it was a shock to see her hair coming in as gray bristles. Not that the length was a shock. It was more the color. She'd always dyed it before, Clairol # 54, Ash-Blonde.

My best friend got it. He lived on the street next to ours. His name was Stanley Fields. He went away to the Air Force just about the time I was going away to college. On my birthday—this was in my freshman year—I got a letter from him saying he'd gotten this intense headache and now they were saying he had a brain tumor.

All I could think at the time was, God, Stan's going to die, and he's never even been on a date, he's never even gotten laid. Even with him being in the Air Force, it was something I was pretty sure of. Back in high school, when the two of us had gone, looking for something to do, we'd usually just end up at some restaurant, stuffing our faces, staring at the girls we knew we wouldn't meet.

Once—I remember this now—once when he'd gotten a new BB-gun we went out in his backyard and hung a Playboy centerfold on a tree. This was on a summer day when his mom and dad were both at work. The closer we got to the intimate parts, the better the score.

I didn't think it was all that funny, but he was laughing his head off, really enjoying himself, as we took our turns. I guess maybe there was some sort of aggression in there that I hadn't really seen in Stan before.

Stan didn't just keel over and die, though. His illness was agonizingly long for all of us. The tumor in his head was in a place they couldn't operate without making hamburger meat out of his brain, nor could they really do much radiation without frying it, so he just sort of vegetated on medication, grew all puffy and pasty. He didn't have a life anymore. I'd go over there and visit him, with this mutual friend of ours, Dennis Needleman. Dennis was always the one to coax me to go over there. I just tried to shy away from it, would always turn my head away as I drove past Stan's house, afraid that his parents or brother would see me. Ashamed that I'd sort of cut him out of my life. But I was still living, going to school, meeting girls. My life was going forward and his had just sort of stopped before it had started.

I vividly remember the last time I saw him. His mind was going slowly. He couldn't remember things anymore. His mother had made a plate of cookies, oatmeal I think. Dennis and I sat around the kitchen table, cookies in hand, while Mrs. Fields briefed us on Stanley's condition. Dennis, a little guy with big energy, nodded his head, acting concerned, maybe acting a little too much—he was destined to be a salesman—hungrily wolfing down cookie after cookie, as Mrs. Fields told us about the tumor size and location, the medication and treatments Stan was on. "There's not much they can do for him now, except make him feel comfortable." It had been a couple of years since the whole thing with Stan had started and Mrs. Fields looked about twenty years older. She'd never seemed old before, a little on the heavy side perhaps, but she'd always looked youthful, pretty in the face. I didn't like to look her in the eyes. She was the kind that could, would, if given the opportunity, challenge you directly. "Bob Hartfield doesn't ever come around anymore," she said, "even though he and Stan were in the band together, they were best friends." It just added to my guilt. I hadn't seen him in what, a year? I couldn't look her in the eyes. Suddenly, her hand was on my shoulder. "It's nice to see you boys. I'm sure Stan will be glad to see you both again. Hold on, I'll get him."

The cookie tasted like chalk in my mouth. My stomach was gurgling like a washing machine. I wanted to bolt on out of there.

And when Stan came in the room, it was a shock. He'd grown even bigger and rounder than he'd been the last time I'd seen him. It was like his body was trying to reproduce itself, only both bodies were in the same skin. And he had that glazed expression on his face, and a thin line of drool coming down from the corner of his mouth (not that that should have been too much of a surprise—he'd always had a bit too much spit).

"Look who's here to see you." Mrs. Fields said. "Your friends have come to visit."

He could hardly talk. He was obviously under the influence of some very strong drugs, but there was something else going on too. He couldn't think, the tumor, as it grew, was taking over Stan's life.

He sat down at the end of the table, lethargically, like something out of Night of the Living Dead.

"Have a cookie, Stanley. Here." She reached out and placed one in his hand. He obediently took it and placed it in his mouth. But it sat there for a moment, like he didn't know what to do with it.

"Chew, Stanley."

He began to chew.

"So, how's it goin', buddy?" Dennis said, smiling, placing a hand on Stan's shoulder. For all the times I despised the way Dennis put on his act, dealt with the world in his dishonest way, I envied him now, wished I could put on a face and be happy. But, it just didn't work for me.

"I...." Stan uttered. "Okay, I guess."

"They treating you all right? Keeping you busy?" Stan's live-in nurse, Anna, who spoke little English, came into the kitchen for something just then. She said "Hello," and then she was gone.

Dennis, who always got to flappin about that, but never actually got any—no girl would take him seriously—got to flappin about Anna.

"Does she treat you right? Sneak up to your room at night? Huh? I'll bet she makes you feel better old buddy, huh?"

"Dennis." I said. He'd gone too far.

Suddenly, Stan looked across the table and stared at me.

"Who are you?" he said.

I didn't say anything. Dennis looked at me, then leaned toward Stan, speaking too loud, like the problem was with his hearing.

"It's Sam," Dennis said. "You didn't forget your old friend, Sam, did you?"

"Who?"

"Sam. Don't you remember how the three of us used to run around the city, the good times we used to have?"

I didn't really remember many good times, just bad times, sitting around wondering why all the other guys were getting all the girls, but if that's the way Dennis wanted Stan to remember it....

"Sam," Stan said, still staring at me, like his eyes forgot how to blink.

"That's right, Sam," Dennis said. "Your old buddy, your old pal."

Suddenly, Stanley, this immovable mass, moved his hand out across the table to me. "Nice to meet you," he said, meaning me to shake it. He was like a big dog.

Dennis gave me another look, then turned back to Stanley. "You don't understand."

I inhaled, took Stan's hand in mine and shook it. "Nice to meet you, too," I mumbled.

When Dennis caught up with me, I was past the slide, past the baseball diamond, sitting on one of the benches in the dark, remembering old baseball games.

"You can't let it get to you," he said.

"How can I not?"

"You still have your life. We just have to do the best we can for him, be his friend, while we can."

"I can't," I said, looking out toward center field, remembering standing out there in my green and white uniform, the oversized baseball mitt on my hand. "I just can't."

"Think how you would feel."

"I know, Dennis. You're a good guy, for all your faults. You're stronger than I am though. I just can't do it anymore."

And I didn't. After that I would come home on my short trips, asking my parents for any news about Stan, but never took up my mom's suggestions that I go and visit him. I couldn't shake off that blank stare of his that time, the way he'd said "Who are you?," as if ten years of growing up together had been wiped out, just like that.

Dennis' brother died, too. Dennis' family lived three blocks from us. I was at their house when they were sitting shivah. Dennis said it would be all right, but I wasn't sure. I told Mrs. Needleman how sorry I was, even though I never really knew Dennis' brother much. It seemed to bother me, though, more than Dennis. He was joking around, laughing when we went up to his room, like nothing was different. He and his brother hadn't gotten along too well, I guess.

Ned had thought Dennis was a little twerp, which he was. I put up with him more than anything, the way he'd walk right up to girls at the mall and start trying to pick them up. It was all pretty embarrassing, and after we were leaving, the girls would always be laughing. But he tried to be a good friend, once let me sleep in his basement when I came home from college, had gotten into a fight at this party, and was too wrecked to go home. And another time he'd had a surprise birthday party for me, only no one showed up except my college roommate, Paul, and these two twins who I used to work with at Walgreens when we were kids. Now that was embarrassing. In the end, Paul and me just went out to the bars together to celebrate. Very depressing. Another time, when I was out of school, had a job at a toy store, and Dennis had a job doing something at a downtown hotel, selling convention space, I guess, he set me up with this girl who worked there. She was real thin—had only cheese crackers and Diet Coke for lunch—with a pretty smile. She was black, lived on the Southside, where I'd always been taught a white guy shouldn't be caught alone at night. I'd moved out of the house then, had my own place, and she said she'd come over to see my place. I think she was afraid what the people in her neighborhood would think. Anyway, she never showed, she stood me up.

The problem with Dennis was he was always putting on, trying too hard to get everyone to like him.

We lost touch, though, after a while. It was inevitable, I guess.

A couple of years later I heard that Stan died. I heard it from my parents. I didn't go to the funeral.

They're shutting up Stan's house, too. They're making four square blocks of people who've spent their lives there pack up and leave. My mom and dad. Where will they go? They're calling it a disaster area. Tell me about it. And soon it will be gone for good, they'll tear it all down and the federal boys will come in with their weird beekeeper outfits, walk around the rubble with their fancy detectors and take soil samples, just like Neil Armstrong and Buzz Aldrin the first time they landed on the moon.

Okay, it's a disaster area, it'll be in all the papers in screaming headlines. But all I'll think about then is my friend, Stan, staring, just staring at me with those watery eyes, and asking, "Who are you?"

The Duke of Broad Street

Since Julius Wolsey had arrived in Rochester he'd slept under the Broad Street Bridge.

It had been over twenty years since he'd set foot in this town. As a boy he'd come with his father to this bridge to fish every Sunday afternoon. He'd stick his hand right into the cool dirt and grab the wriggling worm, threading the strange rubbery life up the hook until he could push it no more, then throw his line with the bobber and little round lead shot weights down to the gray water until it landed so far below with the slightest of splashes, barely making a noise. And he would huddle up next to his father wearing the scratchy red and black plaid jacket, the rich woody smell of his pipe tobacco surrounding him, to gain a little bit of fatherly warmth. Now, years later, so many years after the old man had died, so many lives removed from his youth it seemed, he slept under the bridge for lack of anywhere else to go, hugging himself through the night to stay warm.

No matter where he was, he always liked to have a place, even such a dirty, dank place as this one, to call his own. On some days, his better days, he would get lucky and find an open door to an apartment building and would sneak in and hole up in a place where he couldn't easily be found. There he'd fall asleep indoors for a change, at least until he was thrown out. Sometimes he'd be lucky enough to find a building with access to a boiler room or furnace area, or even a heated basement, though those were far and few between. Sure, he could always sleep at one of the flophouses, the mission houses where they would give you a bed for the night if you were a good boy and said your prayers and showed your appreciation and didn't bring in any booze, drugs, or women. But that wasn't for Julius. He didn't like anyone telling him what to do, especially not those self-righteous types. Pray to what God? he would ask them, and laugh. And they, with their white collars, would feed him the company line, telling him that Jesus had died for his sins and that he could be saved and guarantee his reservation in much more luxurious accommodations after this life if only he believed this and said that, to which Julius would laugh some more, wondering aloud if this God of theirs, this savior of saviors, was so good and so fair and so sympathetic and loving, if He cared so much, why would He wait until Julius was dead to give him the good life? Wasn't that just a little bit sadistic when all he really wanted was a warm place to sleep, a place to shit, food on the table and a hot shower once in a while? Was that too much for any loving parent to provide for his child? But that conversation, of course, would get him nowhere and would not only raise their tempers but his as well, watching their hypocrisy and self-righteousness, and mock shock when he would open his mouth and yell profanities at Him, at their God (because he sure as hell wasn't any God of Julius's!). And, in the end, he would just wind up out the door and back on the streets anyway, one way or another. So why go through all the trouble and humiliation? For what? They had nothing to offer him, nothing at all.

On this particular day, Julius had slept under the bridge and was, in fact, just pulling himself up off the canvas bags he'd placed on the cement floor that was covered with broken glass, discarded food, and newspapers. He hadn't seen or heard a rat all night. Maybe that was a good sign. He'd hardly noticed the pains during the night either, and had, in fact, slept almost straight through the night. Standing in the empty doorway to his private room, he watched the gray river emerge from the blackness, beer cans, bits of wood, styrofoam cups, and ducks all floating under the bridge, his bridge, and disappearing from his sight like they'd never even existed. And then he stepped forward onto the pavement to greet another day.

Natalie was talking with her friend, Rona, over their cups of cappuccino and latte at the Starbucks where they met every morning. They were recent college graduates, former roommates who had been unleashed on the world. That's how they liked to put it.

Rona was talking about her latest clothing acquisitions and her new Lincoln SUV. She sipped her double mocha cappuccino, smiling across the table at her friend, Natalie. Natalie was drinking a light raspberry cream latte without the cream and was nibbling on a croissant. She needed a new car, but couldn't afford one. Unlike Natalie, Rona didn't know squat about struggling—she'd had everything handed to her by her daddy on a platinum platter since she was a toddler. And for some reason they got talking about fathers. It started when Rona said she'd like to go somewhere, Paris maybe. She'd never been there.

"Paris?" Natalie said. "I'll never get to Paris."

"Hey girl, maybe I can get Daddy to finance the two of us for a trip there." Rona said, taking a nibble from the corner of her scone and setting it back down on her napkin quickly.

"And how are you going to do that?"

Rona smiled wide and twirled a yellow ringlet of her hair with her index finger. "Oh, I have my ways."

"Your ways?"

"It's like I know certain things about him that he doesn't want other people to know."

"Like who?"

"Like who? Like my mom for one."

"Oh, those kinds of secrets. He's got a girlfriend?"

"A girlfriend? If he had only one it wouldn't be too bad."

"And your mom knows nothing about it?"

"She just doesn't want to know."

"So why would your knowing about it be any threat to him?"

"Thing is, he doesn't know that she doesn't want to know. And, besides, if I confront him out loud, in front of her, how is she going to ignore it then?"

"You're vicious, Ro."

"A girl does what she has to do sometimes." Rona picked up her coffee cup and whispered over it, "Ooh, look what just walked in, Nat. I'd do him in a minute. Right on this table."

"Ro, you're so naughty. What would your daddy say?"

"Screw Daddy, I want what I want."

"Well, your father is a good looking man. I never told you, did I, that when we were in school together I had a slight crush on him."

"Natalie!"

"Well ... what can I say. He's cute!"

"Yeah, but my dad, really. Yuck!"

"At least you have a father to love you."

"Well, sort of. He isn't my real father. He's my stepfather. And he loves me all right. He loves me about as much as one of his sports cars. Like a possession, I mean."

Well, it's better than nothing, better than a dad you never knew." Natalie balled up her napkin and held it tight in her fist. "I guess I must have had a dad. People like me just don't happen out of nothing. But what if? What if I wasn't the product of sexu-all intercourse, but just appeared out of nowhere? By immaculate conception. Like Jesus."

Rona almost coughed up her cappucino. "Yeah, right. You. Little Miss Innocent, immaculately conceived. How ironic that would be."

"I don't see anyone calling you Virgin Mary, either."

"Yeah, but I was never as wild as you were."

"Oh, yeah, right. Who did it in the Ladies' Room at Mario's with Frankie Dugan? While his girlfriend was right there in the other room? It sure as hell wasn't me!"

"I was really really drunk that night. We both were."

"O—kay. Nice try, hon."

"Besides, the thought of possibly getting caught makes me hot."

"I rest my case."

"And what case was that?"

"That you're the wild one."

Rona blew a yellow curl up off her forehead. "Okay, okay. Can we move on, please?"

"Yes, please. Anyway, I've got to get to work. Duty calls."

Rona looked at her watch. "Jesus, I didn't know it was so late. I've got to get going too. It's been loads."

"Yeah, loads," said Natalie, grabbing her purse off the chair beside her, and rushing for the door.

Julius was sitting on the sidewalk overlooking his bridge, staring at the water below, smoking a butt from his butt collection. He kept all his used butts in a plastic bag in his coat pocket and took one out as needed to get a few puffs in as his addiction required. A mild, but, expensive addiction it was, too. He'd taken more than his normal two puffs and kept going this morning, not caring about preserving anything, a butt much less himself anymore. He smoked the butt down to the nub, then flicked it with his thumb down into the water where it barely disturbed the surface. He pulled his notebook and pen out of his backpack, and flipped open the book, staring at the empty page. Then he looked down at the gray water below, trying to put some thoughts together in his head. The ducks were swimming around in the river like it was their own private cesspool. His mind wandered. He wondered how it would feel to break the surface. Just close his eyes, spread out his arms and fly down to the icy water. He imagined the soothing, numbing feeling, as he hit the water, taking away his current pain—the physical, as well as the harder, mental pain, accumulated over the years. There were ex-wives he didn't know, and children he knew even less. He had Maggie's phone number, ripped from a phone book, folded neatly in his pocket, but he wasn't quite ready to use it yet. Maybe he wouldn't have the balls after all.

He was, or at least had been, a real musician once. A guitar player. There'd been a band, about twenty years before. They'd called themselves The Dukes of Night. There'd even been a record that had gotten air play for a while. But after that, nothing much else. People didn't buy their records anymore and the band split up. There'd been four of them. He'd lost track of them all. Gary Rhodes, the singer, Bobby Simon, the bass player, and Wes Waltrip, the drummer. He stared at the water, wondering about them, thinking, they're all probably respectable now, lawyers, or accountants, or managers of grocery stores, things like that probably, with wives and ex-wives that they actually keep in touch with, and mortgages and cars, and lives.

The ducks down below him swam around in little rows. Thinking how easy it would be if he had a gun. He could pick them off one by one. Thinking about the guys. How easily they'd fallen in line. They'd been like him once, a rebel, with something to say. He stared hard at his empty page, trying to think of the right words to put down, to capture the feeling, the moment. But his hand started shaking and his mind was racing. Maybe he didn't have anything to say either. Not anything anyone wanted to hear anyway. He closed the notebook and put the cap back on his pen, placed them back in the pack and struggled back to his feet.

His stomach growled. His hands were still shaking. The shakes went away sometimes, but they always came back, it seemed, like a loyal, but unwanted dog. He'd retrieve his guitar from that bush down by the railroad tracks and work the corner by the mall for a while, maybe scrape up enough for some food and a bottle of something to stop the shaking.

Natalie was walking with Douglas Feiffer to the mall for lunch. There was a little sandwich shop there that they frequented. Natalie never ate much. Usually just soup and some crackers, trying to keep that girlish figure girlish.

Douglas had a crush on her, but wouldn't admit it. He would stammer when she was around. It gave her a sense of power which, at first, stunned her. That a man would react this way to her. It was almost comical at first. It hadn't happened to her much in her life. She'd always been overshadowed in the men department by beauties such as Rona, not that she was jealous of her for that. Blondes always seemed to get more attention. And Rona had those big boobs. (She called them Daddy's Christmas presents. When the guys stared at them too long in the bars she would say, point-blank, "So you like my daddy's Christmas presents?") Natalie wondered if guys would look at her more if she had boobs like Rona's.

As they walked toward the mall there was a man playing a beat-up guitar, standing against a wall with his guitar case open. There were some coins thrown in the case, but not many.

She diverted her eyes from the man and moved to the other side of Douglas, away from the man, as they approached the part of the sidewalk that he was occupying. Why did they have to display themselves on the streets like that anyway? It made her so uncomfortable. Why couldn't they just ... go ... someplace! It was very annoying.

And what annoyed her even more was how Douglas pulled her by the hand toward the singer so they were standing right in front of him, and Douglas sneered and laughed at the man who, with scraggly beard and hair that flew wildly in every which direction, played on, eyes closed, seemingly oblivious to the people watching him and Douglas' antics. The man strummed his guitar, and in a surprisingly good, if somewhat raw, voice sang the words to While My Guitar Gently Weeps. Natalie stood there for a second, staring at the man. For an instant, she saw something familiar in the man's face. His eyes were watery, sad looking. Or was it just the song? He was looking above the flow of people passing, staring at the sky as he strummed his guitar. His jeans were dirty and torn and there were nickel-sized holes in his flannel shirt. Still, there was something about him that transfixed her. The slunk back look, the way his eyes stared out at nothing, at the sky, the way he howled out the words made her think of some sort of animal lost in the woods, something to be feared, yes, but also to feel sympathy for.

But then his gaze went directly from the clouds to her: he was staring without blinking, and a chill ran through her body, but she didn't look away. There was definitely something eerie about his look. He was probably dangerous, living on the edge. But there was something, a soulful mournfulness in the well of his eyes, too. And, for that brief moment, when their eyes locked, she was drawn to him in a way that she could neither explain nor rationalize. She stepped closer to him, hardly even aware that Douglas was still holding, clinging to her hand now, holding her back. She stood inches from the man, staring at him for a moment, as he opened his mouth, letting the words spit forth, the grizzly appearance of the hairs on his chin softened by the lucidity of his look, of his voice. Mournful like the cry of a lone wolf, separated from his pack. She opened up her purse and the pocketbook inside of it and pulled out a bill, a twenty dollar bill, and dropped it, watched it float like a fallen leaf, into the man's guitar case.

"Natalie!" Douglas said, and tugged her away from the performer, and, still locking her hand in his, said, "What are you, out of your mind? Giving a guy like that twenty bucks? He know the next place that bill will see is the liquor store."

She tugged her hand out of his grip and stopped walking.

"How do you know that? You don't. Maybe he's just some guy down on his luck. Did you ever think of that?"

He stood there with arms crossed in front of him and shook his head and smiled. "You're more naive than I thought, if you believe, if you really believe that."

"What if it were you, if you lost your job, your wife, your ... family? How would that make you feel? What would you do? What if they laid you off at the only job you'd done for twenty years? What if they closed the plant you worked at and you had nowhere to go? You'd be lost. Wouldn't know what to do. And maybe after a year or two of looking for a job you couldn't find anything outside of working at fast food restaurants and you'd grow tired, real tired of it all. Maybe you'd just give up. Maybe that's what it is. It's not him at all, it's us. Where's our humanity? Maybe he's given up on himself because we've given up on him and others like him."

"Whoa," Douglas said. "Where the hell did all that come from? Who would have guessed that little Natalie was a liberal dressed in conservative's clothing?"

"I care about people, so that makes me a liberal?"

"Hey, I care about people as much as anyone. But you think handing this guy twenty bucks is helping him? Come on, wake up! You think all these people shouldn't try to help themselves, but we should just hand them everything they need? What's that going to teach them? Self-sufficiency? Somehow, I don't think so."

She couldn't stop thinking of the guitar player, the way he'd stared so deeply into her eyes with his mournful gaze. It was like it was etched into her now.

"Okay, I'm naive. But I'm human. And if he buys a bottle, anyway, so what? If it eases his pain, gets him through the day? Maybe working at the accounting firm, doing books for rich people for ten years has made you lose something of yourself. Well, I'll tell you one thing, Douglas. It's not going to happen to me."

"Natalie, stop this," Douglas said. "We can talk about it over lunch."

"Get your own damned lunch. Douglas. Somehow, I'm not hungry anymore."

He lowered his arms to his side, straightened his back, and raised his chin. "Fine," he huffed, then turned abruptly and walked toward the mall entrance.

She walked back to the wall where the man was playing his guitar. He was staring up at the sky again, looking like he wasn't there, wasn't anywhere at all. There was something about those eyes, that face. Even the voice held something mysterious but familiar about it. She stood there another minute, during which time he kept looking up to the sky, oblivious to her or the presence of any of the other occasional watchers who would stop for an instant, then decide that they had better things to do. Then she headed back for work, her head spinning, sick. What was wrong with her? She didn't take an interest in those kind of people. "Low-lifes" she'd called them herself, as recently as last week.

It had been one of those late night soirees at her friend, Janet's apartment. They'd been drinking wine, too much, not that that was all that unusual. Talking about their lives. How old they seemed all the sudden. And about how different life seemed to have turned out so far than what they had expected when they were younger, even when they'd still been in college. Natalie had said how she'd always imagined she'd get out of college and be handed this big fancy job, with the large office and the oak desk. Not wind up in some cubicle being a glorified secretary, answering calls for her firm's partners.

"Not me," Janet had said. "I always figured some day I'd wind up on some street corner, penniless, with a tin cup or something."

"You mean a low-life."

That's when Jan had ripped into her, asking where she got off calling people that just because they were different from her, asking her why she thought she was so much better. It had ended badly with Natalie walking out in a huff. But the next day she'd started thinking about what Janet had said. Was that how people saw her— as this insensitive, snotty kid? Who shit on anyone who was different from her?

She left work early that afternoon, telling her boss that she wasn't feeling well. And she wasn't. Something was troubling her and she didn't know exactly what. But she knew it had something to do with that guitar player.

That night she had a date with a man named Geoffrey. She wasn't sure why all the men she was interested in or who were interested in her always used their formal first names. It was her first time out with Geoffrey, who she'd met at the gym where she worked out occasionally (more than occasionally recently as she'd become fixated on attacking the flabbiness of her thighs and arms). He was in an aerobics class with her and had his eye on her the whole time she was enrolled in the five week class, only working up the nerve to ask her out after the class was finally over. They'd had a cup of coffee, but this was their first official date.

They were sitting at Le Cremery, the latest sensation, eating cornish game hens in some sort of orange sauce, having a pleasant conversation, getting to know each other. A movie was planned, something with subtitles, no doubt. Geoffrey wanted her to see this great film—he actually called it that, a "film"—from this Italian director named Facciano, or Pacciano, or something like that. And maybe after that, who knew? It depended on how the night went. Natalie was somewhat taken by Geoffrey's blonde hair, muscles, and general good looks. He had a way of combing his hair so that it fell at an angle over his forehead that she liked and had big blue eyes and dimples. He looked like some sort of Swedish god, an icon of health. It was only when he opened his mouth and talked in that mush-mouthed way of his, exhibiting all the falsity and pretentiousness of his wealth—which, of course, was the real reason her mother liked him—that she realized she couldn't stand him, not as a person, anyway. Still, it was fun being with him, despite his shallowness, his talk about stocks and bonds—who gave a flying fuck really, but it was his job, what else did he have to talk about? But why did she feel at twenty-two she had already missed out on something important, something irretrievable, that her life was passing by right before her eyes?

She was walking with Geoffrey, his arm woven through hers, on the way out of the restaurant, when she saw the man again. It was him. She was sure of it. He was not panhandling this time, but just standing in a doorway, smoking a cigarette, watching them as they passed. She looked at him for a moment, then prodded Geoffrey with her elbow. "Let's go," she said, not looking directly at him again. It was eerie. She felt like he'd been standing there waiting for her, like he was following her or something. But that was ridiculous. Why would he be following her? Because she had given him twenty dollars and thought, maybe, that there was a lot more where that came from? No, it had to be a coincidence. She was just being paranoid. How could he have followed her anyway? It was crazy. Still, she shuddered as they walked and wouldn't look back until she was safely inside Geoffrey's car. She looked out the window into the darkness, but there was no one there. No one at all.

So, how'd your date with Joffrey go?" Rona asked, sipping her cup of raspberry double mocha latte, and, with a quick jerk of her head, flipping a long, dangling curl out of her face.

"Oh, all right," Natalie said, staring down at her apple tart, trying something different for a change. "He's no Vincent Van Gogh or anything."

"Huh? You mean like he wouldn't cut an ear off for you or something like that?"

"Something like that. But there was something funny. I didn't tell you about this. This guy. I saw him when I went to lunch with Douglas the other day."

"Oh, yeah?" Rona said with a smile.

"No, Rona," she said, shaking her head. "It wasn't like that. He was ... a bum. And then there he was, last night in a doorway, smoking a cigarette, just staring at us."

"Creepy."

"Yeah, I know," she said, staring down at her cappucino, looking for her reflection in its caramel-colored surface, but it was nowhere to be found.

He showed up at her door one rainy Sunday morning. She was stepping outside in her robe to pick up the paper. She didn't expect to find him sitting there on the sidewalk, back against the bricked wall, his tattered blue-jeaned legs stretched out on the grass, smoking a butt like it was no one's business. Right next to her "Welcome" doormat with the rubber daisy in the corner. She hesitated for a moment upon seeing him. He looked over and jerked to his feet, then, on second thought, reached back down to pick up the paper, and offered it to her. She stood there looking at him, moving her hand back to her robe, making sure it was securely shut.

He stood there, smiling a crooked smile and narrowing his eyes at her in what she perceived to be a lewd manner.

"Whatssamatter? What are you afraid of? I got your paper for ya. Don't ya want it? It's a perfectly good paper."

"To be honest, you scared me. You look so ... dangerous." She was sorry the moment the words left her lips but there was no taking them back.

He laughed for an instant, then stopped, looking right at her seriously with his dark eyes.

"I am dangerous," he said, puffing the cigarette out the side of his crooked smile. "But I'm also your father."

She stood there stunned, as he pushed open the door and walked right by her into her apartment, and sat down on the couch.

"Got anything to drink? Preferably hot? It's a bitch being outdoors in the rain. You know. Cold rain, down on my head, I am all alone?' Crosby Stills and Nash? Great song. Fucked up bunch of guys, but great song."

She just stared at him with her eyes wide open.

"You're my father?"

"So-called. Not much of one I've been, I know. Sorry about that. Haven't been in much shape to be much of anything the last fifteen years or so. Do you got some beer or wine, or something?"

She stood in front of the coffee table with her arms crossed in front of her. "How do I know you're my father, and not just some ... some guy saying he is?"

"Oh, I'm him okay. Maggie told me about you. I called her up. On the telephone. She told me you was here. And if you need more proof, you have a tiny little oval-shaped birthmark on your left butt cheek. How would I know that if I weren't right there when you popped out?" He stretched his leg out, laid it across the coffee table, like it belonged to him. "And, have you looked in the mirror lately? That oughta tip you off right there."

She sighed, staring at the man, finding it hard to believe that he was her father. Not even remembering what her father looked like. This man could be anyone, some hustler looking for a free meal, a place to stay. She was trying to remain calm. Maybe if she closed her eyes, if she didn't say a word, he might just go away.

"Maggie told me about you, really. Your mother. Sorry about that twenty you gave me. I'll get it back to you. Amazing girl you must be, givin' twenties out to bums like me. You didn't even know, did you? You had no idea."

"You knew it was me?"

He pulled a torn, faded wallet out of his back pocket and pulled out a photo which he placed in Natalie's hand.

"I been carrying this around a few years. Your ma sent it to me a while back. Looks just like you, don't it? Only you're much prettier now," he said with a crooked smile, before taking the photo back and placing it back in his tattered billfold.

"I meant to bring it back to ya, that twenty, or at least a piece of it, but it goes so fast when you got nothin'. You understand." He shoved the wallet into his back pocket. "Although lookin' at you good, maybe you don't. You don't look like someone who's missed a meal lately."

"Well, thanks a lot!" she screamed. She'd meant to keep her composure, keep the mask on, but she couldn't help it now. He was like a needle clumsily looking for a vein to pierce.

"No, I don't mean it like that. Not that you're fat or anything. You see why I am the way I am. Got no sense anymore. If I had a shoe worth putting on, first thing I'd do would be to stick it in my mouth. I'm just a dumb slug."

"Julius. You're name's Julius, is that right?"

"Yeah," the man said. "Sometimes they call me Julie, but I don't like it much, don't like being called by a girl's name."

"And my mother gave you my address?"

"Well, not exactly. She told me about you. I looked you up in the phone book."

"So, what do you want?" She was stepping back toward the kitchen, closer to the phone.

"What, you're not glad to see your old Papa? I thought I asked you if you had a beer? What kind of hospitality is this? It's like an old family reunion."

She stared at the man for a second, then exploded. "Reunion! Give me a break. You leave my mother when I'm two and I never even see you again until now. And now you just decide to drop in and say hi, how about a beer?"

"And, that's a problem? Wanting to get to know my daughter after all these years? Regretting all the shit I've done and been through? I thought they said it was never too late?"

"Who said that?"

"They. You know 'they,' meaning the ones that ain't me. Obviously. Haven't been one of they for a long time. Was one once. For a short time. Had a real life, real job, real kid. A few of them, in fact. Different lives, different jobs, different kids. It was like another lifetime ago."

"You have other kids?"

He laughed, looked up at her, past her. "You don't know the half of it sweetcakes, what a fuck-up your old man is. Left seed here and there, not quite sure where anymore."

"Oh," she said, crossing her arms in front of her. "So, is that what it is? You wanted to see what your seeds sprouted into. That's all I am to you?"

"No, no, Natalie, you got me all wrong. I wanted to see you, to see ... ah, what's the point. You can't go back to the place you fucked up so bad in the past. I should know that." He was sitting on the edge of the couch now, rubbing his temples with his left hand.

She took a step closer to him, but stopped, watching him, wondering who he was, what he was doing here after so long, this stranger sitting on her couch.

"I just want you to know one thing, l'il girl," he said not lifting his head from his hand, but stretching right arm out, pointing at her without looking at her. "You were the first one I tried to find. My first born daughter. My first major screw-up."

"Oh, so I'm a screw-up? Is that what you're telling me?"

"No, no, Natalie, cut me some slack. I'm the screw-up, everyone knows that. That's a given. My screw-up was running away from you and your mom. Running scared, that's what it was. I wasn't ready for that, for a family, responsibilities like that, maybe never was, never would be. Tried it again elsewhere. In San Diego, Austin, Baton Rouge. But it never seemed to pan out. God made me broken. Missing something. The pieces it took to be a good man, a good husband, a good father." He looked up at her now, his eyes red and she could see how sad a man, how broken he really was. He'd given up on himself, just like everyone else had. She almost felt sympathy for him, for this man who had made her mother so miserable and, to a lesser extent, in the vacuum left in his wake, had made her miserable.

What did she owe him after all, after all these years? Nothing, not a thing. He was the one who left when she was just a baby. He was the one who'd never sent her a letter, who was the one missing at her birthday parties, at Christmastime when fathers should have been around, he was the face in the frame in the hallway that eventually disappeared. She didn't know where it went. For years her mother thought he'd be coming back. But finally, when Natalie was about twelve years old, the picture had disappeared once and for all and his name was never mentioned again in their house.

And now, after all this time, after the wounds had healed as best they could, what right did he have to come back and tear them open again? Why was this something that was up to him, for him to control? She didn't have to let him come back, to be here talking to her. He'd been so thoughtless and heartless to let them take him for dead all those years, why should she give him an ear, or even the time of day? He couldn't make her feel anything now. She was a wall, she was a rock.

"So what was it that screwed you up so bad?" she said, walking back to the kitchen. She needed something, some coffee or something to wake her up from this nightmare. "Was it booze, drugs, a combination?"

"I dunno, both I guess. It became a habit. Sometimes you get in these loops and you can never get out of them. Not alive anyway."

"Loops."

"Yeah, loops. Why ya think I'm fruit loops?"

"Drugs, alcohol. You just gave up."

"Yeah. Gave up. When you lose something, when you lose everything, your family, your job, your dreams, what do you have to live for? Only I've never had the courage to put an end to it properly, y'know?" He was sitting on the couch now, his head in his hands. He was sniffling like he was crying, but she wasn't sure. She couldn't see his face.

"And what about me? You know how long I cried? But I gave up, finally, thought, I don't need that, I'm never going to have that. I had to go on. That old thing about someone being dead to someone, well, you were, you are. You think you can just waltz back into my life after all this time, just like that? When you were so heartless, so cruel? You know you've got a lot of nerve. You didn't lose anything! I was a baby, a goddamned infant and you just up and walked away like I was an old shoe or something! Never writing, never calling, never nothing! Like I was never on your mind at all, like something you conveniently, almost thankfully, forgot. You couldn't handle the responsibility. Boo hoo. Make me cry. Just think of your little infant daughter crying, and growing up alone, wondering who her father was, where her father was, and why she didn't have a father to play with, to sing her to sleep at night, to do ... to do ... all those things that fathers are supposed to do with their daughters. You didn't lose anything. You chose to lose Mom and me. That was your decision."

He looked up suddenly, staring at her with his dark eyes. His face shone with tears. "You're angry. And I don't blame you. You have a right to be."

"Goddamn, you're a psychologist and a lawyer, too! See what we missed all these years of you not being here? You're goddamned right I'm angry. You took away something, a lot. You took away my childhood. Because maybe you're right, maybe you are a loser. But not because of what people think about you, but because of how you are. You're so selfish and cruel! How could you leave your baby daughter! What kind of man are you? It's not that you're no good as a father, as person, whatever. It's that you made yourself that way by what you've done."

"I told you I'm no good!"

She walked into the room and couldn't contain herself. She stood right in front of him, feeling the fury building inside of her and getting ready to escape. "That's bullshit, my God, that's so much bullshit! That's a fucking excuse for what you did to other people. You cry about it all the time I bet, what you did to us, to your other wives and children, don't you. You're so weak and helpless. Bullshit. You are what you do in this world, you make yourself what you are by your actions. By running away and not facing your life, you're nothing but a coward. Why didn't you do something about it ever! Why?"

She couldn't help herself. She broke down then, put her hands up to her face to cover the tears.

She felt his hand on her and jerked away and looked through her wall of tears at him and shouted. "Get out of here! Get out of here now! Why did you follow me, why did you come here today? Get out! I never want to see you again!"

He stood there, looking at her, a foot away from her, his face a stone. A sad stone, to be sure, but a stone.

He turned then and walked slowly toward the door. She stood there, not saying a word, watching him walk, watching his back as he pulled open the door, went through the doorway, and closed the door gently behind him, not saying anything either, not looking back at her.

And then there was silence, like he hadn't just been there in her living room. Like he'd never been at all.

She called her mother, who told her, "I didn't give him your address. He called me, that's all."

"What did you tell him about me?"

"Nothing. I told him you lived here in town. I figured you were adult enough now to deal with him. Not that I wasn't worried about it, about how you would react to seeing him. I should have called you and warned you."

"Mom, he told me he was dangerous. And, to be honest, he scared me a little."

"I'm sorry, Honey. I'm sorry he came to see you. I'm sorry he upset you, but, believe me, he's no danger, not physically anyway, to anyone but himself. He likes to put on that hard ass, I'm tough, rebel crap. Dangerous, yeah, like a bad movie or yogurt that's curdled. It might make you a little queasy, sick to your stomach, but truth is he's just a little boy pretending. It makes him feel like something to be bad. To be a rebel. He never really grew up, that's his problem."

"Did he come see you?" Natalie asked.

"Yes. Last night. Even though I told him not to."

"What did he want?"

"Want? I have no idea what he wanted. He told me how sorry he was. Like I hadn't heard that before. A hundred times. A thousand times."

"What's he doing here?"

"What's he do anywhere? I don't know. Last night was only the second time I've seen or heard from him since you were a baby. Something must be going on, though. I don't know what. It's got to be more than wanting money. He talked about wanting to change. What a laugh."

"Why?"

"Him change, after all these years? Being a bum is all he knows. It's what he is now."

"So, you don't think someone can change?"

"Someone, maybe. But not him. Once a drunk always a drunk. That's what your grandmother always said. She never did like Julie much."

"Julie."

"What?"

"Nothing. It's just ... you called him Julie. Even though he never liked that name."

"And ..."

"And nothing. I was just remembering that."

"O-kay. So what did you do? What did he say to you? What did you say to him?"

"I basically told him to go to hell. Oh, Mom, I blew it."

"Why? Because you were angry with him for never being there for you, for never even having the courtesy to let you know him, or if he was even alive? I don't think you blew anything, Hon. The man's a blight. A blight on everything he touches. You're the only good thing that ever came from that man. At least with me."

"But Mom, after twenty-two years my father shows up at my doorstep and what the hell do I do? I throw him out. You know how long I wondered about him, about who he is, where he is, if I'm like him."

"Don't worry, Baby. You're nothing like him."

"But Mom. What if he doesn't come back? What if I never see him again?"

"It'll be his loss, Darling, believe me. That man's nothing but trouble. Harmless, maybe, but still trouble. Everything he touches turns to shit."

The next afternoon she went to lunch alone, telling Douglas that she had some shopping to do and wouldn't have time for lunch. Shrugging off his requests to tag along, like waving off a fly.

She wasn't even hungry, anyway.

She walked down the sidewalk as she normally did, but slowed down when she got to the corner where he'd been the day before. All that was in the spot where he'd been was a brown paper bag with some sort of bottle in it. She crouched down and reached tentatively for the bag, opened it up around the neck of the bottle. She carefully peeled the brown paper away from the neck of the bottle to reveal the contents. It was a bottle of MD 20/20, something she remembered from college that her roommates and her had drunk once—never again after that. It had stained the floor and destroyed her Sunday morning, she remembered that, one of the worst hangovers she'd ever had. And the nickname of the wine came back to her then: They called it "Mad Dog." A fitting drink for her father, not that she could be certain this had been his. She gently lay the bottle back down in the spot where it had been.

She stood up and peered around the corner, expecting to see his gap-toothed smile, expecting him to jump out and say "Surprise!" like she was a girl again, like he was her father, a father, again. Closing her eyes, imagining she was seven-years old, the birthday that he'd had written to her about, that he had promised to come see her at. But he had never shown up. And when she opened her eyes there was nothing there, a sidewalk full of people she didn't know walking away from her and toward her, but not him, not the father she didn't know.

It went on for a week, then two. She searched for him on her walks to lunch, turned around suddenly when she was walking in the city, thinking she saw him in a doorway, behind a tree, just out of sight. Was it her mind playing tricks on her or had she lost him for good?

He finally showed up again at her doorstep one morning as she was leaving for work. She opened the door and there he was, standing there, looking totally defeated, like the all-time loser of the world, blood was caked on his chin, one eye was puffy and almost closed. His beard was at least a week old, with speckles of red and gray. She was so happy to see him, even if he was in this shape, that she wanted to hug him, but held herself back. She smiled in spite of herself. It was like she was getting a second chance.

"What happened to you?" she asked, crossing her arms in front of her, and trying to place a more serious look on her face, not wanting to give away her sudden buoyant feeling.

"Got rolled for half a bottle of wine and a five dollar bill. They smashed my guitar to pieces, too."

"Who. Who's they?"

"Punks. Young punks. One had green hair and twenty piercings all over his face and the other had pink hair, the eyes of an animal." She wasn't ready for what happened then. She wasn't ready for this poor, broken soul, who just happened to be her father, to fall to his muddied knees and wrap his arms around her legs, and start blubbering, his scratchy cheek hugging her legs.

"Please, please, you gotta help me. I can't do this anymore. I know you don't owe me anything, you probably hate me, and with good reason, but I can't do this anymore."

Any hardness, any resistance she had for him then broke away. She put her hand gently on his back then and tested, stroking his curved back through the fabric of his red and black checked flannel shirt. Then she bent down and put her hands under his armpits.

"Come on," she said, and started pulling him up to her. "Come on inside and rest."

She called in sick that day, and sat in a chair, watching this stranger, this man, her father, sleep on the couch for half the day.

Then she fed him, let him borrow a razor, and let him soak in the tub for almost half an hour, listening outside the door quietly as his soft, mouse-like moans came like whispers of peace through the door.

"So he's living with you now? At your apartment? Doesn't that make you nervous? I mean, Natalie, he's a ... how do I put this ... a homeless person, for Godsakes."

"He's my father, Rona, no matter what I might think about him." She sipped her mocha cashew cappuccino, staring blankly out the window. "What is a homeless person, anyway, but a person without a home? I mean if either you or I didn't have a home, we would be homeless, too." There was a sea of suits walking by and in the middle of them an older woman in fur walking a cocker spaniel with its nose glued to the ground.

"Yeah, right. That's so profound. You sure you weren't a philosophy major and not a business major at school? You're missing the point. He's not just homeless, he's..."

"He's what?" Natalie turned suddenly and glared at Rona.

"Oh, come on, Nat! You told me yourself! You said he was an alcoholic, a druggie, lived on the streets. For godsakes! He told you he was a dangerous man, didn't he? How's that supposed to make your living with the man make me feel comfortable?"

"He's harmless. That's what my mom said."

"Yeah, she said that. But did she tell you to take him in to live with you? I mean he's your father and you haven't seen him in what? Twenty years? Without ever sending you a card or calling? I mean, come on, what does that tell you about the man? He didn't care about you for all those years, and now that he needs something he shows up on your doorstep! Can't you see that?"

"But what? He hasn't asked for anything."

"Wake up, Natalie. He's a bum!"

No matter what she said, she knew she could never convince Rona. But she had to say it anyway, maybe more for herself than anything else: "You don't understand. He wants to change, he wants to know me. That's why he showed up. He wants to know me."

"You have him what?" her mother asked over the telephone.

"Sleeping on my couch."

"Oh, no, Natalie, you have to get him out of there. He's not exactly the kind of person you can trust."

"But, Mother, you yourself said he was harmless."

"He is, he was, normally, believe me. But he hasn't been normal in a long, long time. It's the booze and the drugs. They speak for him. Oh, Baby, I'm so sorry he's shown up like this. It would have been better if your father had died or something. Not show up like he has, shell of a man that he is, after so many years. Maybe I should come over to talk to him."

"When was the last time you saw him before now?"

"Fifteen or sixteen years ago. He showed up on my doorstep. Begged me to give him money. You'd think he'd have a little dignity left after the way he used to abuse me. He threw me down the stairs once in a fit of rage, did I ever tell you that?"

"No," Natalie said, inhaling deep, then exhaling, saying: "you didn't."

"Not that he's necessarily a bad man. Inside him somewhere there's a heart. If only he could get off the booze. But he's too weak maybe for that. It's been too long. The bottle is his mother, his wife, his family to him now. It's sad but I'm afraid it's true. He's too far gone."

"Mother. How can you say that? No one's ever too far gone. You can't give up hope like that!"

"Oh, my Darling, you're so young. You don't know how many times I tried with him, tried to get him to clean up. He would promise, and then, a week later, fall into his old ways again. He'd be gone for days at a time, then show up looking like he'd gotten run over by a train. And the men, the ghosts he'd bring home sometimes ... there was not a spark left in their eyes. They were the junkies, the lifeless, the walking already dead. It's not me that's given up hope. It's him. He's given up life, his own life."

"Then why did he come back? After all these years?"

"I don't know. Maybe you can find out. Just be careful with him, Baby, that's all I can say. He can hurt you without even knowing he's hurting you."

"You don't think he would hurt me physically, do you?"

"No, Baby, not physically, not usually. That's not the way he operates. But the other is worse, much worse, believe me. The knife to the heart, once it's in you can't pull it out again."

That night she came home from work and didn't know where he was. At first she was afraid he had left. But then she heard a noise in the bathroom. She slipped off her shoes, and padded softly on the brown shag carpet in that direction. The door was open. Two blue jeaned legs were dangling out from the opened cabinet under the sink and there was a metallic scraping noise.

"Julius?" she said, He jerked and banged his head on the bottom of the sink, let out a scream, swore, then pulled his head out of the space and rubbed his head.

"Sorry," Natalie said, shyly. She felt like a little girl again, staring at her father, her daddy. There were fleeting, foggy memories of a scene something like this. Her as a little girl in a dress, a special blue dress. Looking down at her father, sprawled down on the floor with a tool in his hand. Like now, like the way he, her father, lay on the floor before her now, a pipe wrench in his hand.

"I found these tools in your closet. Thought I'd give this clog in your sink a shot. I think it's okay now, though I'm not sure I am."

"Thanks," Natalie said, her heart starting to fill with something she wasn't sure she wanted to let in, remembering her mother's words. She stood there for a moment, staring at him, her hands clasped awkwardly before her. What did she know of this man? And what of the memories? They were more like a dream she'd had long long ago. She turned then, suddenly, and left the room. "I'm going to make dinner," she said, feeling his eyes on her, the eyes of a stranger.

It was nothing fancy, hamburgers on buns. Frozen french fries thrown from the bag into the oven. But he seemed to savor every bite. Pouring gobs of ketchup onto his plate and daintily swirling the fries in the pool of red. Thoroughly getting into the moment, enjoying the experience. But, why shouldn't he? It must be wonderful to sit down at a table, in a heated place, where he was welcome, to eat, without having to watch his back every second, as Natalie imagined he would have to, on the streets, in the soup kitchens where he went, or whatever. His hair was a tangled mess of curls on his head. His face was riddled with black and gray dots of beard, even though she'd bought him a razor, shaving cream and blades. Shaving was a thing he didn't seem to have much time for. Or combing his hair. Or brushing his teeth—his teeth were browned like wood and his breath was bad, like a dog's breath. Why couldn't he even take care of himself in the most basic ways? What was it about his life—when he'd had a life that was so terrible—that he had fallen to this?

A drop of ketchup was stuck on the corner of his mouth. It looked like blood. He chewed, looking right at her, but not really seeing her, it seemed. It was more like a foggy look, like he barely even recognized her. The food, however, he gave his full attention to.

He was looking right at her, but when she said, "Julius, you've got something here," pointing to the corner of her own mouth, he said "Hmmm?" and looked at her, really looked at her all of the sudden, like he'd just seen her. Then he looked down again at his plate, and back up at her. This time his eyes seemed empty. She wanted to know where he'd been.

"What were you thinking about?"

"What? When?"

"Just then. Before I said anything. I was watching you and you looked like you were thinking about something."

"I don't know. Nothing. I just sort of fade in and out sometimes. It's hard to explain."

"Are you here now?"

"Yeah. I'm here."

"Good. Because I need to ask you something."

"Okay. What?"

She leaned back in her chair and tilted her head down, staring right across the table into his foggy eyes.

"Why did you leave us? Why did you leave Mom and me when I was little? And never come back?"

He put his half-eaten hamburger back on the plate, and looked down at it. "It's no use talking about it now. It was so long ago, like a different life. What good can come from talking about it now?"

She got mad then, banged the table with her fist before she even knew she'd done it, and, in the same moment said "Because I need to know, Goddammit!"

He stared at her with his eyes wide (in shock, in fear?) studying her face, rubbing his fingers together gently, forming a steeple with the finger tips. "Okay, all right. You're right, you have a right to know. But truth is I don't know why exactly. It's just things took a turn for the worse for me. Lost my band, lost my job. The drinking,

I couldn't handle it anymore. I was a bad man, no good to anyone, not to your momma, not to you. Spent all the money on booze and gambling. And I was mean, heartless. I didn't think I was that way, but I saw myself becoming that way. I saw it in her eyes, your mother's eyes mostly. If I raised my hand, made a sudden move, she jumped, she flinched. It was fear in her eyes, that's what it was. And it made me sad, down in the core of my heart, sad and desperate. And you didn't deserve it. No one deserved it. I didn't want to do that to you anymore. It wasn't fair. You were so young and innocent and hopeful. You always had that loving little girl smile on your face for me when I came home half-loaded. Of course you were so young, you didn't know. You'd lift your little hands high to the sky for me to grab you up and take you in my arms. But I sloughed you off, ignored you. And you cried. I was a mean man. Good to no one. Believe me, you were better off. And I yelled at, hit your mother. Who could live with that? I couldn't. Why should you have to? You deserved better. So I left, to leave you with a better life."

Natalie rose from her chair, her eyes wide. "A better life? You really believe that's what you left us with?"

He peered at her from atop the temple he'd created with his fingers.

"You know how Mom had to struggle to keep us fed, to get me through school? You know how hard it was being four years old wanting a father and not having one? Do you know how cruel kids can be? I'd go to school only to hear that my daddy was a drunk, a no good drunk who ran away with some other neighborhood drunk. Because he didn't care about me. He didn't love me."

He closed his eyes then and rested his chin down in his folded hands. "It's not true. I did care. I always cared. That was why I left."

"Because we deserved better than you."

"Yes," he said, his eyes still closed. Tears were starting to wash down his cheeks. "I loved you. I always loved you and your mother. It was me I didn't love."

She went to him them, despite herself. She walked that long walk around the table and gently put her hand on his shoulder, then hugged him from behind, placing her head against his back and closing her eyes. "I missed you so much," she said, the tears coming to her eyes now. "I still do."

He was lying on the couch, watching soap operas, sipping a beer, reading a newspaper. It had been a week since his daughter, his treasure, his savior, had taken him in, and now he was living the life, the good life. Just like he was part of it all again. A television in front of him. A beer. His feet up on the coffee table. Heat and indoor plumbing. Even a refrigerator with food in it. Not much but some. How had he lost all of this? And when? It seemed too long ago now to even remember.

One Life to Live was on the television. The irony, he thought, chuckling to himself, closing his eyes, and folding his hands on his chest. How many lives he'd led, and now it was all coming to an end. Just like that. It was way the chips fell, the way his chips always fell. But when would he tell Natalie, because he had to tell her. It wouldn't be fair not to. She had a right to know. She had a right. He took a deep breath and floated on that cushion of sleep, as the dull constant throbbing pains throughout his body continued, they always continued. He deserved it, he figured, he deserved all God could dish out to him for all the pain he'd cause to his daughter and the others, all the others, in his life.

It could have been an hour, or a day or two or more, and he wouldn't have known the difference. Time had stood still for him. He couldn't tell one day from the next. But it wasn't an hour, it wasn't a day—it was a week later, two weeks after Natalie had taken him in. He was on the couch again, asleep again, trying to bury the pains in his side and in his stomach with sleep. The sound of the key rattling in the lock brought him to. He'd learned over the years, the many years, the price of being too light a sleeper out there. That he was safe now, not sleeping in someone's doorway, not being stirred awake by some cop's foot or night stick, didn't matter. He would never in his life sleep soundly again, that he was sure of.

She came, a bag of groceries cradled in her arms, her key chain dangling from her mouth, as she banged against the door and bobbled from one foot to the other.

"Could I get a little help here, please?" she said.

"Oh, sure," Julius said, throwing the pillow off his chest and jumping to his feet. He stood next to his daughter ("his daughter," how strange the words sounded!) awkwardly for a moment, not knowing what to do. Then she said "Here," and shoved the bag into his arms which he almost dropped, but caught hold of just before it fell. He stood, inches from her, just looking at her, not believing that this was his daughter.

"Do you want to put those away?" she asked. He just stood there. "In the kitchen?" He moved suddenly, woodenly toward the kitchen. After closing the refrigerator door, he moved back toward the couch and collapsed on it.

She stood in front of him, arms crossed, and asked "Have a rough day?"

"Huh? No. Fine day. Relaxing. No problems."

"So, what is it you were saying last night, that you've been saying every night, about wanting to do something to improve your situation?"

He sat up. Put his arm up behind him, and scratched his head.

"I'm looking for a job," he said.

"You are."

"I want to. I'm going to."

"And when is all of this going to happen."

"Soon. Day after tomorrow."

"No."

"No?"

"Not the day after tomorrow. But tomorrow. You're going to get up, take a shower maybe, have a cup of coffee, get dressed and go out there, start looking."

He laughed. Couldn't help himself. The thought of it seemed funny, him, unemployable him, looking for a job.

"Uh, yeah. Or you can pack up your ... your ... backpack and hit the pavement again, sleep under the bridge again, if that's what you want. There are no more free lunches. Do you catch my drift?"

"Look, I can no longer work a job, go without a drink for eight hours than I can have a baby. Don't you understand that?"

"And that's all you've got to say? You want it to be that way forever?"

"No. I don't want it to be that way. What do you think? But do you think I have a choice?"

"Yes," she said, crossing her arms in front of her. "You do."

"Aw, come on. Grow up. You don't think I've been a druggie and a boozer for twenty-five years because I want to be?"

"At some point you must have wanted to. And after that you still did to some extent or you would have done something about it."

"I can't. Can't you see that. I need ... I needed help."

What did he mean by that, needed? She looked at him standing there, leaning against the wall almost looking like he were a ghost, without substance. Just a shadow on the wall.

"Then someone needs to help you. If you're willing."

He smiled. "Who? Who would help me?"

"Me. I'll help you."

"You. But I'm beyond help now. It's too late." He bent forward and hugged his arms around himself. His teeth were chattering. He looked pale, she thought. After a moment the shivering stopped and he stood upright against the wall again.

"Are you all right?" she asked. She'd thought it was from the drink, from his generally bad health. But maybe there was more. She really didn't want to know, but held her breath for a moment and asked anyway. "What do you mean it's too late?"

"It doesn't matter. And why would you want to help me, anyway? What have I ever done for you? Besides leave you and make your life miserable, fatherless. I never was a father to you, never knew how to be. Never knew how to live at all, really. Forgot how. How do people live? How do they manage? I forgot how a long time ago."

"Tell me what you meant. When you said it doesn't matter anyway."

He smiled the broken smile of a broken man. "It's the cancer. Found out last month at a clinic. Cancer in my pancreas. Funny, I'm not even sure where that is, what it does."

"And there's nothing they can do about it? You should be in a hospital or something."

He looked right at her then, his eyes wide, begging. "If you want me to leave, I will. You don't deserve this. I left you alone in life and only return to see you before I die. Selfish, I know it is."

"But, there's nothing they can do? What about chemotherapy or radiation treatment?"

He shook his head and looked down at a spot in the floor in front of him. "Nothing, there's nothing they could do. It's gone too far, been left too long. When you live on the streets you get used to the pains of life, even the wracking, earth-jarring pains. But this was worse, this was something much worse. By the time I got into the clinic to see what it was. I was already gone."

She didn't know what to do. He was still an odd presence, a stranger in her home. She went to him then, walked across the long kitchen floor and wrapped her arms around him. He stood there stiffly at first, resisting, then loosened up and let her hug him.

She moved him into her bedroom, let him sleep there while she took the couch. Her mother and Rona, couldn't believe it, that she would do that for this man. But we all deserve a place to die, she told them, don't we?

She brought him in to see her doctor who could do little but shake her head and give her a slew of prescriptions for pain killers. That was all she could do, she said, apologizing, and offering her help if Natalie thought she couldn't deal with the situation any longer. But, she told the doctor, she was determined to do what she could for as long as she could. He was her father, after all, she said, the words sounding strange coming off her tongue, but light and sweet at the same time.

She brought him meals in bed. She brought him pills and water.

"You shouldn't be doing this, you don't owe me any of this," he would say, but she would shush him, tell him to stop. He was her father, she said. That was exactly what she told him.

"There's no reason," he replied, "there's no reason for anyone to love me."

"Maybe that's what's wrong with your life," she said, "maybe that's what's been wrong all along. You didn't have anyone to love you."

She got up from the chair beside his bed, the chair that had been permanently glued to that spot and hugged him gently, not wanting to hurt him any more than she knew he was already hurting, the tears cascading down her cheeks.

"Natalie, this is insane," her mother whispered after leaving the bedroom. They'd greeted each other cautiously like distant relatives or acquaintances, like people who'd known each other vaguely in another life as, indeed, it seemed it had been.....another life. She'd touched his hand, his shoulder, asked him politely how he felt, kept the talk superficial, thinking, what can be gained by getting into it all now, after all this time? The damage had long been done. And now there was nothing more that could be done to fix it, to fix anything.

"But, Natalie, what are you going to do when he can't help himself anymore, when he can't go to the bathroom by himself, or eat, or bathe? What are you going to do then? He needs a nurse, but of course you can't afford that, or he should be in a hospital, somewhere where they can take care of him."

"Take care of him why? So he can die?"

"Die in the most comfortable situation possible."

"This is the most comfortable situation for him. You should see the way he looks at me now. I can see the love in his eyes. The way he smiles at me. I don't want him ..." (she dabbed her eyes with a tissue—she was so emotional all the time now) "... I don't want him to die alone."

"I know, Darling, but ..."

"No," Natalie, said, pushing her mother off her. "No, Mother," she said holding her arm in her hand. "You don't know."

But it did get harder, it did get more than Natalie could handle. And one day, with the doctor's help, an ambulance pulled up to her door to take her father away to a public hospital for terminal patients. It broke her heart, it wasn't what she wanted, but what other choices did she have?

She accompanied him in the ambulance, his figure gaunt, the cheek bones visible now, his face white. He would come in and out of consciousness, but she sat beside him, holding his arm lightly. "I'll be with you, Daddy," she said, feeling that, once again, she was the four-year-old daughter with her eyes raised up to the skies. "I'll be with you till the end."

And on one cold still, but sunny day, in November, winter's chill nipping the air, she was there as her father's last breath passed, sitting beside him, lightly holding his arm in her hand. "Natalie," she thought she heard him say, just before he left, turning his head toward her once last time, "Daddy's got to go." Then the breath left him for good.

The church was mostly empty at the funeral, just Natalie, her mother, and Rona, who'd seen Julius on a couple of occasions after he'd come for his last stay.

At the cemetery it was just the priest and them. Natalie wept and her mother and Rona put their arms around her, led her to the casket where she took one red rose, kissed it and bent down to place it on the black casket raised up in the plot. "I missed you, Daddy, for so long," she said. Her mother patted her back gently, and the three of them moved slowly away, back toward the car. "I love you," she whispered softly, so that no one else could hear, "I love you, Daddy."

Mitchell Waldman's fiction, poetry, and essays have appeared in numerous journals and anthologies. He is author of the novel, *A Face in the Moon*, co-editor, with his partner, Diana Waldman,   of the anthologies *Wounds of War: Poets for Peace* and *Hip Poetry* and is Fiction Editor for *Blue Lake Review*. For   more information, visit his website at: http://mitchwaldman.homestead.com.